Manhattan
Manitoulin

ALSO BY BONNIE KOGOS

MANITOULIN ADVENTURES
I Was Mistaken for a Rich, Red, Ripe Tomato
(2001)

MANHATTAN
MANITOULIN

BY BONNIE KOGOS

Scrivener Press

Library and Archives Canada Cataloguing in Publication

Kogos, Bonnie
     Manhattan, Manitoulin / Bonnie Kogos.

ISBN 978-1-896350-47-9

     I. Title.

PS3611.O465M36 2012   813.6   C2012-901091-X

Book design: Laurence Steven
Cover design: Chris Evans
Photo of author: ©2012 David Beyda Studio

Published by Scrivener Press
465 Loach's Road,
Sudbury, Ontario, Canada, P3E 2R2
info@yourscrivenerpress.com
www.scrivenerpress.com

We acknowledge the financial support of the Canada Council for the Arts, the Ontario Arts Council, and the Government of Canada through the Canada Book Fund for our publishing activities.

For Polly, Fred and Nancy
with love

Chapter One

"Ladies, you won't believe the magnificent boulders on Virgin Gorda! You've all done well this week," Lily Gardner said proudly. "Keep feeling your way into these tropical islands!"

"Lily, haven't we seen enough for today?" the Philadelphia voice whined.

"You haven't given us time to smell the frangipani!"

"Lily, our notebooks are full!" Her seven ladies of various ages stood under the shade of a canopy like wilted flowers, watching Speedy's Ferry rumble into the port of Road Town on Tortola. The glamour of the British Virgin Islands was lost on them today. They had known the Familiarization Trip would be rigorous, learning about hotels and beaches on Tortola, Jost Van Dyke, Necker, Cooper, and Peter Islands. When they returned to their stateside offices, they would send their elite clients to the delights of these oh-so-lucrative destinations. It was another workday for Lily, who knew the sixty BVI islands and inlets, depending on the tide. She knew the eighteen marinas with every type of boat available to tourists. She didn't know all of the nine hundred boats available for charter, but she knew the yachts that were so grand they made some BVI resorts look small. For the delight of snorkelers and scuba enthusiasts, there were wrecks, flora, fish, and coral formations to hypnotize any diver. She loved selling the British Virgin Islands.

"Lily, we inspected twelve hotels today. I know you keep saying success as a travel agent comes when the client is happy—not us," Janie blurted. "But my feet are killing me!"

A young sailor sauntered by, wearing pressed white shorts and a tight shirt, one of the hundreds of powerfully built deckhands working on mega-yachts anchored in the harbours. Lily watched as he captured her ladies' full attention. Lily knew the confidence of the deckhands' muscled bodies, living on plush yachts, running away from the bitter cold and boredom of Britain and Sweden, South Africa and Holland. Deck fluff needed no explanation. The ladies were delighted unabashedly in the parade of men and women with long hair and, ah, the smiles of the young. Lily knew she had her share of good looks and good men. *No, not enough good men.* But this day in the Caribbean Paradise was all business.

And she knew her business. Her sharp awareness of hotel enhancements forged longtime friendships with the hoteliers. The head of the British Virgin Islands Tourist Board often drew on Lily's extensive knowledge of his territory, referring other travel agents to her tour to orient them to the hotels, boats, and beaches they would book for their clients. Lily set the pace, making sure they inspected every worthy hotel, met each manager and gathered brochures for their notebooks. Despite thirty years experience booking yachts and upscale hotels for her own clients, she felt in the summer of her life. The BVI, by far, were her favourite islands. People from around the world vacationed here. One movie star might step off his yacht, docking to eat Caribbean rock lobster freshly grilled outdoors at the famed Anegada Reef Hotel, while another might retreat to a private villa at the Little Dix Bay Resort.

The highlight each day was a festive lunch overlooking BVI turquoise waters, each day a different restaurant tried and tested. Today, the ladies inhaled the scent of frangipani in a vase on the table as they dined on baked fish, rice and salads, fresh bread and iced tea. There would be no rum punches at lunch, though Lily did grant them the right to dally in the gift shops before shepherding them back to the bus. Only after dinner might they take a quick swim and then sink into lounge chairs under palm trees with a glass of wine. Lily smiled to hear the secrets, stories and lies about where they had traveled and who their clients were, confiding voices playing counterpoint to the sweet rolling surf. Most withdrew at dusk to their rooms. This trip she was dealing with reliable troopers. No professional rivalries, no drunks at night, and no native hookups to rescue.

They watched the ferry docking, the people spilling off the afternoon boat to shop in Road Town. She looked forward to astonishing the ladies, showing them the world famous Virgin Gorda boulders and "The Baths." Years ago a local goat-herder had told her, "Dem's God's Marbles, Lily. They bring us visitors and dey green dollars."

"All aboard!" The ladies piled onto the ferry, mingling with locals, and took their seats. As they pulled away from the dock, a deckhand beckoned Lily forward to the wheelhouse. Captain Malvin George grinned when she entered. "Good day, Miss Lily!

You still our ambassador. How many millions you book this year to our territory?"

"Seventy-five honeymoons, Mal, five family outings, and three business conferences," Lily said, sighing. "And I'm not tired."

"You so like my daughter Winsome. Work too hard. Time you had a man!"

"Too busy, Mal," Lily said, putting down her notebook, and looking out onto the horizon.

"Can't be travelin' all your life," Captain Malvin said. "You know my Winsome marry last month. You gettin' older, chasing 'round dese islands. Her Clyde have job in Canada. Missus and me just back from Sudbury, up in Ontario, see where she be livin'."

"I'm happy for Winsome," Lily said with delight. She wondered what it would be like to change her life as radically as Winsome had. Her life, she admitted to herself, was not perfect. Lily had gaps, loneliness, impossible standards; she knew she fell short. She smiled. Well, she was short. Five feet three.

"We glad to find big Caribbean population in Sudbury, so she not be lonely. Others from down islands," he said, easing the ferry wheel with his gnarled, competent hands. "An hour and a half from Sudbury they drive us to Lake Huron. Nice cold island. Winsome make me swim in fresh water. Be freezin'!"

"Hot islands are my specialty, Mal," Lily asserted, smiling at him. So homebody, hardworking seamstress Winsome had found herself a husband. How many men had Lily met over the years? She had dated New York doctors, lawyers, and advertising men, interested in their own careers, as she'd been, honestly, in hers. It was much more tempting to travel for a week to Hong Kong inspecting hotels and meeting fascinating people, than to cook dinner for a suit. She'd traveled to ninety-two countries and thirty Caribbean islands, and had a stove in her kitchen that was never used. Her stocks and bonds were growing and Winsome had found a husband. Lily didn't need one.

Forty minutes later, Captain Mal interrupted her thoughts. "Yes, Miss Lily, cold island be extra good for you." He chuckled, drawing down the engines, pulling into the town dock.

Disembarking, Lily saw her regular driver, Gafford, waiting by the dock to take them to the bus. "Miss Lily, here we go again," he said, shaking her hand. He loaded the bags onto the bus and drove the ladies up the hill to check into their rooms at Virgin Gorda's Little Dix Bay Resort. An hour later they convened on the large verandah overlooking the bay to have British Afternoon Tea, pinkies up, eating cucumber sandwiches.

"Back into the bus," Lily decreed with an eye on the lowering sun. Collectively, they sighed, gathering up again. Gafford drove them up the mountain, past dizzying views of the sea, and down to Gunn Creek where a boat waited to take them to the north side of the island. After inspecting the elegant Biras Creek Resort and its buffet dinner, they returned, sleepy, to fall into their beds, dreaming of honeymoon suites and bougainvillea-draped windows with panoramic views of the Caribbean.

Five days of this dizzying round of lunches, boats and hotels, pocketbooks burgeoning with brochures and ever-thicker notebooks, they were glad for the last working day. They sauntered with Lily onto Dock B of the Virgin Gorda Yacht Harbour. Noticeably tired of Lily's thoroughness, the ladies allowed their gazes to wander to the bare chests and the long legs of the young sailors. Tourists dawdled in the café overlooking the harbour, and Midwestern accents drifted in from chartered boats coming into dock, oh, so ineptly. All types sailed here; the charter business thrived. But the BVI was changing, growing ever more upscale, with more cell phones and internet. She might need new islands to sell. She paused at the thought, staring at a red-hulled sailboat where a young deckhand in shorts, with disheveled blond hair and smooth, muscled shoulders, sanded a handrail. The life preserver lying on the deck bore the name *Northern Loon*.

Lily caught his eye. Something about a parade of women sporting new vacation outfits, scribbling frantically in notebooks, must strike him as comical. She winked at him, thinking, ah, another hunk, line and sinker!

After inspecting three-mega yachts at the dock, meeting the captains and first mates, and collecting more brochures, the ladies happily returned to Little Dix for a last swim, and to shower and pack. By mid-afternoon, her agents stood at the town dock, more than ready to return to the States. "I'll miss you all," Lily, said with respect and affection. One handed her a gift certificate to a local jewelry store.

"We listened to everything you told us, Lily!"

"I'll *never* forget this trip!"

"Where's my sunscreen?"

Captain Mal, in the wheelhouse, raised his hand in salute to her, and the ferry departed for Trellis Bay, seabirds calling shrilly in its wake. Lily stood and watched the empty water at the dock. Now what? Was she hungry? No. Swim? Shopping on her own? There was a new jewelry store … She ambled back up the hill to Little Dix Bay Resort, surrendering to the lush Caribbean flowers and verdant palms as she let herself relax after five days "on." Lily loved the bright floral arrangements that changed each day in her room. She found technicolour everywhere in the Caribbean, the azure sea, red, pink and green plants, the blue sky above. Her hammock on the veranda beckoned, and she melted into it, swaying away from deadlines, routines, faxes and telephones.

When she awoke, it was dark. Beyond the large glass doors, a fat golden moon was rising above the sweet curve around the bay. Silver light danced across the water towards a lone sailboat anchored beyond the reef. A man and woman in a dinghy rowed together, their laughter floating up to her across the water. Lily watched them from her balcony for a while, and then went into her room, turning on the radio.

It was an old Jamaican song, "Take Warning, Ya Betta Take Warning," a mighty Calypso beat. Lily closed the curtains. She danced around the room by herself. You had to be silly sometimes. The song ended, and the next was slow and dreamy. She looked at the empty king-sized bed. Why did they always give her a king-sized bed? This bed should be for Dahlia and Stuart, her sister and her husband, long married, working hard at careers and raising their children. They were the ones who needed to vacation in this room. She threw the six pillows on the floor. Not tidy. She put them on a chair. The king-sized bed was like a landing field, with nobody to land with. She didn't care. She had it all.

It was dinnertime but she didn't feel like being a single woman at a single table after the week of cheerful chatter. On the bureau she spied yet another gift box of Godiva chocolate truffles and a bottle of red wine with two wine glasses from Pamela Flax, the reservations manager. Five chocolate truffles and two glasses of wine would precisely do for dinner, she decided. Lily allowed herself to soak in a bubble bath. She dried off with a luxurious oversized towel, put on her white silk nightie and slipped into cool sheets. A creature of habit, she moved to the left of the king-sized bed.

Chapter Two

Lily awoke late the next morning. She made two leisurely cups of coffee in her room, took a swim, and then a quick shower with perfumed soap, and dressed for lunch. She knew every person she met, from the hotel's general manager to the gardeners, as she wandered over to the open-air restaurant. Denver, the waiter, who was getting grey around the temples, smiled and led her to a table. He brought her customary single glass of crisp, white Chardonnay. "I ordered lobster salad, your usual, Miss Lily."

Travel brochures were stacked neatly in her bag. She didn't take them out. Pamela looked into the dining room, spying Lily, who smiled and beckoned welcome. Pamela made Lily look like a champ when Lily booked Little Dix for her clients. They had lunch, giggling over the eccentricities of tourists and travelers. When lunch arrived, each picked up her fork, saluted the other, bit, and savoured a perfect piece of Caribbean rock lobster tail.

After lunch, Lily strolled down the hill to Spanish Town, gazing at the Sir Francis Drake Channel sparkling sapphire beneath the spiked, gray mountains of Tortola. She crossed the parking lot and through coconut trees to the Virgin Gorda Harbour docks. The boats strained at their lines, impatient to be let out into the wind. On Dock B, she walked past *Northern Loon*. The day was hers.

"I saw you yesterday." The young man stood at the bow of *Northern Loon*. His broad smile and easy style beckoned her.

"This is a lovely boat."

"Thanks. Gotta say I'm working hard at it. I've been aboard a few months. I served in the Navy. Now I'm taking time off 'til I decide what to do next." He was eager to have some new conversation. "I've been sanding this rail for two hours like a dumb Englishman who doesn't know how to come out of the sun! I heard you talking to those ladies yesterday, teaching them how to charter boats. Would you like to come aboard and have a look at her?"

"Do you take charters?"

"Oh, no, she's privately owned."

Lily looked around the dock, packed with sailors and strolling tourists ogling the boats, as she was. Mid-afternoon; it was certainly safe. Lily had inspected so many sailboats and power boats professionally for so many years. She'd always had faith in her ability to shriek in high C at any moment.

"I'm Bart. What's your name?"

"I'm Lily." Bart moved surely to the stern and extended his hand. She kicked off her sandals, knowing better than to board in street shoes, and stepped gingerly.

"Thanks," he said. "We protect our varnish." He gestured for her to sit, and she sank into large cushions. She leaned back, felt the subtle rocking of the yacht and closed her eyes, loving the warmth of the sun and the gentle rush of water against the hull.

She was tired. She sighed luxuriously, and then opened her eyes. She didn't want to be rude. "Thanks for letting me sit a bit. Where are you from?"

"The fine State of Virginia and glad to be here," he said, poking a polishing rag into his grimy shorts. "I heard you telling those ladies yesterday about chartering around the islands. When we finish all the work on *Northern Loon*, we'll head south. I'm learning every day—sanding, varnishing, and navigation. This ketch is a beauty to sail. What exactly do you do, Lily, when you're not guiding lady travel agents?"

"Today, nothing," she said. "But that's what I do, lead travel agents around the BVI and then go back home. My business partner and I book clients around the world. I love boats, but I'm too busy to sail. Isn't that ridiculous?"

"It sure is," he said with a lazy Southern drawl.

"Taking peoples' money and booking their vacations, that's serious business. You have to know your clients and the right match to the captain and vessel."

"Would you like to come below for a look? You'll like this one." She nodded.

"Mind your head and climb down slowly." He led the way down into the dark interior of the sailboat. She followed, balancing herself on the lowest rung of the ladder. Lily stood to look in. She found the galley pleasingly spacious and comfortable, with a clean sink and a stove. Bananas and apples hung in a gauze sleeve. In the main salon she saw three couches in green corduroy, books along the side, and a large table strewn with charts. Two oil paintings were mounted on the far wall, fir trees on rocky hills, blowing in a swift wind. The yacht was obviously privately owned. A dream boat. All it needed was a gorgeous captain. Unless he'd won the lottery, Bart was not able to afford it.

"So you'll be sailing around the BVI?"

"Yup, snorkeling, diving, and then cruising down islands."

"It sounds like a magical adventure. Do you cook?"

He laughed. "And clean, do laundry, and fix the toilet when it gets stuffed."

"Don't you have time limits, just sailing around to islands?" Always gathering information, Lily stopped short.

"We'll sail when all repairs are made. The owner's a Canadian fellow. He's taking a nap…" Bart raised a finger to indicate quiet.

"How old is he?" she blurted. Oh, that was rude.

Bart didn't seem to mind. "Fifty."

"Fifty years old? Just the two of you on the boat?"

"Yup, he just got a divorce, sold his business. That's enough to make you go sailing."

A deep voice called out, coming from the back cabin. "Hey, Bart, I overslept. Bring me a cup of coffee?"

Lily froze, suddenly feeling like an intruder.

"Sure, Will, coffee's made." Bart turned to the galley to pour the coffee into a large mug. He opened up the cooler, took out milk, poured it in, stirred it, and handed the mug to Lily.

"You bring it to him," Bart suggested quietly, his eyes dancing with mischief. "Have some fun!"

"I can't barge in!" Her face reddened as she held the mug in one hand, her other hand on the ladder.

"Go. Mind the back step into the aft cabin." She slowly edged her way toward the master stateroom. She knocked twice on a wood panel by the open door.

"Bart, since when do you knock?"

"I'm not Bart!" She paused and waited a minute, in case he might need to cover up. Who knew what he was wearing? She waited another minute.

A deep voice grumbled. "Who's this?" Steadying the mug, she took a breath, put her shoulders back, and carefully stepped into the aft cabin.

Blue eyes gazed up at Lily as the seemingly naked man reclined on his bunk. "I have shorts on," he said to her unanswered question. Then she saw worn khaki shorts half-covered and above that, a startlingly handsome naked golden-tanned chest. His disheveled blond-gray hair was splayed on the pillow. His white teeth gleamed through a slow smile on a rugged, bemused face as he propped himself up on an elbow and reached for the coffee. His eyes assessed her in surprise, sweeping from her face, down past her blue shirt and shorts, finally lingering on her thighs and calves before finishing at her bare feet. They returned to her face, brimming with a pleased curiosity. Here was a self-contained man, secure in his boat, in his world.

"Here's your coffee. I shouldn't be interrupting you. You're resting." She held out the coffee mug to him, but he simply stared at her.

"Bart, where'd you find this lady?"

Lily held out the coffee and gazed at him. He stared back with a relaxed intensity as he lay in his bunk.

"If you don't drink this coffee, I will," she stated, New York City cab-driver style. Surprised at the crispness of her voice, she softened. "Where may I set this down for you?"

"Clear a spot on that table. Move those books," he said, shaking his head. He sat up, resting against the pillows, his feet still relaxed on his bunk. The cabin was square, with two large single beds across from each other, the other one covered with charts. Small lamps with fluted shades were built in, and books crammed along two small shelves. He was a reader. A large hatch above let in fresh breeze, and a wooden dresser to the right was covered with books.

She cleared the books and set down the coffee mug. "Since you delivered this coffee," he said, his voice still bemused, "would you like to have some?" He leaned forward to pick up the mug and took a long drink.

"Thanks, I live on coffee."

"Move those charts off that bunk, then and find a seat." Trying to appear nonchalant, she sat across from him on the other bunk. She crossed her legs.

"How do you take it?"

"What?"

"Your coffee!"

"A little milk."

He called out, "Bring the lady a cup of coffee, one milk."

"Yo!" came an answering shout from the galley.

"So what brings you to my boat?"

"Bart invited me. I'm a travel agent," she explained. "I told him I specialize in chartering sailboats and motor yachts in the BVI. This is a beautiful boat."

"I knew it would have to be a second home if I was going to spend time here."

"You've been on boats a lot?" She kicked herself, mentally. A stupid question.

"I grew up on Lake Huron, sailing the North Channel. And I've family along the coast of Nova Scotia and Newfoundland. Had lots of boats." The coffee seemed to be waking him up. "You sound like a New York TV detective show. I know where you're from!"

"The most busy, sophisticated island in the world!"

"Crowded, corrupt Manhattan?" He laughed. "It's a damn zoo!"

"I hope you're not a snob," she said, annoyed. "Where are you from that's so terrific?" Suddenly, she didn't like him, but coffee was coming.

"Bart, I think I insulted the lady. Cut some rhubarb crisp and put it on a fancy dish for the lady from New York City. It'll sweeten up her disposition!"

"You've rhubarb in Virgin Gorda?" Lily was startled. "My Aunt Bea has rhubarb on her farm in Connecticut. It's my favourite in the summer."

"I've a patch at my farm in Ontario. When I come down here, I bring a taste of home."

Bart appeared, handing Lily a small dish of flaky rhubarb crisp, napkin and fork. She placed her coffee on the small table and noticed the sterling silver fork was inscribed with a fancy initial M. She took a bite, her mouth savoring a perfect sour sweet tang.

He laid his mug aside. "Do you like it?"

She put the fork down, nodded, and took a slow sip of coffee. She looked at him, alert to her. She wanted to touch him, to slide her hand along his shoulders and across his chest. She sat up straight. She took another bite. What was she thinking?

"What are you doing in Virgin Gorda?"

"I've worked for the BVI Tourist Board for years. I teach travel agents about the hotels on Tortola, the inns on Jost Van Dyke, Virgin Gorda and Anegada, Peter Island and Necker Island." She took a breath. "I make sure we don't miss a thing. It'll take them a week to recuperate. My work is all Caribbean, hotels, chartering sailboats and yachts. I know about almost thirty Caribbean Islands, places you'd love to see," She abruptly closed her mouth.

"You're still leading your tour…" he smiled, his amusement clear.

She looked at him with resignation. She must stop selling, especially to someone who didn't need to be buying.

"So you know the BVI and the other islands as a travel agent, but not as a sailor?"

She nodded. He took up a chart and pointed, "When the sails are up, driven by a fine wind, there's nothing like it. One of my favourite anchorages is by Norman Island, calm and serene. The stars and moon reflect on the water, that's how clear it is. The breezes are soft, and with a fine glass of wine, you can sit and wonder at the night."

"You have the soul of a poet. I don't know Norman Island. There are no hotels there."

He smiled. "It's not every day a pretty young lady walks, unbidden, into my cabin. And you like my rhubarb!"

Though his aft cabin was spacious, it felt suddenly too intimate. The reason people came to the tropics was to be outside, Lily knew. But here they were, very close. And he sure wasn't moving.

"I'm swooning over your delicious rhubarb crisp. And thanks for your compliment. I *think* I'm younger than springtime, but I'm not." She should be more positive. This fellow was good looking, well-spoken. She prayed she didn't appear scattered. There was silence as they gazed at each other.

"I have a hundred acres of bush land that follows a lazy river on another island up north. Farmer Grey's cows graze on the back forty. But I've given myself time to explore, and sail down these islands."

"It must take courage to just sail away...even though this is a beautiful boat!"

"Only time and money," he said. Bart appeared again, this time bringing an open bottle of chilled white wine, and two glasses. He poured silently and retreated quickly, a gleam in his eyes as they met Lily's.

"May the wind be at your back." She toasted this unknown mystery of a man with the unexpected glass of wine, smiling.

"Do you sail?" he asked.

"No time, too busy." She sipped the wine and finished the rhu-barb crisp. "Maybe an afternoon to meet the captain and crew and see how they'd be for clients. Do you know the Caribbean?"

"I've sailed down island many times. I'm leaving Virgin Gorda tomorrow."

Without losing a beat, she said briskly, "Well, I'd better go so you can get on with your day." She put down the plate and wine glass, stood up and paused. "I've never," she said slowly, "not," she paused again, "been introduced to anyone in bed before!"

He laughed, set his wine glass down and offered a large, cal-loused hand. "I'm pleased to meet you, Miss New York City. I'm Will, owner of the *Northern Loon.*"

She instantly felt his warmth and a desire not to let go, but she did. "Thanks for the rhubarb, the coffee and the wine. I'm Lily, owner of nothing, no boat, only extensive knowledge about traveling the Caribbean. You didn't tell me where you're from?"

"A beautiful island in Ontario. It's called Manitoulin." He reached for a chart of Lake Huron, and gestured toward a shape that spanned most of the northern half. "I always go home to the island. You have to cross an old swing bridge to get over there. And once you do, life is never the same."

"My friend told me about a cold northern island only yester-day."

"Cold compared to these tropics, maybe. I have an old farm-house there. How do I find you again, Lily?"

"I'm staying at Little Dix." Her voice was on fast forward. "My sister is Dahlia Gladiola. We were brought up by our flower-crazy gardening mother, Violet Rose. I wish I could convince my sister Dahlia and her husband Stuart to vacation here in my ridiculously huge room. I could treat them, but they're so busy with careers and raising two kids. Why am I telling you this?"

"Because you love your family. Are you ready for another debatable name?"

"Sure!"

"I am Willard Knot Mudge. The Third."

She put her hand to her mouth. "That's a good one!" And giggled.

"So you understand," he said. She nodded. "I'm Lily Hyacinth Gardner, and I'd like to hear about Manitoulin Island. I do specialize in islands...but I've got to go."

The only sound was sea water lapping at the boat, the boat rocking slightly. Then he nodded. "Maybe we'll meet again."

"Perhaps." She bid Bart cheerful thanks and good bye, went up the ladder and slipped her sandals on at the dock. Bart simply smiled.

CHAPTER THREE

THAT EVENING, THE BATH & TURTLE PUB at the Virgin Gorda Yacht Harbour would be packed with bodies dancing sensuously to hot reggae by a local steel band. Lily must take herself there tonight to see friends, have a drink and a dance. Meeting Willard Knot Mudge was simply an interlude. She met so many people, mostly on the run, short conversations, on a plane, sitting on a bus, walking on a dock.

Speedy, the owner of the ferry, car rental agency and most everything on Virgin Gorda saw Lily enter and gently touched her hand. She liked Speedy, a respected businessman, and she booked all her rental cars with his office. She was delighted to dance with him, feeling the music, her spirit and body racing with the sultry night and a Caribbean beat. From the dance floor, Lily caught a glimpse of Will sitting nearby at the bar. His broad shoulders were encased in a well-used brown plaid shirt and his blond-grey hair was parted on the left side. He was watching her. When the dance ended, she melted away through the crowd toward Will, unable to take her eyes off him. He gently took hold of her arm. Not speaking, he gestured with his head toward the door.

They walked down the dock, not speaking, and she smelled his aftershave. Something spicy. The old guard, sitting by the red Queen's Post Box on the main flagstone path of the marina, raised his hand in greeting.

She left her sandals on the dock and carefully stepped aboard the boat. For the second time today, Lily sank into the soft cushions. Will methodically untied the lines that held the sunshade in place, rolling back the awning to show the full yellow moon hanging low in the Caribbean sky.

"I'll make you my special drink," he said, returning to the cockpit, and climbing down into the galley. She heard the sound of chopping ice. Emerging above, he handed her an enormous plastic glass. "I call this a Manitoulin Sunset Smoothie. It's got cranberry, orange, rum and a twist of lime."

She sipped it, relishing the sweet, bright taste, the touch of sourness across the tongue. It had enough rum to stagger Captain Morgan. She asked, "Where's Bart?"

"Visiting another boat, maybe for the night, so we have privacy for now," he said cheerfully, raising his glass. "To what we love the most!"

He sat down close to her. "That was my father's toast, one of the favourite things that I remember about him. He was a doctor, serving in the Canadian Air Force. He was killed when his plane was shot down while delivering medical supplies."

"I'm so sorry, Will," she said. Her own beloved father had died suddenly, of a heart attack, too young. "Yes, to what we love the most."

She raised her glass, and sipped.

"But what we love the most often changes," she added thoughtfully. She mentally catalogued what she loved the most: being valuable to her clients, her community of good friends, having the love of her mother and her sister. In all her years of dating, she had never had a man she could love the most. She said to Will, "I love playing the piano and singing classic Broadway songs. My dad played every night in our home after dinner. I keep meaning to buy a piano, but I'm so busy working I've never found the right one. And I like dark chocolate, traveling, reading, and shopping with discounts."

"Like isn't love," he said. Then he smiled and relaxed against the cushions, closer to her. "I'm a shopper, too. Everything on this boat's discounted."

"Nothing I see is discounted about you," she said. "Will, what do you love the most?"

He looked at her and then glanced out at the rising moon. "Sailing in the Caribbean is unbeatable, and I've taken this break to start a new life, retired, no ties. But there's no place like Manitoulin Island. In winter, icicles hang from my door, and turn pink in the sunset. I can take my snowmobile and skim for miles across the clean-swept white frozen bay. The ice is three feet thick. That's safe enough to drive your car on. The air's clear and crisp, the island spacious, with an ancient history. There's a place called Sheguiandah where scientists have found evidence of a nine-thousand year old culture. Manitoulin is a place where life persists."

"And you love it," Lily murmured, enjoying the deep sound of his voice, a charming, polite Canadian. He was not a New York City empty suit. She looked at Will's rugged face in the moonlight. He seemed earnest about beginning the next phase of his life after, Bart had said, a divorce. More than half her friends were divorced in New York City. Hearing about the ex-wife would take away the tranquil mood, she decided. She would enjoy this privileged sense of sitting with him on his glorious sailboat, and the smell of him next to her.

"This drink's the colour of a perfect Manitoulin sunset in summer," Will said, leaning closer. "If you're lucky, Lily, one day you might travel north and see a real sunset there. We get hours of extraordinary colour on summer nights. Northern Ontario is God's country."

"Tell me about your family."

He smiled, settling back. "You want to know about my ancestors, the Knots and the Mudges? They were among the first European settlers on Manitoulin. The Mudges waded ashore, carrying their belongings and a prize piano from Europe. My grandmother played that piano. Lily, we were there before electricity. My Uncle Mudge swears we were pirates and bootleggers, but who wasn't in those days! We had to become respectable, turning into teachers and farmers. Now I'm divorced. I have one daughter, Laura, happily married and living in Vancouver."

"Are there any other women in your life, Will?"

"Not now. *Loon* takes all my time, and gets cranky without enough attention. That's what we're doing now," he said, and took a deep pull from his glass. "Anyone in your life?"

She shook her head no. Will quietly reached for her hand and held it. She felt the calluses across his palm. She felt herself redden and blush in the night. His hand was so warm. "I've never booked any clients north of Toronto. I'd be lost in your Northern Ontario, break a nail and die."

"You're obviously a big city girl."

"Yup, a Broadway babe, that's me. You talk about Manitoulin as if it's magic. Believe me, Will, I know magic. It's what I do, deliver a dream, make people happy," she said.

"I'm still trying to learn that! Last week, I turned fifty. This entire year of sailing is my birthday gift to myself, to explore new islands and horizons. I'm glad to have Bart. He's a great deckhand, smart and strong. When we're on passage between islands, I don't like to single-hand. In rough seas, we handle the boat well. When we anchor in other harbours, Bart and I take turns guarding the boat. We know all about the dope runners and theft on the high seas. Security's paramount. The sea offers plenty of human danger. Here, let me refill your glass," he said, getting up and stepping below to the main salon. The notes of Handel's *Water Music* drifted dreamily up to the cockpit. He climbed up and handed her a freshly filled glass, sinking into the cushion next to her.

"Will, I like this Manitoulin Smoothie. I feel so smooooth…"

From *West Side Story*, she sang, "I feel pretty, oh, so pretty! I feel pretty and witty and gay!" He laughed, charmed, then leaned toward her, looking into her eyes, her face, silently asking for permission. Casually, carefully, he picked up her bare feet and placed them on his lap. She laughed, expecting a kiss. She was a little nervous, but also captivated, to be touched, again, his warm hands caressing her feet.

"Lily, what about you?"

"I told you I love music, singing and playing the piano. I wish I had more time for it. After college, I worked for my dad's art business, made so many travel arrangements for his staff that I went full-time as a travel agent. Sending people to the Caribbean has been my specialty for twenty-five years. I love my work."

"Have you been married? Kids?"

"Neither. I fell in love with work and travel and life in the big city." Lily chuckled. She stopped, took another sip of the Manitoulin Smoothie and went on. "Will, in my twenties, I had all that youth and beauty, which everyone, young, seems to have. I couldn't decide if I wanted to marry the president of a company or become the president! I got engaged once, to a dentist from Boston. A good guy, but I knew I'd always be an adjunct to his life." Lily twitched with the memory. "My sister Dahlia's been lucky with Stuart. He's easy going and loyal," Lily said, wistfully. "Dahlia's smart. She teaches English, directs plays for her school, she knows how to clean, wash, dry, make jam, iron and sew, referee games, and she drives a stick shift."

"Are you jealous of her?"

"I'm crazy about her."

"Don't you do those things too, cook and sew?"

"I hire people! I have coaches for everything," Lily said, laughing. "And I get paid to travel!"

"Sounds like you have an exciting life."

"I'm in a relationship with my cell phones, two computers, my clients and the office." She stretched against the cushions.

"The only lady in my life's right here," he said, patting the wheel with his other hand. She followed his gesture, gazed up, mesmerized by the moonlight shining on the water. "But it doesn't stop me from putting my arm around you."

"You're the captain," she said dreamily, meeting him halfway, nestling into the comfortable crook of his arm. Stars twinkled, a thousand jewels in the sky. Will leaned over, his lips full and rich, and kissed her gently. His other hand enveloped her shoulder comfortably. She tilted her head, closed her eyes, inhaled the fresh scent of his skin, and savoured the touch of his lips. Will's tongue lightly played against hers. It was a give and take so generous that it profoundly triggered her breath and her heart. They lingered gently in the power of each other. Startled by the immensity and fullness of the kiss, both leaned back.

"I wish I didn't have to leave in the morning for Toronto," Will said, not happily. "I have spring projects lined up with my Uncle Mudge on Manitoulin. I've been here most of the year, meeting all kinds of women, traveling the islands. And I meet you the afternoon before I leave."

"I should let you get some sleep." Was she being rejected? "I can get a taxi."

"I don't need sleep. You don't need a taxi."

Under the brilliant Caribbean moon, Lily was next to a man who sent heat through her body that she hadn't felt in years. She'd heard plenty of satisfied clients talk about the benefits a vacation had brought them, under their Caribbean moon. She listened to the water lapping against the sailboat. She felt restless, eager for more. But...didn't she always have to be the careful one? Who was she becoming? Who was this person and what had she done with Lily Gardner?

"Will, would you please walk me up the road?"

Will pulled away reluctantly. "Of course, and you'll be thinking of me all night."

"I'm sure of it," she admitted, looking up at him. But she slid out of his arms, slowly balanced herself up, and stepped carefully out of the cockpit up on the deck and off the boat onto the dock. She slid on her sandals and waited. They walked off the pier, nodded at the sleepy guard, and crossed the empty parking lot. To prolong the night, they slowly ambled up the hill, feeling breezes blowing from the Sir Francis Drake Channel. Will reached for Lily's hand again, affectionate and strong. Could she let herself know more of Will Mudge? In a few hours, he was flying north to the dangerous wilderness of Northern Canada, to wild animals and frozen lakes. Bears. She imagined there were bears. Walking alongside him, she felt petite. Why was she so intrigued with him? This was simply one of those Caribbean fantasies that bubbled up in his presence this lovely evening. Or perhaps, she thought, Manitoulin Sunsets.

The wind suddenly blew cold as they reached the top of the hill. They walked through the main gate at Little Dix, greeting another sleepy guard, and their feet crunched on along the gravel path under fronds of bougainvillea. This man would soon be gone. Not yet.

"How do you get to Manitoulin?"

"Tomorrow I fly to San Juan, then to Toronto, then north to Sudbury. I'll drive an hour west, and turn left at Espanola. Go south to cross the swing bridge onto Manitoulin. Stop for coffee. Drive an hour more along the north shore of the island and arrive at my farmhouse. The town's called Kagawong."

"A long way," she said, standing in front of her door. She put her arms around his waist, resting her forehead against his shirt. He wrapped his arms around her, leaned down and kissed her softly. "Are you sure you don't want me to come in?" She opened the door. He looked past her into the luxuriously appointed room. She stepped back. He caught the message and withdrew from her embrace. He started to walk away, then hesitated and turned back to her.

"Thank you for your company, Lily," he said, and then walked down the path very slowly, the damn gravel crunching under his feet. The overgrown path to the main road concealed his departure.

At the door, Lily made herself stand straight and tall. One of her many New York behavioural coaches had taught her to take a deep breath, stand tall, to feel and show strength and dignity. There were plenty of beautiful women for him to meet in the Caribbean. And she had everything. Lily turned and went inside. A pretty, flushed woman looked back at her from the mirror. She had enjoyed meeting a man from Manitoulin and hearing his stories. And tasting sweet kisses. She smiled.

Pink oleander blossoms in a vase on the dresser gently brushed her cheek as she slowly closed the door to her room. She heard the quiet surf.

CHAPTER FOUR

LILY AND HER LONGTIME BUSINESS PARTNER, Alexis Barnes, sat in the office they shared in their New York City travel agency. Their window boasted a view from the 45th floor—a view they seldom saw. Each had a thrillingly messy desk, three phone lines and two computers. They faced away from each other, always talking at the same time. Lily had told Alexis about meeting Will, but they were so busy in the office, she hadn't spoken more about the stranger. She picked up the next phone call.

"I'm at the Dubai airport; my computer bag's been stolen!" a corporate client shrieked. "Help me!"

Alexis, at her desk, soothed her own distressed client. "Sam, I'm sorry your girlfriend skipped. Don't cancel her ticket home; you need to know more. I'll wait to hear from you."

"Lily, a policeman found my bag. That was close! Bye!" Lily winked at Alexis, both ringmasters on the travel circus today.

"Yes, Mrs. Goldhar," Alexis said, taking the next client. "I booked forty seats to Paris. You have twenty double rooms at The Plaza-Athenee Hotel in October."

"This is Lily, how may I help you?"

"Am I interrupting?"

"Isn't all life an interruption?" She laughed.

"That's debatable." the voice said, amused. "This is Willard Mudge calling from Manitoulin Island." Lily drew a sharp breath, placing her heels squarely on the floor. "That was a nice evening we shared on *Northern Loon*. My uncle and I have finished our projects. I'll get to the point. Perhaps you'd like to come north and visit Manitoulin? It could be another island under your belt! If you fly to Sudbury, I'd pick you up. My island's beautiful in June."

There were three beats of silence. At dinner last week, Lily's three college friends, Brenda, Charlotte, and Treva, had listened over Chinese food to Lily weave the spell of Will Mudge.

"You don't know anyone that he knows," said Brenda, the lawyer.

"Come on," Lily protested. "We were wild when we were younger."

"Not now, we're hanging onto forty," said Charlotte, the doctor. "We must stay safe."

"The man must have a credit rating, history, background we can check," stated Treva, the banker.

"Will, I'm in the midst of booking a huge business conference in San Francisco. Would you consider stopping in New York?"

Another three beats of silence. She almost laughed out of nerves. Will Mudge was simply an idea. "Naw, I hate cities. Maybe another time. We'll be in touch. I enjoyed having you aboard *Northern Loon*. Wildflowers are blooming along the Kagawong River. Too bad you'll miss it."

Nibbling tuna on rye from the deli downstairs, Lily phoned a travel specialist at the Canadian Consulate. Between bites, she flipped the atlas to the Great Lakes. "Look for the island at the top of Lake Huron," Marie directed. "It's there, all right. Manitoulin's the largest freshwater island in the world. Its eighty miles long and thirty miles wide, covering 1,068 square miles. It has one hundred and eight lakes; Kagawong's among the largest. The island is mainly limestone. It's said Manitoulin's made up of one-third good land, one third rock and one third water. Tourism's marvelous in the summer. Our family has a cottage on Silver Lake."

"Stop already with the travel brochure, Marie," Lily said. "From New York how would I fly there? Toronto to where?"

"You connect in Toronto and fly to Sudbury. A Northern mining town. Astronauts practiced in Sudbury. They thought the landscape was like the surface of the moon."

"So, is Manitoulin Island really magical?"

"The island is dreamy, romantic. Crossing the swing bridge is mystical every time." Marie's voice was coaxing.

"Marie, stop with the sell," Lily protested. "I know magic. I make magic!"

"Lily, you haven't been there. Or you can tell your clients to drive north from Toronto to Tobermory. Then they take a ferry called the *Chi-Cheemaun*. It crosses Georgian Bay and lands on the south shore of Manitoulin. My husband and I cross this way. We eat leisurely dinners by sunset, and we have to swim it off. We watch deer drink at the lake."

"I can't stand this fairy tale," Lily said.

Marie laughed. "Think about winding country roads, wide green pasture land, leaves shimmering in the sunlight. If you cross the old swing bridge to Manitoulin, you call me."

"Sure, sure," Lily said.

❧

Lily's pal Pamela at Little Dix knew everyone and every thing on Virgin Gorda. The Yacht Harbour, a multi-million dollar operation, had five long piers housing private sailboats and motor yachts with ample space for charters. The shopping centre boasted three restaurants, a bakery, a laundry, music store, dive shop and the main office of the harbour master. Sprinkled among the constituency of Virgin Gorda were the best confidence men in the business. Drug dealers, subtle with their nighttime drops from down islands into the string of uninhabited small islands, seemed to fit seamlessly into the economy. They didn't fool anyone for a second and were well known to undercover police.

"Pam, would you check out the owner of *Northern Loon*? Slip 48 when I was there."

A day later, Pamela told her, "M'dear, Captain Mudge pays his bills on time. Nice Canadian man, reserved. This'll cost you five bookings."

The San Francisco business conference took Lily's total attention. She'd hoped that if Will took the trouble to phone, perhaps he might reconsider coming to Manhattan. It wasn't going to happen, she knew. A week later, the phone rang.

"Will Mudge here, Lily. I hate your city. I will be heading south and I don't mind booking a flight to New York for a few days. Would that be all right with you and would you arrange a hotel in the neighbourhood? Next week?"

"You want to shop the boat stores," she teased.

"That's not the only reason I'll be taking on the dangers of New York. I want to hear you sing and play the piano," he said. "Now, nothing fancy!"

Surprised, delighted, Lily cleaned her windows and the small kitchen she never used. She bought pink lace underwear at Lord & Taylor. She would practice being soft, girlie and sexy. She would take him on the Circle Line boat cruise around Manhattan Island. She made a list of the boat supply stores. A walk through Central Park would drive a Canadian sailor crazy, a guy with forty flowered acres of his own down by a river and cows grazing on the back forty. Good thing the fine restaurants sold take-out cuisine that she could buy in advance and simply take out of her refrigerator.

Chauffeur Denny Jones, whom Lily hired frequently for her corporate clients, offered to drive her in his black stretch limousine to Newark Airport. "I'm grateful for your business, Lily, so this ride is on me and I'll have the ice bucket full."

Lily waited impatiently for passengers to disembark from Air Canada Flight 762. Will, looking rumpled and wearing that same brown plaid shirt, awkwardly greeted her at baggage claim.

"Lily, you look different."

"So do you," she said. They waited for his bags to come around on the carousel. Will piled them on a cart and followed her through the exit to the passenger loading zone. A black stretch limo purred to a stop in front of them. Denny, in his black hat and black suit, jumped out and put his hands on Will's duffel bags.

"Hey, what do you think you're you doing?"

"Mr. Mudge, I'm driving you and Miss Gardner to the city." Denny tipped his cap. Will peered, eyes sneaky with suspicion. "Are you are putting on a New York show for me?"

"I am!" Lily said, smiling, as Denny strained to lift the bags, and could not. Will picked them up them easily and slid them carefully into the trunk. They got into the limo to the sound of Johnny Mathis crooning "Chances Are," the sound mixing with the moneyed scent of new leather. "Will, would you like a rum and coke?"

"That seems like an excellent way to enter Manhattan," he said, settling into the deep leather cushions.

"Denny drives all my business clients," she said, opening the ice chest, clinking in three cubes. She poured Will a drink, pinky up, and handed it to him. He took it and belted it down.

"Pour me another, would you?" he asked, as Denny expertly navigated the New Jersey Turnpike. She understood. She too felt shy, a world away from Virgin Gorda. A few days with Will, but nothing could come of this. Enjoy the now of it. In the mirror, Denny winked at her.

She poured a generous second glass and handed it to him.

"To what we love the most," Will toasted, raising his glass and sipping slowly. Loosened by the comfort of the limo and two rums, he told her about his farmhouse in Kagawong that always needed some sort of repair, about his Uncle Mudge and Aunt Molly, the projects with Uncle Mudge and the boat tools he hoped to find in New York. "What I dislike about the city? Too much consumption, too much garbage," he said. She simply nodded. No Central Park for him.

Cold chicken salad, fresh steamed asparagus, crunchy French bread and iced tea, was lunch delivered up from Sarge's Delicatessen. She set it on the table. "After lunch, I'm taking you on the Circle Line boat around Manhattan to see New York Harbour, the East River and the Hudson. And I made a reservation for you at the hotel next door."

"Good," Will said. "I'm kind of surprised to find myself and your apartment so comfortable. Uncle Mudge told me I needed to be open to new experiences. He said I needed adventure and not the sailing kind."

"To Uncle Mudge," she toasted with her iced tea.

The June weather in New York City provided clear skies and a smooth ride upon the Hudson and around to the East River. After dusk, the Statue of Liberty's torch beamed across the Hudson River.

Will and Lily sat at the stern of the sightseeing boat, watching a glorious pink sunset behind the Statue of Liberty. As the night sky darkened, the lights of New York City shone brightly. They talked easily, of inconsequential things, and before they knew it, the boat docked. Somewhere between ship and shore, Lily knew she was in love.

They made their way east toward 10th Avenue. The smells of oil and burnt metal wafted out of a dozen automotive chop shops. Sharp river breezes channeled off the cliffs of the New Jersey Palisades. The drone of the heavy traffic up and down the Avenues was punctured by catcalls. Abrupt blasts of car horns serenaded the scantily-clad women who strolled down the sidewalks. Some leaned provocatively against darkened doorways. Passing them, the brisk pace of their stride did not abate until they reached the golden lights of the Landmark Tavern.

Lily and Will were ushered past the dark wood of an age-polished bar and the antique mirror that rose to meet a tin ceiling sculpted in the style of another century. They were given a cozy booth, and two glasses of merlot materialized.

"New York harbour's bigger than I realized, tankers anchored here, cruise ships docked at the piers, and room for sailboats to tack," Will said. "This was a fine afternoon."

"I appreciate seeing the harbour through your eyes, Will."

"You've the brownest eyes, Lily," said Will, reaching for her. Lily held his hand for a moment, feeling his strength and tenderness. Wanting more for herself, she took her hand away, stood up and excused herself. She was back in three minutes.

"I cancelled your hotel reservation," she said, sitting back down.

"I was hoping you would." Their dinners arrived, breaking the moment. The waiter placed freshly caught Maine scallops sautéed over penne before them.

"So far New York City and the harbour's not too bad," he said. "I don't care for Toronto either, although I made my money there. Sudbury's too damn busy."

"Not too bad? You Canadians say that all the time."

"We don't want to startle anything," he said. "I just mosey along."

"But you have a life full of adventure and travel, Will. You said you live in the bush, track deer, sail around Manitoulin, Lake Huron and the Caribbean."

"My money's invested well. And my daughter Laura married last year, so I'm pleased. My work is done," he said. "Though with kids, you never know…"

"I made a list of the boat provisioning stores for you," she said. It was getting late.

Will hailed a taxi. In the back seat, his arm curled around her shoulders. Silent, they were driven through Broadway, with its billions of dollars of bright lights, signs and throngs of people. "Too many people, too much for me," he said. "I'm a simple backwoods Canadian guy."

"Oh sure," she said, and laughed. "Ha!"

Returning to the Victorian brownstone, Lily fumbled in her purse for keys while Will glanced protectively up and down the street. They stood in the small wheezy elevator. Will's eyes locked on the certificate of inspection. The superintendent had polished the old brass fittings, cherished Victorian relics of the past. Out of the elevator, Lily felt Will's presence behind her as she unlocked her front door. She had one key to open the main door downstairs and two keys at her door. This was the locked-up city. Yet, she knew her seduction as the sweet, sultry fragrance of pink stargazer lilies that had opened in the afternoon greeted them as the door swung back. Will's bags were still in the living room.

"Would you like cognac?" she asked, heading for the small bar.

"Are these family heirlooms?" Will asked, browsing the living room. He picked up an African wood sculpture. "Cognac's great. What's the story?"

"Aunt Bea, she's the rhubarb queen," Lily said, pouring cognac into a glass. "I arranged her trip to Africa, and then had to go with her, and helped her write a book."

"You brought back an ebony three-headed woman with a big belly?"

"We gathered 250 recipes from ten African countries." A breeze filtered through the living room from the open window. She handed him a copy of the book.

"So you cook?"

"I write about cooking."

Will glanced at it. "Your name's not on the book."

"She didn't like to share."

"Neither do I." Will put the book down, walked to Lily and lowered his face to hers. She raised hers for a lingering kiss.

"Sit awhile, I'm feeling shy." He sat down. After a few moments, neither was interested in sitting as he kissed her again. And again. He got up, took her hand, and she led him to her bedroom.

A Manhattan summer breeze, agreeably soft through the open window, moved through the room over the queen-sized bed. Will sat on the end of the bed with Lily and slowly unbuttoned her blouse. He leaned over and kissed her neck tenderly. She closed her eyes, curled into him, and together, they leaned back. She reached for the buttons of his shirt. He helped, taking it off and dropping it on the floor. His wide chest intoxicated her with his scent. He was ready for her. She kissed his shoulder. He was hers tonight. He traced the outline of Lily's breasts with his hand, and moved across her body, ever so slowly. As if remembering how.

She could hardly stand it. He seemed sure of himself, touching her slowly as if she was the first woman of his life. Her excitement rose as she caught her breath, and then sighed in pleasure with him. Will explored her neck and her breasts with his tongue.

"You're beautiful."

"So are you." His touch was gentle, as intimacy began to transform them. The thought crossed her mind that she always built in romance for her clients, couldn't find it for herself, and now here was Will, with a will to please her. This wasn't about any island, hot or cold, at all. She sighed, wet with wanting him. Her hand slid down his belly and he was hard, yes, strong, round and beautiful to her touch.

"It's been awhile," she confessed softly.

"For me, too," he whispered. The dance of their love-making began, gently, little by little. By then she was so eager, pulled by his smell, his taste, besotted by the way he looked at her and held her. Lily helped Will put on a condom, in unspoken agreement. He kissed her neck, her breasts again, making her wait and want. When they both felt ready, he fully entered her. Their movement together rocked and swelled, sweet heaven, as Lily breathed in Will, kissing his mouth, feeling wet and strong, rising with him, rolling with him, and Will reaching bliss inside her. At the same moment, both stopped, holding back. No words were needed. Taking it slower, building to ecstasy, until she couldn't hold back. Waves exploded through her body, as he joined her, powerful within her.

They stayed entwined, their senses heightened, peaceful, and Lily felt waves of contentment. Forgotten, remembered. For twenty minutes they lay together, silently, flooded in each other's aura, basking in a glow of well-being.

When Will reluctantly got up to go to the bathroom, Lily jumped up and ran to the kitchen. She opened the refrigerator and took out a chilled bottle of Dom Perignon and brought two glasses. "This is to celebrate your arrival."

"Our arrival!" Will got into bed, smiling. "This has been a big day and I'm jeezley tired," he said, wiggling the wire off the cork, which hit the ceiling and bounced onto the bed. She laughed, holding the two fluted glasses. He poured, and they toasted each other.

"To courage, braving New York City," she said. "You can sail the seas, live in the backwoods of Ontario, and you made it here!" She was giddy.

"To what we love the most," he said. The chilled bubbles of champagne danced in her mouth. His presence not only filled her bed, but her apartment.

The next day, Will and Lily walked around the South Street Seaport and took a sail on a chartered schooner around the harbour. Lovely June winds blowing, sails were up within minutes, and Will asked to take the helm, while the captain told jokes. Other tourists sat enjoying a sail around the Statue of Liberty. Will was so competent, ably steering the boat through busy harbour traffic, that the captain offered him a job.

"No thanks," said Will.

On the third morning, Lily asked, "Do you like *anything* about New York?"

"Well, traffic's lousy; people move too fast, it's noisy. I like waking up with you and watching the sun shine across the buildings. Your apartment's so old, your floors creak. And I'm aghast at your kitchen," he said, gazing at its dinky four by six feet space.

"But it has a window. That's everything in New York," she said.

"You've never used your stove," he challenged.

"That's right. Maybe you'll teach me?"

One afternoon he found his way to Macy's and came back with new pots. "Lily, you're spoiled, always out to dinner, ordering up!"

"Thirty restaurants thrive in the neighborhood, open twenty-four hours. They all deliver," Lily explained. "I choose from major food groups, Chinese, Italian, Mexican or Indian."

"We didn't have fast food when I grew up," he said. "All our food was slow."

"Where did you eat?"

"A place called home."

Will's reserved Canadian manners made getting around New York City ridiculous. Where was his direction finder? One morning, she watched him from a block away as he stood on the corner, staring at the map. A person stopped to help. She saw him say, "No thanks," and he declined three other people. She wondered if he'd ask a New York policeman for directions. She had gathered that he had a stubborn, masculine streak. If he could read a nautical chart, by golly, he could surely wander busy streets by himself, seeking out more boating tools for his heavy tool box.

"I found every boat store on your list," he said proudly, carrying in boat tools and stacking them in her living room. "Philosopher Louis Pasteur said, 'Chance favours the prepared mind.' Very important to have the right tool," he murmured, steering her to the bedroom.

Will's four-day visit turned into six. On the phone with the Virgin Gorda Yacht Harbour, he left a message for Bart: "Captain Mudge is detained in New York City."

Bart phoned back. "Detained with monkey business, boss?"

"A happy captain means a happy boat," Will told him.

On the last morning, Will hailed a taxi at the corner of her street. He loaded his heavy duffel bags into the trunk. He held her for a moment, the morning sunny and bright. She fought a looming sense of bleak loneliness.

"Lily, it's been wonderful. Thank you for everything. It's clear to me you belong here managing things. This city will never be part of me. If we see each other again, it'll be places other than here. I'm always looking over my shoulder. At home, I see fields, cows, deer and the bay. On the boat, I hear wind and water."

She nodded dumbly, helpless against her newfound passion for him, his full-bodied manhood and tender loving that had filled her body and her home for days. Or was it simply fabulous sex? Oh, straighten up, Lily.

"I like you, Lily, a lot, but I'll never be back to your city. I'll be in touch."

When a man said he'd be in touch, forget it, she knew from her years of dating. He leaned over, kissed her cheek, got into his taxi, and looked straight ahead as the taxi turned the corner. She drew a deep breath, drew back her shoulders, stood tall and whispered, "Boobs up!" She was Lily Gardner, the tough, strong travel agent.

CHAPTER FIVE

AT THE NEW YORK PUBLIC LIBRARY, Lily took out *Exploring Manitoulin*, by Shelley J. Pearen, whose family had lived on the island since 1864. Manitoulin was not gentrified like Nantucket or Martha's Vineyard off the East Coast. Manitoulin, isolated in winter, was busy with campers, cottagers and sailors in summer. The bucolic island was settled by the English, and had Aboriginal reserves. It boasted vegetable farms, and farmers raising cattle, sheep and chickens. The waters provided perch and whitefish. She read about the Ojibwe, the Odawa and the Pottawatomie tribes as aboriginal settlers on Manitoulin. Will had spoken his piece. She could fly north to Manitoulin any time by herself.

Meanwhile, she sent her clients to the Caribbean and Europe, while Alexis arranged business travel for large corporations. Each of them specialized; together, they were a well-oiled machine.

"Lily, you're staring at the walls again," Alexis said, as Lily pulled her gaze away from the BVI poster of a sailboat in a cove. "We think we get men all figured out? We never do! Forget this guy!"

"I don't like unfinished."

"Maybe it hasn't started? Where's it written any of us has the right to be comfortable? Don't confuse the pursuit of happiness with the promise of happiness," Alexis said.

"You're pontificating again."

"It's easy, girlfriend, when it isn't me." Alexis was sympathetic.

Three weeks passed without a word. Lily couldn't help that she wandered into Goldberg's Marine Store on Fifth and 37th Street to look at books about sailing in the Caribbean, heavy foul weather gear, compasses, and ships' clocks. She skimmed through the classic Chapman's textbook on sailing instruction and bought it. She wondered if anyone else, pretty or otherwise, had wandered aboard *Northern Loon.* Will said he was a simple Northern Ontario backwoods country boy. Believe him. She remembered resting against him in bed, and she tucked away the tourist photograph of them together on the Circle Line boat, with the Statue of Liberty in the background. They were too opposite. Onward. He was another pearl in her necklace of very interesting men.

A week later, the phone rang at Lily's office. "Bart says I've been cranky since being in New York. If I don't smarten up, he'll fire me! Think you can take to ocean life for two weeks?"

"Two weeks aboard? What if I'm lousy and seasick?"

"I'll throw you overboard, save you and put you back on a plane. To understand sailing, you've got to sail and live aboard *Northern Loon.* And Lily, captain's orders: no inspecting hotels, only me!"

With romantic conspiracy, Alexis and Lily juggled their work schedules. Alexis, five years older than Lily and unhappily single, believed in snatching every romantic opportunity. "Of course go, for two weeks," Alexis instructed. "But check in or I'll worry that he did throw you overboard."

Sitting at JFK airport, Lily felt set in her new Ralph Lauren navy blue double-breasted blazer, her white blouse and short, pleated red skirt. She catalogued the items in her duffel: Dramamine, three new bathing suits, a flimsy nightgown, sunscreen, shorts and tops that matched and five pairs of sandals. She flew into San Juan and transferred to the local feeder to Virgin Gorda. The plane circled over the rock-speckled, green hills of The Baths. She fidgeted as the pilot banked on the final approach to the gravel runway, before swooping up again in a familiar move. A man ran out of the terminal to chase the goats off the runway. The pilot came around again, landed and taxied to the tiny sun-bleached stone building.

Slouched against a pole, Will waited, wearing a white shirt, blue shorts and those scuffed docksiders. She waved at him, but first had to register with BVI Customs and Immigration. Cleared, she eagerly walked toward Will. He doubled over with laughter. "Too fancy, Lily, you don't belong on my boat." He shook his head. "This wasn't a good idea. I better drop you at Little Dix with the other beautiful people."

"You have an elegant boat," she said, feeling deflated after her glamour only moments before. But, he *had* said "beautiful." She was pathetic.

"You're out of place in my life style." He eyed her duffel bag with a wry grin.

"I promise I brought crummy clothes." She reached up. "You haven't kissed me hello."

"I'm not into public display."

He looked one way and she the other, and they did not speak in the taxi that took them to the harbour. When they reached

Northern Loon, Bart greeted her effusively, but cast a dubious eye upon her finery.

"I'll get ice cubes from the chandlery," said Will. "Unpack in the aft cabin. I emptied the top drawer for you."

Bart took her duffel down the steps to the back cabin. "I'm pleased to see you again, Lily. If you need anything aboard, don't hesitate to ask. Boss wants you to have flippers, snorkel and mask. Size seven? Boss says if you don't relax, I'm authorized to put Dramamine in your drink. Rum and coke and a quiet anchorage will settle you right down."

"Thanks, Bart." She pulled clothes out of the duffel.

"We've got a storage locker in the yard. You'd be surprised what you can leave ashore."

But what if she needed to escape, get off at another island? She folded up the offending blazer, T-shirts with too much glitz, and two pairs of sandals, and put them into the duffel. She silently laughed at her first lesson of the sea: wear crummy clothes. She tucked her more casual tanks, shorts and swimsuits into the drawer, while Bart took the rest of her life off the boat to storage. She glanced at the shelf above the bed. A steely black handgun lay near Will's books and reading light. Her self-assurance evaporated. She'd be alone at sea, with two men and a gun.

"You're looking at a Glock 9 millimetre," said Will, standing silently behind her.

"I got rid of the fancy clothes. Still going to use that?"

"Only if you don't do what your captain tells you. It's cocktail hour. Get settled, put on your shorts, a crummy shirt and come above."

"Crummy it is," she said. In the cockpit with Will and Bart, Lily drank delicious Manitoulin Smoothies, and they ate perfectly grilled snapper. The sun set red behind the Tortola hills. Lily gazed

longingly at Will through three Manitoulin Smoothies, fire growing within her.

"Bart, go have drinks at the Bath & Turtle. Take my credit card."

Bart couldn't get off the boat fast enough. Will brought the
glasses down to the galley and left them. He led her to the aft cabin.
Northern Loon gently rocked beneath them.

🪶

"Wake up, Lily; it's your first day in paradise. We aim to pam-
per you," Will said, standing over her. Her eyes opened, and she
smiled, stretched and sat up, grinning. She took the cup of coffee
in a red mug on a small polished sterling silver tray. The sun filtered
through the screened porthole. Lily looked out. "Hey, we're not at
the dock."

"We motored to Norman Island. You were dead to the world."

"Looks like the BVI poster at my desk."

She heard bleating. "Sheep?"

"No, the island has wild goats on the hill, great fish and turtles
below."

"Will, I studied *Northern Loon*. She's designed by Germaine
Freres, a famous naval architect. She's overall 50 feet in length."

"Lily, this is a vacation, not a test," Will said, severely, but his eyes
twinkled. "I'm taking you to a tiny island that's almost not on the charts.
No hotel, no goats, great snorkeling. It's called Fallen Jerusalem, the
one I told you about when we first met. The rocks are flat and shine in
the sun. They resemble the actual roofs in Jerusalem."

"You're my destination!" she said, joyfully, handing Will her
empty cup, and bounding off the bed before he could grab her naked behind. She slipped into the aft head, stood at the marble sink
counter, brushed her teeth, and looked in the mirror at the relaxed
glow on her face. She put on her red bathing suit, anointed herself
with sunscreen, went on deck and was handed into the dinghy.

They skimmed over pale blue waters with a full picnic basket, towels and snorkel equipment. Reaching the tiny island of Fallen Jerusalem, Will cut the motor and threw out the anchor. The dingy bobbed gently on the waves, as he helped her adjust her new mask. "I've snorkeled before, Will. I'm comfortable in the water." She put on her fins and slipped over the side into the warm clear water. As teenagers, she and Dahlia had swum across Lake Winnipesaukee at Camp Glory Days in New Hampshire. It had been glory nights for the counselors, but Lily and Dahlia had been too young to know that. She floated, gently scissor-kicking her legs, gazing at the bright sand on the ocean floor.

"Lily, take off your suit. Swim naked," Will said, already in the water. He immediately threw his suit into the boat. Like a seal, he grinned, and dove effortlessly to the bottom of the cove. She watched him move gracefully, her attention focused. This sight would be hers for two weeks. She must pay attention to breathing. He surfaced, holding a pink conch shell. "It's for you," and he put it up into the dinghy.

She wiggled out of her bathing suit, tossed it into the dinghy, allowing the warm Caribbean water to caress her skin. Like the touch of silk, the water passed gently over her breasts, around her nipples and between her thighs. She liked the fit and feel of the mask tight around her head, and the breathing tube, providing her power to concentrate on watching bright purple sea fans that beckoned towards a bank of red brain coral. Had the Caribbean Sea always been this colourful? Why had she been so fevered inspecting hotels, and not snorkeling more, drinking more smoothies? Lily's eyes followed a glittering school of small yellow fish below. Will swam naked next to her, pointing toward a large turtle hovering nearby. It was so close; she wanted to laugh, not wanting the turtle's mouth getting too close to Will.

Will popped his head up. "Take three deep breaths. Dive and see what you can pick up on the bottom." She drew in three times to inflate her lungs, and aimed for the shallow sandy bottom, which glistened with sunlight. She saw a sand dollar, clutched her treasure, rose to the surface, and handed it to Will.

"You show promise," he said. They swam together, slowly kicking, over abundant sea life, until he glanced at his watch. He signaled their return to the dinghy.

"You've always got to be smart with the ocean, the currents and tropical sun. We need to drink water, have lunch and rest. Can't let our picnic lunch go to waste," Will said, hoisting his naked well-arranged poundage up and over into the dinghy. Lily inspected the rope lines around the side of the boat, wondering how she was going to get her naked self up into the dingy. At the third attempt, she flopped in, backside and legs askew, relieved Will's attention was devoted to unwrapping turkey sandwiches. "I am a fish out of water," she said.

"Cover up against the sun, Lily. Use more sunscreen. Here's iced green tea, pickles, coleslaw, napkins and toothpicks. Bart thinks of everything."

They sat, towels around them, having lunch.

"Will, this is my new definition of heaven." She bit into the turkey sandwich deeply, tomatoes, lettuce and mayonnaise dripping onto her towel. She sipped iced tea and gazed at the shining rocks on Fallen Jerusalem.

When they returned to *Northern Loon,* Lily learned how to take a fast freshwater shower. Water on, get wet. Water off. Soap up as far as possible, down as far as possible. Then wash possible. Rinse fast.

On deck, Bart made smoothies for them and went to check if there was mail in the Chandlery. He was back too soon. No lingering at the pub. "Boss, urgent message. Laura's flying in. Bad fight with Tim."

"I better call; maybe I can defray any damage." Will got off the boat and she watched him walk hurriedly off the dock to the Chandlery. On this boat, for two different reasons, these were the two lovely men who had picked her. She looked out at other boats in the marina. Lily sighed; just one night and day with Will, and here was another woman taking his attention.

"Boss likes you. Me, too, Lily," Bart said. "I want him to be fulfilled. It means getting laid and being loved."

"You don't mince words."

"Boss is fifty, funny and fit for an old guy. I admit I picked you off the dock."

"You're unquestionably loyal," she laughed. "And I thank you."

"Maybe he can keep his daughter in Vancouver."

Gone twenty minutes, Will stepped back into the cockpit, shrugging unhappily. "Both Laura and Tim have high-powered jobs. He's on his way to Beijing. Can't or won't take her. They never have time for each other. She's so angry. And she's flying here tomorrow."

"Shall I disappear to Little Dix?" Lily asked, the ever-accommodating travel agent.

"Bart will keep her busy. We'll sail to Anegada and have lobster," said Will, unwrapping steaks he had picked up in Tortola.

That evening, Will and Lily lay comfortably entwined in the cockpit, looking up at the stars. Bart disappeared again. "I never mind if Bart stays out all night," Will said. "Even when he sleeps in the fore cabin, the boat shakes with his snoring; you can't imagine the energy..."

The weather was clear from Vancouver to San Juan to Virgin Gorda the next day, allowing Laura's on-time arrival. By dusk, a tall, disheveled young woman in her late twenties walked along Dock B, followed by a taxi driver with her duffel. A large pocketbook hung askew over her shoulder, and she held a small, half-empty bottle of Crown Royal, the top off. Will hurriedly got off the boat to greet his daughter.

"You're here! Glad to see you, honey. Come aboard."

"Bottle top's gone, Daddy, help me finish it. I'm beat. Maybe I'll spend a month here!"

Will hugged his exhausted daughter, and helped her aboard. He took her bags. "Laura, this is my guest from New York, Lily Gardner." No hand was offered. "You need a cleanup, dinner and sleep, Laura. You've got the fore cabin," said Will.

Lily spoke up. "Nice to meet you, Laura. You need time to get settled. Will, I'm going to visit Pamela. Her house is nearby." This time, fast, Lily jumped off the boat, knowing Pamela always opened her door to her.

It was past ten when Lily returned to the boat. *Northern Loon* was shaking with the thunder that was Bart, snoring in the quarter berth. Small snores also came from the fore cabin. She found Will in bed, reading, plugs in his ears.

He looked up. "I put a clothespin on Bart's nose last week. It didn't help. And now Laura… You'll need ear plugs," he said, handing her a pair. She took them, then wiggled out of her shirt and shorts, took off her underwear and snuggled in, next to him. A breeze fluttered through the open air chute. He closed his book, snapped off the reading light, and held her.

Lily saw that it was simple. Laura found refuge with her father. Will was distracted with too much on his plate. Loving his daughter, unhappy that she was unhappy. So while Will took Laura snorkeling or hiking, Lily stole away one afternoon after another to have lunch with Pamela or other friends in town. One afternoon, she and Bart hiked up Gorda Peak. Another day, they walked to the Copper Mine. She developed great respect for Bart.

"Will's a quiet, complicated man, who keeps his secrets. It's hard to get to know him. Stay the course, Lily," Bart told her after three beers.

One afternoon, over drinks, Lily was able to chat with Laura about their respective careers, Laura's in human resources, as a manager in Vancouver. But the subject changed to snorkeling, which was fine with Lily, who got too wound up when talking about her career.

"Daddy, sail me to Anegada. We must have lobster!" It was an order. Will smiled and saluted to his daughter. Under full sail, *Northern Loon* enjoyed the rollicking waves on the approach north to Anegada as the wind puffed intermittently against the sails. Lily sat in the cockpit, balancing herself as the boat heeled over. Will sat at the wheel, his hair flying, his hands barely moving as the wind shifted. "I might sail *Northern Loon* up this summer, but she's easier to store here. Someone get me coffee?"

Lily took his empty mug and climbed down into the galley.

"I'll take care of Daddy," Laura said, standing below in the confined space. She grabbed the mug. The boat heeled over sharply in a gust. Lily fell back against the steps.

"This is a one-butt galley, Lily," Laura said. She filled the cup and bounded up the companionway, handing the half-filled cup to her father.

Lily slowly climbed back up, retreating to a corner where the dodger shielded her against the wind. Her morning cereal struggled in her stomach. Was she queasy, with the boat heeled over so far, or was it Laura? Where the hell was the Dramamine?

"Lily, would you like some iced tea," Bart asked. "That always settles you!"

She said no, held on topside, and threw up all over the deck.

"Not that way, Lily!" Will pointed in the other direction. "Leeward, leeward!"

Laura gave her a brief glance, and a small smile.

"Sit back, Lily," Will consoled her. "The waves will take it away. Rinse your mouth with some iced tea."

That afternoon, *Northern Loon* anchored in the bight at Setting Point on the south side of Anegada, along with other sailboats and mega-yachts from all over the world. Anegada Reef Hotel offered their celebrated grilled rock lobsters and dancing to reggae at the bar on the sandy beach. Will and Lily got in the dinghy and tied up at the dock.

"Something going on between you and Laura?" he asked Lily.

"She knows the boat," Lily said.

"I've reserved a room for us tonight. The youngsters can sit all night on the wooden stools at the bar, drink and meet everyone."

At dusk, the four stood at the Anegada beach bar. Bart loved every minute: "I know some of these sailors. Boy, do they tell tall stories and lies!"

"Bart, you just want to get lucky, back at somebody else's boat, eh?" Laura teased.

"Laura, you are so Canadian, and yes," Bart grinned, "if you weren't married, just one year younger and I was one year older…"

"You kids stop that," Will said. "Lily and I are checking in to the hotel. Order us lobster tails and white wine. See you in two hours."

"Can't I come take a shower, Daddy?"

"On the boat, Laura. Boat's yours."

At the bar, Japanese and Spanish travelers chatted with South Americans and French. Different accents and languages drifted through the air, lifting her spirits. Lily felt much better in the hotel room, after a shower. They'd kissed and cuddled on the bed but forced themselves to return to Laura and Bart on time for dinner under the dark starry skies. Large, succulent white meat rock lobster tails braised over open fire pits, with rice, vegetables, and breadfruit, were served, along with two bottles of white wine. After dinner, Laura struck up conversation with newfound friends on charter. Bart hailed his buddies, other working crew, and laughter erupted in the warm Caribbean night.

With a whispered finger to his lips, Will led Lily back along the path to their room. He locked the door behind them. Near the queen-sized bed, each stripped. Will ran the tub, and sank into fresh hot water. "Get in with me," he invited. She did, his thighs enveloping hers as they faced each other. "Soaking's one of my delights in life. Do my best thinking here," Will said. At the side of the bathtub, he brought forth a bottle of champagne that had been hidden in the cooler under the desk. "I stole glasses from the bar." He popped the cork and poured. "Congratulations, you've made it through ten days with Laura, and you only threw up once. You've showed Canadian restraint!"

Will roused Lily early the next morning to walk with him. The island of Anegada was balm for the soul, miles of white, sugar-spun beaches, and gentle surf in which to refresh any body. "These sounds of the wind, little birds that skitter on the beach and the whispering surf assure me we're on Mrs. God's beach," Lily said.

"With enough sleep, you wax eloquent," he said. "At the farm and on the boat, I'm used to spiritual silence." Was that a hint, she wondered as she picked up shells and bits of coral, stowing them in her shorts' pocket. The point of this beach was surrender to natural beauty, simply listening, strolling on the sand. She watched a sailboat disappear over the horizon. How many years had she spent inspecting beaches on other islands in the Caribbean, learning beaches? Today she was sharing paradise with Will as they walked to the point, where the surf met from the west and south, this seemingly endless, untouched beach.

Back on the boat, Lily found herself admiring Laura's sense of humour. Laura described more of her work in human resources for a large mining company, and she didn't whine about her husband. Laura had graduated from Laurentian University and found the world of mining, its personalities fascinating, its opportunities rewarding. She was sharing more enthusiasm with Lily. They seemed to sigh in some sort of relief and understanding that they had similar talents.

The next day on Anegada, Will excused himself from Lily to take Laura bone fishing in the flats with their guide George. Lily watched as the boat receded along the shore line. She went to the shop to browse. Hubert at the front desk of the hotel rushed to find Lily: "Someone's been phoning frantically for Will's daughter. They'll call back in two hours."

When George's boat returned, she, Laura and Will waited anxiously at the hotel, fiddling through worn paperbacks in the library. The sound of Laura sniffling and blowing her nose was louder than the surf. The office phone rang. Laura ran in.

"Tim?" She slumped into a chair, her head down, clinging to the receiver.

"I can't stand the suspense, boss, I need a beer!" Bart went to the open-air honour bar and opened beer for Will and himself. Telephone talk from Vancouver to Anegada seemed endless. Will drank a second beer, while Lily sat beside him. Was it stupid fighting talk, divorce talk or make up talk?

Finally, Laura stepped from the office, her cloak of loneliness and anger gone. "Daddy, I'm going to Beijing!" Hugging him, she spilled her father's beer. Bart dutifully wiped it up

"Marriage in a state of reconciliation," Will sighed. "We'll sail you to Tortola tomorrow."

"Sail me now!" Laura grabbed his bottle of beer, chugged what was left, and set the empty on the bar.

"No wind, too hot to sail. I had two beers. Anchorages in Trellis Bay will all be taken."

"I want to leave now, Daddy."

"Lily, will you charter a plane for Laura?" said Will. "Take my credit card."

Hubert stood at the door to the office. "She missed the last flight for today, Lily!"

"We've two hours of daylight, Daddy," Laura said. "You know how to sail in the dark! I want to get home to Tim!"

They were lucky to find the last available mooring in Trellis Bay before dusk. At the Tortola airport, due to Lily's travel agency affiliations, she was able to upgrade Laura to first class on her flight from San Juan to Vancouver. "Thanks, Lily. I was a mess. You're okay, " Laura whispered to Lily at the desk. "Please be careful with my father, I don't want him hurt." Her flight was called. Without looking back at Lily, she turned, hurrying to the Gate.

Lily and Will walked back to Trellis Bay. "Lily," Will said, "I'm just going to lie down for a quick nap in the back cabin. I need to restore my equilibrium."

"Of course," Lily said. Bart took them to the boat.

"You still have time with the boss," Bart told her, and took the dinghy back to the dock to find his mates. She smiled, put her feet up in the cockpit and read, Laura's presence slowly evaporating. Lily thought about Bart, a perfect sidekick. Lily liked watching him watch his boss, the manly men who shared the 50-foot ketch. She would have another exuberant night with Will.

With a day left of her trip, they sailed back to Virgin Gorda, to their slip at the harbour. "So captain," Lily asked. "Does this novice sailor pass muster?"

Will put down his coffee mug. "You didn't know that Bart kept putting Dramamine in your iced tea. You were green and wouldn't admit it. You wouldn't ask, so we helped. You supported Laura. You make me laugh, Lily. You're able and humble about getting people out of their travel troubles."

"Did I pass?"

"You're on the crew list."

Bart sat in the bow of *Northern Loon* watching a nattily dressed fellow attempt to nudge his rental sailboat into a berth. The boat bounced noisily off the dock three times before the novice pilot finally succeeded.

"Charterers," Bart said, winking at Lily, who nodded in sage agreement. Will lifted her duffel into the dinghy. She took a last look at *Northern Loon*, the boat that would sail him wherever and whenever he wanted to go.

Chapter Six

"I'm putting the boat up here in Virgin Gorda," Will told her when he phoned her office two long weeks later. "I can't bear to miss summer on Manitoulin. I'll fly north, no stops in New York. Maybe you can come to see the farmhouse and walk along the river with me. One duffel."

"I'll check my schedule and get back to you," Lily said. Who was she kidding?

"You're flying up to sheep and cow country!" Sartorius George, a client, friend and clothing designer, couldn't believe what Lily was telling him as she booked his flight to Paris. "I'll have my seamstress sew you calico overalls for faux-country charm, my *Walking-in-the pasture* clothes for a New York hot-house flower."

"You're such a snob!"

"I'm so talented! You'll love the overalls."

"Why are you my favourite client, Sarty? You're impossible!"

Lily loved the overalls, and the shirt, and the boots, and the jacket. She flew to Toronto and changed to a small commuter plane headed for Sudbury. She peered from her window seat as they descended toward the Sudbury airport. Grey rocks, sand pits, greenish-blue lakes and a million fir trees welcomed her. Sudbury's landscape was deemed ugly, but she saw rugged beauty and knew that Will was waiting for her.

Lily wasn't making a dramatic entrance, though she knew how. Feeling unaccustomed shyness, she was the last to step down from the airplane and cross the tarmac. It was windy and she shivered, wearing jeans, shirt, sneakers, and a light pea jacket, crummy, not designed by Sarty. Rolling her laptop in a bag with small wheels, she looked for the rumpled guy, slouched up, waiting. His eyes were bright with anticipation as he stood by the door. For a day in July, Sudbury was cool enough that even Will wore a jacket. The airport was so…regional, so quiet and empty. Less than twenty people waited for their baggage.

"One duffel, one laptop," she said. She would not utter how worried she was about coming to visit Northern Ontario with the black flies, ticks, otters, snakes, rats, sheep, cows, raccoons, bears and cougars. Perhaps she had read too much. She didn't do bugs or poison ivy. Treva, Charlotte and Brenda had made her promise to check in with the names of the towns on Manitoulin, and give them the numbers of the police stations.

"Will, I need a few minutes to phone my friend Winsome in Sudbury. Her dad, Malvin, is Speedy's ferry captain. Winsome's husband's a chef at the Ramada Inn downtown."

"Is this work?"

"Oh no, I promised I'd check in."

In a minute, she heard Winsome's musical voice. "Lily, you here in Sudbury?"

"I'm at the airport, Winsome, on the way to Manitoulin! How are you?"

"We excited, Lily, baby on de way. You better call me later to tell me everything, you hear! When I tell Papa you be making it up here, he hoot and holler!"

"He certainly will," she said, glancing at the man waiting for her. She loved Will's courtly way of being, no matter how scruffy he looked. He was authentic, slow, and romantic, and soon she would see meadows and country roads.

He carried her duffel outside to his diesel truck. The parking lot was large and empty. He opened the passenger door for her. She jumped up into the seat. He started the truck and turned onto Skead Road.

Lily asked, "Do you think people will know I'm from New York City?"

Will's laughter was merry, his eyes focused on the road. "Only if you talk."

They drove south, through hills covered with pine trees, past swamps and lakes, and through small communities, finally turning west onto Highway 17. It was getting cloudy. He told her about his home. "I've kept every fine old fixture in the farmhouse. It holds the history of my parents and grandparents. The original furniture's still there. I'm the keeper of Mudge and Knot history now. I got us fresh whitefish from the Purvis Brothers, and organic chops and steaks from the Burt farm. Early lettuce, chives from the garden. My pal Muddy's eager to meet you. He's part of the local wildlife."

"And where's the rhubarb?" she asked, not really teasing.

"First sign of spring and there's rhubarb poking its pointy green head up through the dirt," said Will. "Sometimes I can hear the stuff grow."

"Did you know that rhubarb," she said thoughtfully, "is the word for background noise that supporting actors use behind the action of the lead characters in plays? In New York City, the rhubarb's constant with car alarms, honking horns, ambulances, police and fire sirens. It's in the whistle of a doorman hailing a cab, the screech of a subway train, and the constant murmur of a million cell phone conversations."

"Here, when you drive into a ditch, you've driven into the rhubarb. If something's a bunch of rhubarb, it's bullshit."

"My Aunt Bea says rhubarb's a hardy staple of rural life. When she cooks rhubarb, she coaxes the bitterness out of the stalk, and simmers it into sweetness. If you fall into a patch of rhubarb, she says you simply pick yourself up and keep going."

"I wait 'til the rhubarb's ripe, pick it, cook it, strain it, and add the flavour of life, love and sweetness to it," said Will.

"But a patch of sourness can be so deep, how would you get out of it?"

"I put it in jars," Will said, as they passed Nairn Centre. Railroad cars stood idle on the siding in the town of McKerrow. In Espanola, smoke pulsed from the huge stacks of the Domtar paper mill, and she looked down into the Spanish River as they crossed the bridge into town. They drove by shopping malls and fast food shops. He pulled into the line, ordering two large vanilla cups at Tim Hortons.

Will handed her a CD called *Heart's End*. "I want you to hear the music of Kevin Closs, one of my favourite local songwriters." Lily put the CD into the player and the soft sounds of a swingy acoustic guitar, bass, and a gentle voice singing "Outward bound…" drifted from the speakers. The main road became narrower, twisty, and cut through pink granite and white quartz. Lily dreamily bonded with the song, feeling courageously outward bound herself toward a new island. There had to be rhubarb waiting.

At the top of the Willisville hill, rocky terrain spread below, reflecting pink, grey and brown in the sun. They drove past Sunshine Alley and Birch Island, rounding to a long flat road leading to the island.

"I've got friends on Birch Island," he said. "Brave Falcon's my fishing buddy. If there's time, I'd like you to meet him." They approached the North Channel and stopped at the traffic light. The old iron swing bridge stood in front of her.

"The bridge swings on the centre pedestal," Will said, pointing. "You drive across when it's closed, joining the mainland to the island. When it swings ninety degrees, it stands in the middle of the river. It becomes a bridge from nowhere to nowhere standing parallel with the river, and the boats sail through on either side. Then it closes, but only one lane of traffic can move at a time. It makes us take time to pause, and reflect." He looked at her.

She remembered what he'd told her on his boat. *Once you cross the old swing bridge, your life will never be the same.* She gazed across the dappling blues of the North Channel. Well-kept homes dotted the hillside, the land green and trees welcoming.

"Ready to cross the swing bridge?" he asked, when the light changed. His grin was as much challenge as welcome.

"I remember what you said on the boat," she told him. "And I'm here. Let's go."

"The name Manitoulin means 'Spirit Island' in the Anishnaabe language of the Ojibwe, Odawa and Potawatomie people. Local legend has it that Manitoulin Island was the Great Spirit's final project when creating the world," Will told her, easing the truck forward onto the single-lane bridge. "The Creator needed a place, so he shaped a physical world of rock, water, fire and wind. He then breathed life into it and made man, Lily. I believe it, that he took the most beautiful trees, the clearest water, and the cleanest air, and made it Manitoulin." There was a note she'd never heard in his voice.

She gazed out of the truck window. Another layer of learning. She liked the sounds of the names as he said them, Odawa, Ojibwe and especially Potawatomie. She saw boats down on the North Channel. Lily liked the shape of the black girders; the old design of the bridge, robust, like a giant kid had put an erector set together.

"In winter, about 13,000 people live here," Will said. "We're sorry when the kids leave to go to school or earn a living in Sudbury or Toronto. We want to keep young people here. In summer, people arrive from all over the world—tourists and campers and cottagers. The North Channel's a huge draw for sailors. Summer is the busiest season for islanders. It lasts eight weeks and then gets quiet. Traffic lines up for people waiting to cross this old bridge, and each side takes a turn," Will pulled off the bridge, past the cars and trucks lined up to leave the island. "There's a song by Arthur Schaller, called 'There's a Bridge in Little Current.' Maybe I have it at home. I think you'd like it—after you cross the bridge, it has meaning. Here we are."

They stopped in Little Current at the ice cream shop and Lily tasted maple ice cream. Smitten. They drove down Water Street, shops on one side and the municipal building on the other, fifty feet from the North Channel. She looked at the bright windows of Turner's Department Store. Townspeople and tourists strolled along.

"Are they Ojibwe?"

"Some of them, probably from Wikwemikong. They've a population of 4,000 on 100,000 acres. It's the only unceded reserve in Canada. They never signed a treaty."

"May we visit?"

"If there's time. It seems like there may be nothing to do on Manitoulin, Lily, and then there's never enough time. You'll see."

The sun appeared in full shine as they drove west along Highway 540, past the village of Aundeck Omni Kanning, and up a hill where a large blue expanse of the North Channel lay before them. Several boats with full sails dotted the horizon. Hay fields sloped gently down to the water's edge. Wooden fences snaked across the land, picture frames around the waving hay. Round hay bales perched in pastures. The *New York Times* was folded in her pocketbook with the latest Manhattan developments, and she had to finish the crossword puzzle. But the countryside was startlingly green and inviting to her New York-weary eyes. Smitten again. "Please, may we stop to take a photograph?"

He parked on the side of the road while she jumped out. When she got back into the truck, he said, "Listen to Stompin' Tom Connors. He sings 'Sudbury Saturday Night.'" The rousing music ushered them through M'Chigeeng and the long, flat Billings stretch. Sky and fields, beautiful, and then the green metal sign: KAGAWONG.

"On the right is Bridal Veil Falls. Wait until tomorrow, and we'll take a walk and maybe a swim there. It's one of the island's main attractions." They rounded the corner and drove down the hill. The view before them at the bottom of the hamlet was arresting: a blue bay of tiny whitecaps, flanked by green ridges, with mountains in the misty distance.

"That's Mudge Bay, and further out, the North Channel and the La Cloche Mountains," said Will. "Here's where I grew up. My mother and Uncle Mudge raised me. Aunt Molly, his sister, is the best. We'll have a fish fry at their house this week."

"For me to pass inspection?"

"Oh no, Aunt Molly and Uncle Mudge are wonderful. Welcoming. I mean, if we ever get out of bed," he said. He didn't look at her, but the corners of his mouth turned up.

He drove down to the bottom of the hill. The red and white Canadian flag danced in the breeze on a pole at the end of the long public dock. "My farmhouse is up the hill, around the next corner," said Will. "I wanted you to see the hamlet first and I need to get the mail."

He hopped out at a small Canada Post outlet. Lily followed, looking at two hundred small metal postal boxes.

"How are we today?" The postmaster looked at Lily with interest and cheerfully introduced himself. She smiled and held out her hand. Oliver Hill was the first person she'd met in Will's world.

"Thanks, Ollie," said Will, carrying his mail and holding open the door for Lily.

"Always welcome, Will," Ollie said. He turned to Lily. "Will's one of our fine-standing citizens, always available to help anyone on the bay if they're in trouble."

In the truck, she giggled, "Did you pay Mr. Hill to say that?"

Will smiled and was silent. They drove back up the steep hill to flat ground on Highway 540, past houses set back from the road, past fir trees. Will guided the diesel into a grand curve in front of a shockingly decrepit farmhouse. "We're thirteen miles from Gore Bay and fifty miles from Little Current."

The ancient walls of the two-storey farmhouse were...rustic.

It had to have been painted streaky red more than fifty years ago, or never. White ragged concrete patches were obvious on the standing walls. Weeds grew out of the walls. Flower beds in front of the farmhouse were wildly overrun with tall, orange tiger lilies. Lily cringed and covered her dropped jaw with her hand. Will was so proud of his well-tended sailboat, and this *thing* was a ramshackle mess. Bugs, snakes, mice and rats had to live in it with him. Maybe owls, beaver. Toads. Was there a hotel in Kagawong?

"Place needs a bit of work," he said, looking up at it with affection. He hopped out and went to the back of the truck to unload luggage and provisions. He carried her duffel and groceries across the grass to the front porch. An old horseshoe was wired above the door, full of rust. She sat in the truck, aghast. Not smitten. She got out slowly.

"This farmhouse is more than one hundred years old, and has been in our family from the beginning. My great grandfather, Rufus Meander Knot, built it in 1885. The door knobs and windows are original. I have responsibility as the curator and caretaker. It's one of the last farmhouses on the island to have dormer windows. I've got a bumper crop of carrots, tomatoes, lettuce, beans, onions…"

Her contact lenses glazed over. She was speechless. She had to get back to Sudbury, immediately. This man and this broken-down derelict were not for her. "I won't listen to myself," she whispered. This man loved to sail, garden and cook. She loved to shop.

"Be careful, Lily," he said, as she stood on the grass. "A family of raccoons lives under the porch. Step lightly. Sudden noise disturbs them."

"Raccoons?" She tiptoed across the grass, past the open porch, and opened a rusty screen door that clacked shut behind her as she stepped into a mud room. Four pairs of well-worn boots stood in a row. Jackets, hats and gloves hung above. The house was cold. Entering the dark, thousand-year-old kitchen, she sneezed, pulled a tissue from her pocket, blew her nose and clamped her jaw shut. A hand pump stood at an old, dirty, white sink.

"We pump fresh water from the Kagawong River," he said. "But don't worry—the bathroom has running water."

Rustic? Not for one New York second. This was well past rustic. The white kitchen cupboards were thoroughly scratched—did small animals want to get out? Or in? Worn out red-and-white-checked organdy curtains framed each window. A scratched oak table stood in the middle of the kitchen. Grunting noises came from an ancient refrigerator. The original black linoleum counters seemed clean. They shone, but it could have been grease. She turned to see shiny new pots and pans, clean; a sheath of five German-made knives stood erect in a corner of the counter.

She sank carefully into an old wooden kitchen chair that teetered and squeaked beneath her, before she changed her mind and left. How ungracious it would be. Oblivious, Will zipped open her duffel and threw the flap back. She grabbed the golden box of Godiva, opened it and stuffed two chocolates in her mouth. She held the box out to him. Will took a piece, popped it in his mouth. She hoped he hadn't seen the shock on her face. She was trapped.

"I knew you'd like the place. It's one of the last beauties on Manitoulin." He patted her shoulder. He opened the refrigerator and took out a lime and an orange, and set them on the counter beside a bottle of rum.

She tried to give a positive reaction, but none came.

"You're not too chatty about the farmhouse," he noticed, while making the smoothies.

"Do you have mice?"

"I'm rich, so I can afford mice." He turned to her. To the New Yorker it wasn't a joke.

"I need time," she said, getting up. Wandering into the living room, she gazed at two rumpled plaid couches and an old TV set. A dining room led off the living room. Cartons of clothes, dishes, and books were neatly stacked.

"I've been meaning to get those cartons," he said, standing in the doorway behind her with a glass in his hand. "I come in and plunk right down. You'll see. I told you there's nothing to do on Manitoulin, and no time to do it."

He handed her a full glass. She took a large gulp.

In the dining room, there were two enormous gilded mirrors and a formal Victorian dining table with elegant high-backed mahogany chairs the height of formality.

"How do you have these beautiful antique mirrors?"

"Family heirlooms I'm storing for Laura," he said. "This is a relaxed farmhouse. No pretensions."

"I'll say," she whispered. In the corner of the living room, a tiny piano peeked out, hidden behind cartons. Brightened by the sight of it, she stepped over. Growing up at home with her father playing Broadway melodies on their Baldwin baby grand, she had adored taking piano lessons, could sight read and sing. She spied *Johannes Zunipe Sondini Princes Street Hanover Square* in black paint on the yellow wood. It beckoned to her to come and play. Charmed, she touched the middle C. Not in tune. But her fingers wandered over the keys, picking out a familiar melody. "Tea for Two." She slid onto the tiny bench, played chords and sang softly. Part of her mind registered the need for tuning, but her fingers enjoyed the cool smoothness of the old ivory keys and the odd, rich sound of the neglected instrument.

"Lovely, isn't it?" Will spoke from the doorway. "Those are original ivory keys. My grandfather carried this with our luggage off a ship, onto a boat and then a small barge in the bay. It's over one hundred years old. It's spent many winters in the cold by the fireplace."

"You haven't taken care of it," she whispered. She improvised around the tart notes and found the good keys. She made up a song using the good notes. The more she played, the more she got used to it.

She glanced at a carton filled with old, curled sheet music at her feet, "Embraceable You," the Gershwins' 1928 hit, visible a few layers down. Her father had told her that nineteen-year-old Ginger

Rogers had sung it in the Broadway musical, *Girl Crazy*. He'd played it every time her mother walked into the living room. He'd encouraged Lily to sing it when she was twelve years old, telling her she had a fine voice. Lily was chubby, wearing braces, and when she'd sung that song, her father had beamed, saying, "My gorgeous daughter and her voice!" Lily smiled bittersweetly. She played the song through, using every note.

Will stood silently in the doorway behind her until she reached the end of the song.

"My mother used to play," he said quietly. "Sounds good to hear it again, Lily. Even if it needs tuning. I'm pulling the truck into the barn. Don't want Muddy stopping by after playing cards at the gas station in Gore Bay. Tonight's for us."

She began to smile down at her fingers, picking out one more song, got up, and returned to the kitchen. The sheet music would wait for tomorrow.

She picked up her second smoothie. A buzz would help. In the Caribbean, the evenings she spent with Will were relaxed, but she was not at all certain she could relax here. He could not possibly have the second floor renovated. This farmhouse was musty, dusty and rusty.

She was surprised to find the table set with elegant old un-polished silver and Limoges dinner plates, with crystal for wine. "From my marriage," he said.

The bathroom's ancient tub had high clawed feet. She jiggled the toilet lever. It was old, loose, but working. In the corner, an old washing machine and dryer stood, with an open box of detergent. She wandered back into the kitchen. He turned around from the stove and placed his large hands on her shoulders. He walked her to the open screened door at the front of the house. "Look and listen, Lily."

"Someone's crying?" She looked west, brilliant pink dusk shining on the open field.

"Those are Farmer Grey's cows in the back forty." Will opened the door. "Walk with me."

After the aged mustiness of the frayed and decayed farmhouse, Lily smelled fresh, chill Ontario air. Birds twittered in the bushes and the orange lilies by the screened door caught the last of the evening light. The divine part of his farm in Kagawong was sinking in. Three acres of lush grass flourished in front of them, wands shimmering in the wind. She had opened the door, not knowing, and trusting.

She looked up and put her arms around him, feeling him relax. With her finger she took a speck of dark chocolate off the side of his mouth.

"Let's walk to the river so you know what you're waking up to, Miss New York."

"Let's go to bed, Will," she said.

He smiled. "Not yet, honey. You'll develop a feel for the rhythm of life here on Manitoulin." He released himself from her hug and led the way down the grassy hill to the Kagawong River. She wandered after him on the path, each step taking her further from the bustling concrete avenues of Manhattan Island. The Kagawong murmured and chuckled past white water lilies. She clasped her arms around herself. Smitten again. Will hadn't described this country accurately. He stood, relaxed upon his land, seeming elementally rooted. Here he was most himself. Lily stood, enthralled beside the sweetly flowing Kagawong, with clouds above, and hay fields swaying on the other side. She realized that she'd been ensconced, happily, in a global hub, an urban whirlwind, armed daily with her digital communications. She knew she loved it. But this... this was a storybook. The word Sabbath came to her, a sacred place of rest. Perhaps this Kagawong was the key to round out her soul?

"We're imperfect beings in a flawed world," Will whispered, beside her again. "In an imperfect, old farmhouse. But down here, I feel the fields, the water and the sky. There's no beginning or end, no point except to follow the path, to be challenged by it and let it lead." She listened to his words by the water's edge, and to the river flowing past them.

"Dinner's almost ready. I'm broiling wild salmon and succotash with almonds. I set it up while you were communing with the piano."

"I like the way you commune with cooking, providing us real nourishment," Lily told him.

"My daughter says that, too," he said, turning on the path back to the farmhouse. From the river side, the homestead looked better to her, full of promise. Was geography destiny? She had been to so many islands. This was different. "Where's the rhubarb patch, Will?"

"Near the barn. We'll walk there in the morning. We'll need take an empty can and fill it with gravel, to shake away the garter snakes." He glanced back. "They're more afraid of you than you are of them, city girl. It's the bears we worry about. They get into garbage, so we're careful to recycle on the island, keep the dumps small."

In the kitchen she drank more of the rum-laced smoothie. He looked at her from across the room.

"Since you've stood by the Kagawong River and watched it flow, seeing the clouds mirrored, the water lilies, and some fish, can you maybe understand why New York City's so abhorrent to me?"

"As snakes, ants and flies are to me." She took another gulp of her drink.

He laughed. "You're ready for the upstairs. Leave your shoes here. We don't want to dirty the carpet." He sloughed off his worn boots. She made a face of disbelief and stepped out of her Pradas.

"Will, this plaid carpet looks one hundred years old."

"It is. The upstairs is new."

She looked at the knob on the stair door. It was at her shoulder.

"The door knob's set high to keep children from coming up. That's how they did it in the old days." His voice floated down from the stairs above her.

She dragged herself up after him, tired. Could she handle ten days of this, up and down the dark narrow steps, living in a dusty, dirty farmhouse with the ancient bathroom? The washer and dryer had to be forty years old. Spoiled New York, she thought, knowing she was exhausted from the long day of travel, three airports, two countries and this moulding museum.

She climbed onto the top step. Her surprised feet sank into luxurious, white carpet. She looked around at freshly painted white walls. His large bedroom windows looked west over the field. A queen-sized bed, two dark mahogany chests, two night tables with big lamps, and a large closet beyond welcomed her. "Laura sent a new Ralph Lauren bed spread, pillows, sheets and blankets. She wanted you to feel welcome. Across the hall is a room you can use to write. You told me, on the boat, that you wanted to write a book about three sisters from Boston, based on family letters," he said. "Here's a room to begin."

"You remembered?"

"I remember almost everything you've said to me, Lily." His eyes were intense. "And this was after you made love to me so sweetly. I asked what you would do if you had all the time in the world."

"I told you?"

"Yes, and you fell asleep, but I got it."

She peered into 'her' room: the study had a desk, a plank of polished barn wood placed across two crates. An antique chest with a pink marble top against the other wall held a fax machine. The window was a picture frame looking down a path toward the sweetly flowing Kagawong.

"We need to have dinner, and then we can snuggle and sleep. You need energy, and I may keep you up all night."

After dinner, Lily lit scented candles in his bedroom, and she watched his strong, muscled body by candle light while he undressed and came to her. Afterwards, they slept in each other's arms. On one chest stood a bronze art deco statue of a young dancer, slim, graceful, standing on one foot, her other leg pointed forward, arms high. "It was my father's," Will said. "I've looked at that statue my whole life, wondering if I'd ever meet a woman like that, lithe, tender, and beautiful, reaching for me. Here you are, Lily, in my bed."

Honk, honk blared from the driveway below. "Open up, ya big ole fat Mudgester!"

"Muddy," Will yelled from the bed, "go on home! See ya tomorrow."

CHAPTER SEVEN

AROUND LILY, THE NORTHERN ONTARIO DAY was coming to life. Breezes rose up the hill from the river, rustling through the leaves on the maple trees and across the meadow. In the front yard stood a small apple tree with a sturdy trunk and gnarled branches. She picked up the tomato soup can filled with pebbles and made her way to the tree, shaking the can to ward off living things in the tall grass below it. Will joined her.

"My apple tree in this Garden of Eden," he said, kissing her hair. "But you're the apple of my eye."

"From the big apple," Lily said, smiling. He gazed down at her, not looking up as a green car passed slowly by the end of the drive on Highway 542. Lily could see a dark-haired woman watching them from the driver's seat.

"Let's go make breakfast," said Will.

"Kagawong means 'where mists rise from falling waters,'" he

told her that afternoon as they stood at the top of Bridal Veil Falls, on the steel steps that would take them down to the rocks and sand. "We swim here in summer. It's Manitoulin's most beautiful natural feature—right here. Twenty metres to the bottom." They walked down the steps to the edge of the plunge pool, the roar of cascading water lovely in her ears. Across, up the steep bank, she saw two deer, still as a picture. A flock of seagulls flew across, silhouetted against the summer sky.

They ambled along the leafy riverside path to the waterfront, and then onto the Kagawong dock. Will pointed out the Old Mill housing the Rick Edwards Art Gallery and the Billings Township municipal office. Children were laughing on the beach, their mothers talking by the benches. He took her up the hill past Hunt's General Store and into the small, but dignified St. John the Evangelist Anglican Church, which had stood there for over a century. Outside again, they walked to Upper Street and past the library. Summer flowers bloomed in front of old houses, some with gabled roofs. They stopped in at the Bridal Veil Esso Station for coffee.

"Kagawong fools you," Lily said. "It looks a little sleepy, but there's everything to do outdoors." She was charmed by the small-town ambiance, and determined to try everything.

On the second day, she spent the morning writing at her new desk, and then stood at the upstairs window to watch an oncoming rainstorm. Flashes of lightning crackled across the sky. "I've never heard nature sizzle before," she shouted down to Will. The rain hit the ground so hard it seemed to bounce. She could feel the house-shaking thunder through her feet.

"We always lose trees," yelled Will from downstairs. He pulled windows shut as the sky darkened, illuminated sporadically by lightning. The branches of the sweet green apple tree shook in the wind, small but strong. Lily retreated from the window and snuggled under a blanket in the bed. Within thirty minutes, the sky had cleared.

She heard the sound of a car in the driveway and looked out, wondering which of Will's friends had come. A tall, pretty woman stepped out of a new green Ford, brushed her fingers through her long black hair, and took something out of the back seat. She glanced up at the farmhouse window. Lily stepped back quickly.

The front screen door opened. "Will, I missed you. I brought you something!"

Lily could hear Will downstairs, where he'd been on a business call to his stock broker.

"Call you back, Bill." His voice sounded different. Lily tiptoed to the head of the stairs.

"Hello, Carlotta," Will said, with resignation.

"I baked a quiche," she said. "What, no kiss? I want to meet her."

"What difference can it make?" he asked. "Why are you here?"

"All of Kagawong knows she's here. You can't hide her."

"Carlotta, you know I've moved on."

"You think you have."

"I suppose it's better if you meet her in front of me," he said, sighing tiredly. "Lily, can you come down for a few minutes?"

Lily tiptoed to the bedroom mirror to check her appearance. His ex-wife? Wasn't she in Toronto? She applied lipstick and whispered, "Boobs up," her silly mantra for bravery. Downstairs, Carlotta was helping herself to a cup of coffee, as if she were familiar with the kitchen. She turned to inspect Lily. "I heard Will brought home a friend. I'm Carlotta. I made you a quiche."

Lily stopped dead. "How nice, good to meet you," she said, certain she didn't mean a word of it. Will sat at the table in the middle of the room. Lily instantly knew stakes had gotten higher. She had an absurd mental image of two hungry dogs, circling a tasty bone. A gust of wind blew in through the screen door.

"I have two children with Will," Carlotta said, smirking at Will, who flinched and started up out of his chair.

"What?" Lily looked at Will.

"You know that's not true, Carlotta," Will sighed, slumping in his chair.

"Can't I make a joke? We've spent years together. So, you're Lily?" Carlotta picked up her coffee cup and took a sip. "When did you two meet?"

Will glanced warily at Lily, who shrugged her shoulders. "A while ago."

"I'm a Haweater, born on the island. My family's been here longer than Will's. We run cattle in Gordon Township, and own a golf course and land on Barrie Island. When Will's away, I look after the house. Do you like the island so far?"

"It seems lovely," Lily said, working up a half smile to diffuse the icy chill in the kitchen, wishing Carlotta would leave. "You made a quiche. What a nice thing to do!"

"How long are you staying?" Carlotta pressed.

Who was the predator? Lily walked to the pot on the sideboard, poured herself a cup of coffee. She turned, directly in front of Carlotta, looking up at the tall, beautiful, hostile woman. Lily kept her coffee cup clearly on one side of her body, the other arm open. Was there a possibility here for something other than icy? She answered vaguely, "I'm not sure. Perhaps you'll come one night and have the quiche with Will and me?"

She had misjudged. Will looked helpless, sinking in his chair.

"That quiche is for you and Will alone to share." Carlotta put her coffee cup down and brushed her hand slowly over Will's shoulder. "Bye for now, Mr. Will Knott Budge."

Lily and Will were silent until they heard the car door slam and the engine's rumble fade away down the curved driveway.

"I'm sorry, Will," Lily said miserably. "I'll put the quiche in the freezer."

"Throw it out, Lily. It's probably full of poison ivy." He looked weary.

➤

During the following days, Will exhibited stillness and concentration, whether he tinkered with a truck or tractor, or read an instruction manual. Lily poked around the working barn, stuffed with old wooden dressers, an ancient washing machine with rollers, rickety antique chairs, hoes, rakes, trunks of clothes, and paintings done by his mother.

"Someday I'll show you the Sunday Barn, where my mother entertained friends and they had tea and cookies," he said to her. "Forget the Hiding Barn. I've got all kinds of homemade booze in there."

She found an old suitcase with love letters from his parents to each other. He allowed her to open them. At Manitoulin Smoothie time, dusk each day, she read him parts of the letters. He said, "Mom grieved such a long time. I think she died of heartache. Hearing what Dad wrote emphasizes what little I can remember. I sure could write a book about the Knot and Mudge history here, but it's an awful lot. I'll leave the writing to you."

Lily thought of the great aunts whose letters and diaries had inspired her dream to write. "I grew up on Long Island, thirty miles from New York City," she told Will. "We weren't a country family like you, but not city, either. Dahlia and I still call mom 'The General.' Will, my mother's smart and elegant, a crack bridge player and golfer. She presides over her fourteen-room, four-storey house overflowing with clothes, books, antiques, dolls, and furniture."

"Being a pack rat's part of being an islander. The day I throw it out, next day I need it."

"I know sometime soon I'll have to clean out the house for her," Lily said, thinking of the treasures and discards of decades stashed in the corners and closets of her family's home.

In the working barn, Will was comfortable, making business phone calls, faxing contracts, and arranging for boat deliveries. He kept the refrigerator stocked with beer and maple ice cream, and his bookshelf included the five-foot collection of Harvard Classics and the works of Heidegger.

"When I was at school, German philosophy was jammed down our throats, but once I got into Heidegger, all of it began to make sense," Will told Lily as he took down a volume. "The way I see it, he talks about our small existence in the face of death, the temporality of existence. That's why I've got to be my own man. The world's so screwed up. Here, on Manitoulin, life feels good. I'm saving myself for myself. Why not take a look of this, and we can talk about it. We've got to be ourselves, affirming our own being in the world."

"Sure," she said, gulping at having to read all the compendia on the shelf.

While Will was working, Lily would amble along Route 540, avoiding the ditches. A left turn down the hill brought her into Kagawong. Walking on the dock in the crisp wind refreshed her senses. The harbour was filled with small sailboats, and local people sat on benches, their fishing lines draped over the dock. Lily was charmed by the picturesque town. She talked to everyone, from the tourist children playing along the boardwalks to the two old fishermen who seemed to have priority rights to the best spots. She poked around the dock and the boats fearlessly. She would return in the late afternoon, sometimes sweaty, sometimes dry, and one afternoon rather wet. She simply smiled and hurried to her room. Will was too smart to ask why.

"You can't keep her away from us, you dolt," whined Muddy one evening before dinner, standing at the screen door of the farmhouse. It was the end of Lily's first week.

"Get in here, Muddy, dinner's ready," Will said, looking up with a grin. "Juicy beef ribs from the Burt Farm. Lily, this disaster is my childhood pal, the Mudman. Muddy, be polite." Muddy was a short, stocky fellow, with thatched red hair and a great smile. The smoky, intoxicating aroma from the outside grill drifted in through the door as he entered.

"I'm some jeezely hungry," Muddy declared, sitting at the kitchen table. Will staggered to the table with a platter of spicy ribs piled high, and they dug in. It was a Manitoulin feast: ribs with roast potatoes, and a huge salad from the young garden, packed with green peas, lettuce, the last of the radishes, green onions, carrots and tender, early baby cucumbers. This was a celebration for Lily. She had lasted this long on Manitoulin.

"We'll get you Manitoulinized," said Muddy, refilling her glass. "Willy Boy, tonight we let loose and have fun! I brought butter tarts and ice cream for dessert." Biting into a rib, Lily almost swooned. She surprised herself by keeping up with these Manitoulin men. She ate ten ribs. After dinner, Will put on thirties jazz, and poured brandy.

"He likes being called Muddy," Will told her, "and once you're lulled by the name he dazzles the hell out of you with his competence."

"Not much else you can do with a name like Thornton Mudlington," Muddy told her, grinning. "Kids called me Horny Thorny. We lived in Little Current. My dad told me to 'Go West,' so I did: I moved west to Kagawong. I own that little white house overlooking Mudge Bay. When we were twelve, Will and I made dandelion wine. First time we tried our brew, I fell deep into the mud. Took hours to wake up and get out. Name stuck." Muddy took a napkin and wiped a spot of juice off Lily's cheek, endearing him to her. She had a new friend, a man she might have easily passed by on a New York City street. "Most of the time I pay attention to what Will tells me," said Muddy, "stashing my dough in Tortola. Wife's long gone. Didn't like my drinkin'. Girlfriends get smart and leave. I've done all the marrying I'm gonna do. My claim to fame is I can drink with the best of 'em, especially my best pal here, the Mudgester."

Disarmed, Lily laughed delightedly and toasted, "One of my best nights!"

Muddy stayed past the godly hour of nine, he and the Mudgester finishing off the Burt Farm ribs. Lily took a photo of the mountain of bones. She was tipsy, laughing, and it was divine, a secret of crossing the old swing bridge, letting go on Manitoulin. She swayed unsteadily from the table, giggling, and held onto the railing as she climbed upstairs. Once there, she fell onto her bed, still fully dressed.

Dimly, she heard Muddy say, "Your girl's funny. Talky soul, easy to like. She's crazy about you. Assumes nothing. She's a classy drunk. That's how I judge potential women."

A few days later, while Will was in Mindemoya on errands, the green car pulled into the driveway. The tall woman got out and knocked on the screen door, then opened it.

"Will's not here, Carlotta," Lily said, sitting at the kitchen table, writing notes for a travel article. Few of her clients had ever heard of Manitoulin Island.

"I came to see you. Did you like the quiche?"

"We haven't had it yet," she said. "I read in a brochure that you're an artist, exhibiting your oil paintings at the Gore Bay Museum and the La Cloche Country Art Show…".

"Yes, it's a good show. I'm a sculptor, too, wood mostly. I like using a knife. Come by sometime and see my work. My family was among the original settlers on Manitoulin, and I tell our island's history in my work with wood and oil."

Lily slightly nodded her head

"This island's not what it seems." Carlotta stood over her, subtle aggression in her voice. "It's not quaint and hand-crafty. Nor is Will. If you've been raised on the island, and go to school or work elsewhere and come back, you're called a traitor to Manitoulin. I've been accused of taking work from islanders, and I am one. This is not," she finished quietly, "a welcoming place."

As Lily looked sharply at the beautiful woman who stood over her, Will's diesel pulled into the wide driveway. Carlotta stopped talking, went out the door, waved to him, then got into her car and left. She gunned the engine down the wide driveway, past the apple tree in the front yard, and then onto the highway.

He banged the screen door. "What did she say to you?"

"She asked if we liked the quiche. We talked about her art, and how she went off island for college. She likes cutting down trees," Lily answered, frozen at the table. Will turned around and walked out of the house. Through the window, she watched him stride towards the working barn. She felt threatened by Will's obvious emotion, so easily aroused by this local woman who seemed to have standing in the community. Lily breathed slowly. With emergencies at work, she always knew what needed to be done immediately to take care of other people. Here, there was nothing to do. Would this woman keep her from experiencing love and laughter with Will? She shook herself. It was simply a visit.

Lily went upstairs to the phone. Alexis answered from the New York office.

"What's up?"

"I need to hear your voice, restore my balance. How are you?"

"Had enough of Lake Huron's pastoral island? Wearing those funky overalls?"

"We went to an old time church supper, yard sales and a fair!"

"You better be home soon," Alexis said. "Don't get too comfy up there!"

"Not a chance," said Lily. She went downstairs, and saw Will standing in the same spot in front of the working barn.

"You're angry, upset that she stopped by," Lily challenged.

"I'm taking the boat out on the Bay. I'll make salmon sandwiches for us. Get ice…"

Will's small boat puttered out of the harbour. His mouth was tight. Lily eyed him, staying still as they cruised and the sunset spread fingers of pink and purple. After a while, she unwrapped a sandwich, and handed it to him.

"Ta," he said. He opened the bottle of rum, poured a small amount in a large cup, added ice and water and gently offered it to her. They ate in silence, came back to the harbour, put the cover on the little boat and drove back up to the farmhouse.

CHAPTER EIGHT

"I SAW UNCLE MUDGE IN MINDEMOYA yesterday," said Will the next morning, "Aunt Molly's home from Nova Scotia. Dinner with them tonight."

Will and Lily arrived at the Mudge family's large stone home on Whiskey Hill as the sun touched it with golden light. The winter living room held comfortable sofas and leather chairs focused around a stone fireplace. A coffee table was piled high with books. The summer living room overlooked a grand view of the bay. Lily took one look at Everett Mudge and realized he was a man of consequence far beyond the shores of his Manitoulin Island home. The Mudge family's earliest ancestors had settled the shores of the bay, which took the family name, over a century past. Aunt Molly was tall, a lean and elegant sister, who welcomed her warmly.

"Glad to see you dry today, Miss Lily," Uncle Mudge greeted her. "What are you drinking? I have some homemade wine."

Lily blushed as he turned to Will. "This lady talked to me last week at the dock. I told her to go buy worms at Hunt's and gave her my fishing rod to try. She asked me to put the worm on and then I gave her my best spot, right at the end of the dock. A kid walked by with a chocolate ice-cream cone and her eyes just went to that chocolate, no attention to her line. By gumbo, a perch chose her line to end it all. She was looking at the ice cream. I saw the tug. *She fell into the bay!*"

"What?!"

Uncle Mudge guffawed. "She surfaced, spit out water, still holding up the damn rod. Everyone on the dock saw her. But she saw the steps, you know, built in to the dock. Just climbed back up onto the dock like she owned the harbour. That was one lucky fish that got away."

"I'll say it before you do," she cried. "I'm an American moron."

"I would never judge," Uncle Mudge said with a pious smirk, winking at Lily. "Will, she struggled up hard. I heard her sneakers slosh. I thought, 'No fish is in danger when you throw a hook!' But a minute later she reeled in a tiny perch."

"That's why you were wet!" Will realized.

At dinner, Lily learned that Everett Mudge represented the savvy elder generation on Manitoulin. He was self-sufficient, and had lived well and prospered.

"We've been on the Bay since before they brought in electricity," Uncle Mudge told Lily.

"Ev, I've told you not to exaggerate," Molly said.

"Why not! I'm over 90 and holding, sharp as a Swiss Army knife!"

The Mudges seemed to crackle along the road of life. Uncle Mudge had a layered packsack of accomplishments and tricks—a packsack not yet full, he told her. Lily instantly developed respect for Will's uncle, despite seeing him in the same outfit all week at the dock: dark blue suspenders, blue plaid shirt, and green work pants. He bore a comical air that belied his self-proclaimed engineering competency.

He raised an ear of corn to punctuate his conversation. "It dawned on our parents just how bright I was at six-years old. They immediately took corrective action, shipping me off to prep school and then the best university Canada had to offer."

"When you were six?"

"They hoped to blunt his wit," Will said, reaching for the butter.

"Into a dull, safe Ontario squire," said Uncle Mudge. "But I fooled 'em all."

They ate fresh fish, corn, and Molly's eggplant and tomato ratatouille. After a jovial dinner, Lily took dishes into the kitchen to wash. Aunt Molly looked pleased, and they chatted while drying. Lily admired the spacious old house, which was exquisitely well-kept and full of polished antiques. She admired Aunt Molly.

"You come back soon for another dinner," hooted Uncle Mudge from the door as they stepped out into a late night. "So I can make more fun of you!"

Early the next morning, Will took Lily canoeing along the elbow of the Kagawong River, the curve of his property. Lily paddled in the bow and a kingfisher paced them along the riverbank. White waterlilies shone up from the water's surface. As they pulled the canoe up, Will said, "Today gets better. I'm taking you for a ride to Sophia."

"Another former girlfriend?" she asked, daringly.

"Wait," he said, smiling. "I see you don't trust me yet."

"Well, maybe. I'm still waiting to fall into the rhubarb."

"Don't worry, it happens to everyone who lives on Manitoulin," he said, driving west on Highway 540 to Gore Bay. He made a left turn at the OPP building to lusher farmland. Route 6 offered grazing land, cows, sunlight, and pastures. She couldn't take her eyes off the scenery. She wanted to know more about farming here, and aboriginal cultures on the island; she wanted to know more about Will—and, truthfully, where Carlotta had come from. How did people on the island grow up, what beliefs and standards did these Canadians have? What did Will have that so compelled her? His quiet, burly presence in the truck made her crazy. He turned on the road to Dominion Bay and pulled into a long driveway in front of a chalet.

The chalet overlooked the crescent-shaped sandy beach of the bay. It curved wide, with rocks for punctuation, a stunning picture postcard. How had she traveled around the world and ignored Northern Ontario? This past week, she'd gathered brochures and tucked them in her suitcase. She could book families to this pastoral island, quieter, colder than the summer tropics. And they'd thank her for finding Manitoulin.

The hand-carved sign over the door read "Originals by Sophia." A petite, pretty woman, with green eyes and blonde hair, smiled and stepped back to let them in.

"Will phoned, said he had a surprise. Please come in." She was dressed in a peach and brown skirt under a multi-coloured patchwork jacket, startling Lily with her elegance. Lily looked beyond Sophia to see hand-knitted sweaters in ochre, hangers full of patchwork jackets in pale green, and more in blue, sunshine yellow blouses with ducks, and matching shirts. Gold and silver gleamed in jewelry cases. "I make jewelry, paint and sew each winter," Sophia said. "And sell to the summer people. I make coffee, *ja*?"

Lily's eyes danced over a profusion of luxury and colour that would drive Sartorius George crazy. He'd love it all. Her hands itched to try on a jacket.

Will explained nothing, watched for a minute, smiled, and then slipped outside quietly. Sophia brought in two cups of coffee. "He's gone to see Kurt at the wood mill," Sophia told Lily with a gentle smile, as they settled into a corner of her shop. "They'll stand over a saw for hours and say nothing."

"All of this is so lovely! Where did you learn to design?"

"In Soest, near Frankfurt, art school," Sophia said.

"I've been there—a lovely town. What brought you to Manitoulin?"

"We saw an advertisement for this chalet and called the owner in Germany. He came to visit us with photos. Kurt came over and made the deal. This was for vacation only, in summer. But we felt good about being here all year. Kurt made us furniture; he could hunt, and run his log mill. I have my gardens and play tennis. It's been good."

"This island seems magical," Lily confided to her. "I'm not surprised you stayed."

They visited until shoppers began to fill the store. While Sophia served them, Lily browsed through the racks of clothing.

"Try on this cornflower blue patchwork," Sophia advised, handing her a jacket during a moment's pause. Lily chose a hand-dyed shirt to match, and tried the outfit on. Sophia offered a silver necklace with a blue stone. Lily pulled out her credit card.

"Sophia, don't tell me the price, just write it all up. I can walk merrily up Fifth Avenue or on Meredith Street in Gore Bay."

Returning to the store at the morning's end, Will invited Sophia to come with them for lunch in Tehkummah, but she was too busy. At the restaurant, Lily dawdled over fresh baked whitefish on a bed of fresh vegetables from the restaurant's garden. Will was vocal in his appreciation of a huge hamburger with onions. Angela, the owner, came out of the kitchen to offer them the day's fresh apple pie.

"We call her Angel, because the food's divine. I'll have the pie," Will said. "Bring Lily a slice of your Mad-About-Chocolate cheese-cake." During lunch, Will told Lily about his discussion with Kurt, and the project they were planning to enlarge his workshop in the working barn. When the afternoon rush was over, Lily asked for permission to chat with Angela, who was still in the kitchen.

"Okay, it's your socializing-with-other-people-day," Will decreed. "I'll get a few things and meet you in the parking lot. Get your talking done."

An hour later, Lily ran outside. Will was sleeping in the truck, with a volume of Heidegger open beside him. "You see—we have fascinating people on the island," he told her when she poked him. He turned on the engine and sighed. "I get worn out with too many people."

"People are friendly here," Lily said. "I'm interested in learning…"

"Canadians tend to be pretty reserved," Will warned her. "People will tell you everything they want you to know, if you're patient." She nodded wordlessly. She'd buy guidebooks and road maps, learn the names of the inns and guesthouses and restaurants.

"Will, it's beginning to fascinate me how people find, come to, and stay on Manitoulin."

"Take it slow, Lily," he said, and they drove home in silence.

➷

It was the first of August. Lily's visit was coming to a close. She'd been charmed by the two island newspapers, the *Manitoulin West*

Recorder and the *Manitoulin Expositor*, and their stories of small communities. They'd visited Little Current and South Baymouth. She played the little piano every day, part of her hoping that the off-key notes would encourage Will to have it tuned. They'd wolfed down hot turkey sandwiches at a local place in Mindemoya, had pizza in Gore Bay, and tried every restaurant, declaring each one excellent. They had been to the Billings "recycling centre." Will forbade her to pick up anything, no dumpster diving, no matter how interesting. Lily hadn't noticed that she'd run out of chocolate.

At the farm, they sat in wooden armchairs on the verandah, enjoying the breeze that kept away flies. "Will, this time with you has been great." she said. "Have I talked you to death?" Three beats of Manitoulin silence. She smiled.

"Almost, well, yeah," he drawled. "But I like showing you the island. You're direct, Lily. I've never been. I may have another project with Uncle Mudge. Think I'll spend the fall here."

"That's good. You'll miss hurricane season in the Caribbean."

"That's the idea. I'm glad you came. You've made friends in Uncle Mudge, Aunt Molly and Muddy. You've made it through the dead flies in the windows, and you like walking the overgrown path to the river. You let me teach you…"

"I'm fascinated by this cold, summer island," she said quietly. "And I've enjoyed the writing room. I started the first chapter about the Boston sisters last week…"

"Do you think Alexis could carry your work a little longer?"

Lily was packed for tomorrow's departure. "Seriously? Are you smitten with me?"

"Smitten?" Another three beats. "Maybe. You're lively. I like having you here and watching you learn."

Lily sat still for a long moment. Her three beats. She got up and went inside.

Alexis was still in the New York office. "Get this craziness out of your system. When business picks up, I'll need you or I'll kill you."

"You're a true friend," Lily said, gratefully. She had more time with Will. She poured two glasses of Aunt Molly's rhubarb cordial and took them out onto the porch. Unsmiling, she handed one to Will and settled back into her armchair.

"I can stay longer."

"Lily, you don't sound happy about it. Afraid you'll be disappointed with me?"

"Or maybe me, Will…"

"Tomorrow we're getting those tender city feet into walking boots. Sneakers are wrong for the hiking we'll be doing. I'll take you up to the Cup and Saucer Trail."

"You said that once a person crosses the bridge, life changes."

"Has it?"

"I need to ask about Carlotta. Do I have competition?"

"When she and Jordy fight, it's bad. I'm a good listener."

"Jordy?"

"Her husband."

"Her husband! Are you supposed to rescue her?"

"Do I hear jealousy?"

"It's simply research," she told him.

After supper, she walked the path to the river with a wary eye for raccoons, slithery snakes, and frogs. A spark of light caught her eye, and she bent down. In the grass, an old silver fork, tines tarnished, lay waiting to be picked up. It was engraved *The Book Room*. Was this a sign? She pocketed the fork, and later brought it upstairs to her desk. She gazed out the window; the moon was rising. Her mind jumped to the ferry ride with Captain Mal, on the way from Tortola to Virgin Gorda. He'd said a cold island might be good for her.

She called her friend Winsome in Sudbury. "Lily, we two, so far from our islands. You sound happy. " Winsome's lilting voice caressed her.

"Winsome, you're from Virgin Gorda, I'm from New York and here we are, in Ontario. When will you and your husband come to Kagawong? There's so much I want to show you!"

"Ever de travel agent; my daddy be laughing," said Winsome merrily.

Chapter Nine

Lily left Will in the working barn, bent over plans for his new addition, and walked to the library on Upper Street. She found books by Robertson Davies, and soon fell under his spell. Uncle Mudge found her on the dock, reading *Fifth Business*.

"Robertson and I were in school together."

Uncle Mudge hadn't appeared to lie to her yet. She liked the acceptance of her in his eyes. "You've got a good one. I taught him everything he knew about girls." He chuckled, walking away.

The social centre of Kagawong was the post office. Postmaster Ollie Hill offered her conversation and friendship, and Lily found herself there often. "Sit in that corner and chat with me while I work," he invited. His glasses, perched on his forehead, danced in the light from overhead as he separated mail, answered phone calls, and helped people at the front counter.

She sat on an overturned tin wastebasket while Ollie told her stories about working for Lester B. Pearson, the great statesman and former prime minister, winner of the Nobel Peace Prize. He never lost the thread as he sold stamps and weighed parcels. As each person came in, she was introduced as "Will's New Yorker."

Lily enjoyed her small celebrity. A local teacher walked into the post office with a huge laugh and big blue eyes. "Lily, the New Yorker! Come with me to the Esso. I need gas, and we can have coffee. I want to hear about New York City."

Coffee cups in hand, they perched outside the restaurant on a bench overlooking the Kagawong River. Lily hesitated. "You know the score on Manitoulin. I need help."

"I never spill a confidence. Give."

"Chocolate. I'm out of chocolate," Lily confided in dire tones.

"Manitoulin Gourmet!"

In Gore Bay, Lily found the natural food shop and spoke with the old-time, grey-haired merchant, dressed in a blue smock. "The Manitoulin Gourmet stocks chocolate from Switzerland, France and Germany," he told her, drawing her over to the display. "I haven't seen you before."

"I'm visiting," Lily's eyes settled on the shelves of dark, glorious chocolate.

"I was a visitor, too, long ago. My wife Anna and I are transplants. We came to visit, and couldn't leave. We'll never be Haweaters," he said with a smile. "You have to be born here. Are you the New Yorker Carlotta's been talking about? You don't look like you're trying to nab anybody."

Lily met his eyes, stricken.

"That Carlotta. Fine old Manitoulin family, but she's been after him for years. People from Manitoulin tend to know things. My shop's open all year. I hear it all. I'm Chris Brooks."

"I'm Lily." They shook hands. Chris turned, picked up the phone and dialed. "Anna, a new lady in town is in the shop. She talks as fast as you! " He got off the phone. "Anna needs bright company for her head. You're invited for tea tomorrow. Our home's outside of town."

Lily nodded. "Can you tell the fir-tree-and-moccasin telegraph that I don't have airs?"

"Best rumours I hear are the ones I myself put out," he said, wrapping four bars of the Swiss dark chocolate. "You can't pay today. Welcome to Gore Bay."

Lily drove into the Brooks' yard the following afternoon, walked up the flowered path of August, and knocked on the door. Anna Brooks took one look at Lily, handing her a box of chocolates, and laughed warmly. The smell of freshly baked apple tart met Lily as Anna ushered her into the kitchen.

"Chris and I've been wondering how a New York lady copes in that ancient farmhouse." They were off, a breathless ping-pong conversation and recognition of kindred spirits.

"It's a lot of learning," Lily laughed. "Let me tell you this one!" Lily devoured Anna's apple tart and vanilla ice cream. They talked books and island gossip until Lily noticed it was five-thirty.

"We're close by," Anna said. "I always need brisk, peppy conversation. Come again, soon…"

"How was Gore Bay?" Will asked when he came in from the working barn.

"Quest successful," she told him. "Chocolate achieved! How's your design for the addition going?"

❧

"You don't say a bad word about anyone," Lily told Oliver Hill from her wastebasket perch one day. "You're someone people trust. How do you do it?"

His hands stopped momentarily. "People always ask me questions. If you can't say anything nice about a person, say nothing."

They heard Everett Mudge stomp through the front door, muttering as he turned the key to his mailbox. They heard the tear of an envelope. He grumbled, "Another cheque. Eighty thousand dollars! Idiot, I told him to reinvest it." Lily's eyes met Oliver in silent merriment "Every damn day my bonds accumulate, it pays to stay alive!"

"I'd stay alive forever on Manitoulin," Lily said softly.

Jessie Eagle was getting her mail. Lily looked up to meet the Anishinaabe elder's open face and a warm, serious smile. Ollie introduced them. "Ms. Eagle, I read in the *Expositor* about your work on Ojibwe language retention."

"Call me Jessie," she invited graciously.

"I'm learning about Ontario, and reading about aboriginal life. It's kind of magic that I'm visiting Manitoulin. I'm a travel agent from the island of Manhattan."

"It's good that you're visiting in Kagawong. There's a reason you're here on Manitoulin."

"I don't know what it is," Lily confessed. "Will says I'm learning."

"Everybody learns. That's life. The ground is solid, but we move," Jessie said gently. "You'll find your answers. Come visit me in M'Chigeeng."

Lily went back into the post office and settled onto her wastepaper basket. The fir-tree-and-moccasin telegraph was working overtime as one person after another stopped by. Was one New Yorker worth so much curiosity? She tried to disappear into the corner of the post office as Ollie handed Stan Simpson his mail. Lily settled back quietly, thinking about solid ground and where she might find hers...and the wastebasket buckled sideways beneath her, without a sound. Lily gasped, falling over to the floor, her rump lodged in the basket. Oliver stooped and pulled the basket away.

"Is that you, Lily?" Mr. Gladstone stood at the desk, seeing it all. Ollie told her he was a kind, gracious man; otherwise this scene could quickly fly across the fir telegraph!

The next morning, Lily, walking by herself around the bay, met Aunt Molly. "Come for lunch, my dear. Let's have some time for ourselves."

Lily followed her to the big stone house, where Molly set out a lunch of salmon and homemade bread. "You had courage to travel up here, knowing only Will. He took a long time to recover from the divorce. He's smiled a lot since you've been here. This is a Will we haven't seen in a long time.

"He's changed me, too, I think," Lily confessed. "Would you tell me about your husband?"

"Ah, you never know who you're going to fall in love with. I was some lucky, having forty-five years with Horty." Molly's voice caught. "He went with a heart attack two years ago. I miss him every day. I'm glad you and Will are enjoying each other."

"I'm not sure," Lily confessed. "Carlotta stopped by."

"She has nothing to do with you. Enjoy your time here, Lily. I've visited Manhattan. Every island has something for the soul. Time touches this island gently in the summer. Time's more a pat on the head than the usual slap in the face," Aunt Molly said. "If you stay, you'll love autumn: frost at night, crisp days filled with incredible colour, apple picking, pickling, filling up the winter wood piles, all of it works up a sweat."

Will and Lily strolled down Meredith Street in Gore Bay that night, ate dinner at a local restaurant and walked on the town dock. Will checked out the new sailboats and motorboats that arrived daily from Michigan, Illinois, and southern Ontario. Will walked slowly, eagerly inspecting equipment and rigging.

"Sometimes, the people who own the yacht chartering business ask me to take out charterers for a day around the North Shore. It's always fun."

"I like that you're inquisitive about boats, and you talk to all sailors. I'm surprised."

"That's how I learn. You're pretty nosy about people," he said.

She nodded cheerfully. "I learn immediately what kind of trip my clients want, what kind of bed my clients sleep in, double or single, and how much they want to spend."

"It's who you are, Lily, and how you learn," he said. Did she detect a snort?

❧

"Let's get ice cream and sit outside," Jessie said, when Lily sought her out in her office at the Ojibwe Cultural Foundation. She took Lily's arm in hers. They took their ice cream to the bay, where they found a bench.

"Your spirit is fresh, but I see you might move more slowly through this world."

"In New York, we do as much as we can, each day."

"While you're here, accept the rhythm of each day, the seasons, and the people on Manitoulin. Pay serious attention and respect all that's here, all that you're being taught."

"Jessie, what is Gitchi-Manitou? I hear people use the words."

"Gitchi means grand or immense. Manitou means mystery, essence or substance. It refers to the supernatural spirit, the great mysteries around us. I know you feel the beauty and wonder of Manitoulin." Meeting Jessie's dark eyes, Lily needed more. "Mother Earth's bountiful on Manitoulin. From our land and lakes, we've been able to hunt and fish and farm. The Great Spirit is always around us, but she doesn't always yield her harvest easily. We have to earn what we can, work for what we have. It's not easy. Our Anishnaabe communities strengthen traditional beliefs. We believe in the growth and maturity of the individual, which betters the well-being of our people."

"Will's teaching me to learn Manitoulin."

"You don't learn an island. It seeps into you."

Lily drove back to the farmhouse, and put on a shirt and long pants over her bathing suit. Will was working in the barn. She took the short walk to Bridal Veil Falls, where she hopped down the iron steps into the deep ravine. Water rushed from the high embankment, leaping from Kagawong Lake over the falls. Spray fused into a frothy veil. She watched cascading waters rush into the luxurious pool of water. She left her clothes, sneakers and towel on a rock, and sat in her bathing suit in the cold, deep pool below the falls. Her hands made soft circles in the water, caressing the small and large red stones. She raised her face to the sunshine. The water was music. Will was the first one who had told her that the Great Manitou Spirit lived here, where the mist met the falling waters. Local books mentioned this pervading spirit, a gracious sense of well-being and awe, the sound of rushing water cleansing worldly worrisome thoughts. She was opening to this, the sounds, water and air.

After a time, she dried off in the sun and wind, and put her clothes back on over her bathing suit. She walked the path along the stream toward the bay. The small harbour was filled with vacationers' sailboats. The Canadian flag waving in the wind meant much more to her now. She stepped forward—and her arms flailed as her toe caught a rock and she thumped down on hands and knees. She pushed herself up, brushed the dirt off of one knee, and rolled her pant leg up to probe gingerly around the broken skin on the other. She limped, shaking her head at her awkwardness, talking to herself. "Just a bump."

She stopped at Hunt's and bought band-aids, cleaning the blood from her knee at a pump at the beach. She limped back to the farmhouse, swallowed ibuprofen, cut her hand on a sharp knife slicing a green pepper, cleaned it up, and then burned her other hand at the old toaster. Far from city sophistication, instant answers, she had to fall down, get up...learning was bound to come. Will came in from the barn and asked what she was staring at.

"Nothing," she said. He took it as peace.

"Aunt Molly's invited us for dinner tonight," he told her.

❧

"I'm used to being a widower," Uncle Mudge answered Lily's questions. "I like living with Molly. When my kid sister was young, she could shoot a deer, skin a bear, dress a moose, and do it all before lunch!" Photographs above the fieldstone fireplace showed a lithe, beautiful raven-haired woman wearing braids, hunting clothes with leather chaps. "Molly was class, all right. She broke hearts and bent minds while she tried to keep up with me."

"Ev's still jealous of me," Aunt Molly commented, a hint of smile lurking at the corners of her mouth. "Since his wife, Martha, died, the ladies in the Red Hat Society run after Ev. Every week a dish of stuffed cabbage is left here for him."

"Sibling revelry?" Lily joked.

"My brother and I have a running cribbage game. He cheats," Molly retorted, getting up to clear the dinner dishes. Lily folded her dinner napkin, wanting to help, but Molly shooed her away. She went to the porch to overlook the bay, feeling suddenly uncertain. Uncle Mudge got up, following her through the screen door and stood by her.

"Takes courage to come here and be a beginner. I see you've got troubles. Let's take a walk." She trudged after Uncle Mudge up forty large stone steps to the back of the hill. They paused at the top, and as they looked out at the view, her eyes began to sting.

"I was married a long time," said Uncle Mudge, his eyes not leaving the horizon. "I still know nothing, but I can listen." His warmth and silence calmed her, and she felt a tear spill over. He offered a linen handkerchief with the initials EBM, still not looking at her.

She took the handkerchief.

"Get to it, I'm an old man!"

"Carlotta came by the house, bearing a quiche."

"Say no more. When things don't go your way, that's good, too," he said. "Carlotta's been pestering him for years. When she was pregnant with her son, she said it was Will's. But he's Jordy's kid."

"She keeps coming to the farmhouse…"

"Will's too much of a gentleman to make a scene. Carlotta's from an excellent island family. She's had disappointments, like the rest of us. I raised Will after my brother was killed in the war. It seemed to take more time for Will to grieve and grow up. But you can depend on Will. He's a strong guy with principles. Here's the lesson, Lily; you're on a small island. It seems like a paradise, and in some ways it is. But everyone knows everything. You chose to cross the bridge. So get over it!"

"Say something that helps!"

"Go your own way. Trust the universe. Eat a piece of Molly's sour cream rhubarb cake. You'll feel better."

"I suppose," she said.

Back at the table, between bites, Uncle Mudge went on. "Did you know that my sister had an East Coast education? Radcliffe."

"It was a fine time in Cambridge. I loved Radcliffe," Aunt Molly said.

"My mother and father grew up in Boston," Lily said, realizing how desperate she was for any social connection of strength and community.

Will and Uncle Mudge steadily worked through the entire sour cream rhubarb cake. "Molly, don't give me that look," said Uncle Mudge, then turned to Lily. "She'll make us another one tomorrow."

Lily picked up the dishes, careful not to stack, and brought them to Molly in the kitchen. Her father never let his daughters stack dinner dishes in their elegant home. They had to brush their hair and pull it back with a ribbon so he could see their pretty faces at the dinner table, but he'd also demanded a new word from the dictionary each night before they were welcome at the table. Lily thought of her father's pedantic charm as she placed the dishes on the counter. "Molly, someday I'd like you to meet my mom."

"Will's got a spring in his step. I never thought he'd meet anyone nice again. Don't worry about Carlotta."

"This isn't my normal playing field. In New York, I might know how to deal with this."

"Just be yourself, Lily. Will had a long time to choose Carlotta if he wanted her."

"I hear gossip."

"Lily, on Manitoulin you learn fast to keep anything important to yourself. If you speak badly of a third party or you're overheard in a store, it gets repeated. At my quilting circle, I keep my head down, stay serenely uninterested and listen."

It was the first of September. Will was comfortable and Alexis had not demanded her return. Will asked her to stay another two weeks. Alexis said yes. Lily had been quietly writing, inspired by letters written by her mother's Boston aunts. Great-aunt Emma had been a beautiful woman, the first female lawyer in Boston. Her sister Evelyn, an artist, had vowed never to live in stuffy Boston and had fled her strict parents for Paris, where she established herself as a Bohemian writer in a walk-up. Their letters to one another revealed an early twentieth-century world of daring and discovery.

With two more weeks on Manitoulin, Lily drove to Sophia's shop for warmer clothes. When she returned to the farmhouse, laden with sweaters, pants and a silver necklace she would send to Dahlia, Will announced, "We have had a phone call from Mrs. Violet Rose Gardner."

"My mother! Why would she call?"

"She said something about a surprise."

So, Violet Gardner had taken it upon herself to phone Willard. "Did you invite her?"

"I don't think so."

"That means she's coming. We have to trim your hair." Lily was well aware of the anxiety in her voice. "I'll do laundry and try to bake a cake. You should shine your boots."

"Tell her not to come."

"You never say no to the General."

"Lily, no changes, okay?"

CHAPTER TEN

"MY TORONTO FRIENDS TELL ME SEPTEMBER'S an auspicious time to visit Manitoulin." Violet Rose Gardner, the singular and dynamic doyenne of health and wealth, purposeful on the phone, announced her forthcoming visit. Travel times were established. It was the next week, money never an object.

"Mom, would you please bring sheet music for me from Dad's piano?"

"Certainly, dear. How is your weight? Will I recognize you?"

Will drove to the Sudbury airport to bring Violet directly to Manitoulin. It would give Lily's wily mother and Will time to charm each other. Lily prepared the guest room, ironed the sheets, arranged fresh wildflowers in a vase, cooked a turkey, made marshmallow sweet potato stuffing and baked a Betty Crocker chocolate cake, lopsidedly. Maple ice cream would cover that, one step up from ugly.

Will's diesel slowed at the curved driveway. Black-eyed susans and asters waved a greeting in the wind. Lily didn't rush out. She wanted her mother to take it in. Will helped Violet down from the truck, and Lily could see they were laughing together.

"Welcome to Kagawong, Mom!" She hugged her elegant mother.

"Honey, the trip wasn't terrible. Let me look at you!"

Violet allowed her daughter to open the front door while Will unloaded the car. They passed through the mudroom and into the kitchen.

"How quaint," Violet commented, touching the ancient copper water pump by the sink with her fingertips. "Does it work?"

Without waiting for an answer, she continued, "This reminds me of your Aunt Bea's old farmhouse in Connecticut. That farmhouse was putrified, but now it's been purified and gentrified, a colonial farmhouse worth two million. And *that* looks like my mother's stove in Boston, seventy years ago." Lily stood speechless while Violet inspected.

"I'm not judging!" her mother said, her eyes everywhere. "My dear independent daughter, God knows how many men you've dated, rejected—all those nice doctors and lawyers! And to find you here! Look at those gingham curtains—have they been washed?"

"Yes, mother!"

The wooden table had been freshly waxed. Violet peered into the living room. "Nice sofa, comfortable chairs—must have been good fabric, some decades ago. Quite antique, I see."

"Will likes vintage living."

"Your sister Dahlia is so well-married and productive," Violet murmured as she shook her head and moved across the living room to run a finger along the edge of the piano keys. "Ooh, desperate for tuning. And you're my single, career-oriented daughter…"

"Mom, you're here ten minutes…"

"What are you doing on this nowhere island, in this remarkable farmhouse?"

"Please, Mom," Lily begged, and then laughed. Will entered the kitchen. She prayed he hadn't heard Violet's assessments.

"I haven't uttered a word about her suitcases, or her golf clubs," he commented blithely, depositing two suitcases by the staircase. He walked over to stand beside Lily as she hovered in the doorway.

Violet dusted a pillow and sank into the old couch. "Will dear, get me a drink of water. I've got to get these heels off." She slipped her feet out of her expensive Pradas, picked up the *Manitoulin Expositor* from the table, and fanned herself.

"I cooked dinner, Mom."

"You couldn't have. I know Will's done everything."

In the kitchen, Will winked at Lily, who rolled her eyes toward the ceiling. He whispered, "She made you wonderful. Lighten up, have some fun!"

Sitting down at the head of the table, Violet took stock of the meal. "I look forward to meeting Will's people tomorrow," she commented. "I hope one of them plays decent golf."

"Would you like to taste rhubarb cordial before lunch?" Molly Mudge asked.

"Iced tea is good for me," Violet said, after their introduction. Molly took Violet out to the summer porch overlooking the bay. Violet had looked around the large living room. *Relaxed country charm*, her expensive decorator in Great Neck would have called it.

Lily sat across from them, trying to hide her nerves as her mother and Will's aunt took stock of one another. Despite their different backgrounds, she realized, they both had piercing blue eyes that met directly as Molly offered her guest a glass of iced tea.

"Violet, you'll find the amusements here very different from what you're used to," Molly continued in answer to her guest's questions about life on the island. "For instance, I handled a twelve-gauge shotgun by the time I was ten. Shot my first deer when I was eleven. Mama packed a lunch and we spent all day in the woods. I could still hunt if I had to, but I don't climb up a tree stand any more. I like bow-shot venison. It's a better taste than gun-harvested meat," Molly paused. "Besides golf and bridge, what do you like?"

"I do volunteer work at our hospital, enjoy my two daughters, and I'm a shopper," Violet admitted. "I don't care for sitting around. I studied physical education at Sargent College in Cambridge. Golf and tennis are still my passions."

"Sargent? I graduated from Radcliffe," Molly said. "Class of '51."

"I was in Cambridge at the same time! We must be similar ages!"

"We probably are. My husband Horty attended Harvard, engineering class of '42. After the war, we came north for Horty to work in the mines. Sudbury was busy making nickel. This was our summer home. I've lived here full-time since Horty's death. Two years ago, now. We knew each other since we were fourteen."

"I knew my Freddy from childhood, too. He lived in Dunster House."

"Dunster House? Wait a moment!" Molly disappeared into the house, reappearing with a brown, leather-covered Harvard College Yearbook. She slowly turned the yellowed pages as Lily leaned over their shoulders.

"Here." Molly stopped at a page of photos.

"There's Freddy," Violet said, her manicured finger resting beside a photograph of fresh-faced twenty-one-year-old Frederick Islington Gardner with a mustache. Lily gazed at her father's picture. They were silent. "Think Horty and Fred knew each other?"

"There were so many at school, I don't think so," Molly said, paging to the end of the book. "Here's my Horty Farquhar Weathertall. Though everyone still calls me Molly Mudge."

"The family is the Weathertall Mines in Sudbury, famous in this part of the world," Lily said. She did not add they owned half of Sudbury.

"I don't need famous at my age," Molly said. She and Lily's mother erupted into laughter. Lily felt the lovely coincidence with relief. Manitoulin and Manhattan weren't so far apart.

"Ev, come out here, you've got to see this," Molly insisted.

"Can't. Busy," he yelled from the kitchen. "Lily, set the table!"

Gathering utensils from the kitchen drawer, Lily glanced at Uncle Mudge, clean shaven. He wore a pressed jaunty red and tan plaid shirt.

"Take those plates and forks in immediately," he said firmly. She flashed a smile across the kitchen to Will where he was standing over a steaming pot. Will raised his eyebrows at her.

"Violet, ten minutes after I graduated, Horty put a ring on me," Molly said as Lily placed Limoges china and freshly polished sterling silver on the linen-covered table. "I wanted to live in Europe. He promised me London and Paris. But we knew we'd return to Northern Ontario so Horty could manage the mines."

"From Paris back to Sudbury?" Lily asked, eyebrows raised.

"Horty was a man who kept his promises. We had our European life, enjoying the arts, the music. He worked for one of our companies, while I raised our son. He moved back with us. Something about Manitoulin always pulls you back. Johnny lives in Manitowaning, married to a beautiful Anishnaabe girl, Trinity. She's lovely."

"Coming back must have required adjustment," commented Violet.

"The need for Northern Ontario air's never left me. I taught school in Sudbury, while Horty managed the mines."

"I taught physical education. Freddy and I married and moved to New York. We bought a home on Long Island, and raised Lily and Dahlia."

"We moved back to Kagawong, in the end. We had two years here before he died," said Molly, looking away. "It's hard, isn't it, being a widow?"

"Yes, it is. We were lucky to have them," Violet said. "Now I look to the future. And here I am, in my eighties, visiting my daughter who's visiting Manitoulin."

Lily drifted back into the kitchen to investigate Uncle Mudge's progress. He picked up the platter of whitefish and swept into the summer living room to set it down on the table with a flourish. "Violet, sit next to me. Do I understand you play bridge and golf?"

"I certainly do, Everett," she said.

"Those two are off and running," Will's voice came from the door as he entered with another platter.

After lunch, Molly, Violet and Lily strolled along Maple Drive around the curve of Mudge Bay, talking fashion. "Mom, Molly's style is casual. She lives in denim skirts, western boots and plaid shirts."

"I must admit that this style horrifies me," Violet confessed. "But that jacket is quite lovely." Molly sported a softly brushed leather jacket, well-stitched and draping her shoulders but close-cut to her body to keep her warm in the brisk wind off the bay.

"It was made by clothing designer Bruno Henry from Wikwemikong. If we have time, I'll call and take you to see him. He has some lovely dresses and pocketbooks. And Lily, you must take her to Sophia's."

"I will, Molly, though Mom's style is more urban," said Lily apologetically.

"I brought a jacket by Lanvin of Paris that would suit you perfectly, Molly," said Violet, eyeing the other woman. "And you *must* dye your hair. You'd look decades younger!"

"Molly doesn't need to be fixed," begged Lily.

"I like being an elder. I don't need to be made over," Molly said, winking at Lily. "Violet, you'll like my collection of turquoise necklaces and bracelets. I'll take you to the pow-wow at Wikwemikong, if you have time. We'll make a day of it."

"Lily says there's nothing to do on Manitoulin, and no time to do it."

"It's true. I want to take you around. We'll have fun," Molly said.

"If you don't mind my mom correcting you," Lily murmured under her breath.

The date of Violet's return to New York came and went shortly after the pow-wow. "I'm aglow with all I'm learning about the wonderful people here. May I stay longer?"

"Of course, Violet," said Will. He was getting a kick out of Violet, liked her spunk.

"Mom, you must stop trying to correct Molly about her hair."

"She'll wise up. No one need look older, especially Molly with her marvelous energy. We're going to a painting workshop at Rick Edwards' studio. Lily, I see Kagawong's no backwater hamlet. This island thrives with artists, singers, writers and craftspeople everywhere. You only have to look, listen, and be included."

"You sound like your daughter," said Will.

"I taught them to look on the bright side, but I do wish Lily would slow down."

"Ha, you know your daughter," Will laughed.

"You two like picking on me," Lily said. "Molly said I bring New York's brash humour into her life. When Molly hugs me, she stays in close."

Lily's mother looked at her jealously, "And, Lily, don't I?"

Autumn arrived, the shoulder season for visitors, and Manitoulin was busy with church breakfasts and festivals. Alexis allayed Lily's worry about work; the New York office was rolling on without her. Farmers' markets offered fruit, vegetables, honey, baked goods, fish and local organic meat, crafts and artwork. Violet was still there, talking to people from Ohio, Michigan, Illinois and Toronto, cruisers in love with the North Channel, talking about gardening, travel and art. They spent sunny afternoons walking the Gore Bay docks, built to allow walking and looking at the sailboats. Canadian Yacht Charters hosted sailors from all over the world. Lily wondered what it would be like to work there, to show up every day in a booking office, taking care of people again.

Violet took Molly aside. "Please tell me what a Haweater is."

Molly laughed. "In the early settler days, hawthorn trees grew everywhere on Manitoulin. They only go to 20 feet high, in fields and along fences. Their berries grow from green to a deep red in the autumn. The stems have thorns and the berries are tough to pick, but one winter, supplies were almost non-existent and the farmers, to survive, picked hawberries. The berries turned out to be rich in vitamin C, which helped the settlers fight against scurvy."

"But why is it a mark of distinction to be called a Haweater?"

"Hawberries became a symbol of survival and toughness," Molly said. "And so the people of Manitoulin are called Haweaters."

"Do you like them?

"They can be bitter but that's easily fixed. Almost like rhubarb. But, Violet, in order to be a real Haweater, you must be born on Manitoulin."

➤

"By the way, Ev, I play cribbage," said Violet one night after dinner on Whiskey Hill.

"Violet, let's see what you've got!"

"I hate cards," Lily said.

"Honey, it keeps your mind sharp and young. I keep telling my daughters that cribbage is a model for human relations—a game with etiquette and rules," Violet said. "Ev, you've met your match!"

"Harrumph," said Uncle Mudge as he cut and shuffled the cards. He let Violet cut the deck. He divided the cards in half, bent them, shuffled, and then reshuffled them in reverse.

"The guest should deal, but I started."

"You play with Harley-Davidson cards? How long have you had those?"

He dealt to her. "Ah, my lucky cards. A little ragged, but I've never lost a game!"

"We'll see," said Violet, whipping her cards into place. Uncle Mudge glanced up

"My crib."

"I guess I'm superfluous?" Lily asked.

"Go help Molly," Uncle Mudge commanded her. "This is a match of champions!"

Lily retreated to the doorway. Uncle Mudge put down a six. Violet put down a six: "Twelve for two."

He put down another six. "Ha, and eighteen for six!"

"Not for long." Violet put down a ten for twenty-eight, for a go. They laid their cards out. Done with the count, each picked a hand. Violet put hers back down in front of Uncle Mudge: "Fifteen two, fifteen four, and there's no more."

"Fifteen two, fifteen four, a pair is six, a pair is eight, and that's not so great."

They pegged their cards.

The cribbage talk continued as Violet dealt the next hand. Lily didn't understand a word, didn't care. This was an animated, flirty edition of her mother that Lily did not know. At the window, she looked out at the red dusk on the bay, blending into the blue of night. Stars twinkled. Neither Uncle Mudge nor Violet noticed, both intent on sovereignty.

"Mine's great," lorded Uncle Mudge. "Our game'll take longer."

Lily could see he was in fine form as he laid out his hand, and counted.

Violet saw the right jack, called him on it. "Keep looking!"

"Is there something else? I don't have my good glasses on."

"That's not all, Ev," said Violet, coyly. "But I won't take those points from you."

In the winter of their lives, playfully quibbling, they laughed as if it were summer.

⤳

One week later, Alexis phoned, frantic, "Lily, I'm sorry to call. We got a huge booking from the construction company, four hundred clients from the US and Europe to Mexico City. You can go back to Manitoulin later. Right now I need you!"

Will was aghast. "Can't she hire someone?"

"I've already taken too much time. I'll get my mother home and get this work done."

In the truck on 17 east, he said, "You've pulled the rug from under me, Lily. I understand you're a busy career lady, but…" He paused. "I've gotten accustomed to your face."

She smiled. "Can't a person commute from Manhattan to Manitoulin?"

⤳

Lily and her mother boarded the 4 pm flight out of Sudbury to Toronto, and then the 6 pm to LaGuardia. They took a taxi to her mother's home on Long Island.

Lily went to the baby grand piano and played "Embraceable You," and the tones were rounded, resonant and full of memory for her father. Her mother listened from the door of the living room. "I was always happy when you sang and played with Freddy, and I'm glad that you've carried on. If you don't cook, you are, at least, my musically talented daughter!"

"Wait 'til I tell Dahlia you're still picking on me," Lily teased her mother between chords. She chose twenty pieces of sheet music that she might, if asked to return to Manitoulin, take with her.

That night, Lily climbed into the single bed in her childhood room, with the small pink canopy draped above; she looked across at her miniature collection of porcelain, iron and plastic horses. In this privileged suburb, there had been no room for real horses. Her mother came into her room.

"Lily, you know I'm too old to live here alone. I've put the house up for sale."

"For sale? Mom! No!"

"Shush. I've made my decision and it's mine to make." Assuming the appropriate parental position, Violet leaned down and kissed her daughter good night, turned off the light and left the room. In the dark, Lily settled under the quilt that matched the drapes, feeling a pang. Her mother, pragmatic, might be ready to leave this home forever, but Lily wasn't, despite the ease with which she'd been putting down roots elsewhere.

Back in Manhattan, she picked up life where she'd left it, sauntering along Park Avenue, thrilled to look into shop windows on Madison, happy to ride the elevator to the 45th floor of her office building, eager to see Alexis and her co-workers. Alexis gave her the latest gossip and a stack of tickets to book. On Friday, they attended Broadway musical theatre to see a client star in a show. On Saturday, Lily took the train to visit Aunt Bea in Connecticut, presenting Will's proudly made rhubarb preserves. Suspicious, Bea took a spoon, closed her eyes, and took a taste. She put the spoon down.

"Much too runny! When you return, take *my prize-winning* rhubarb preserve to Will."

"You're too mature for this, Aunt Bea."

"Will hasn't learned everything there is to know about rhubarb yet. You must balance the sweet and sour. I speak from experience."

Alexis was thrilled to have Lily back. Three weeks flew by, and Lily settled in as though she hadn't left: exercise class early each morning, shower, and the New York clothes she loved. She was back to planning honeymoons and vacations, now also talking to her clients about Manitoulin for next summer. She caught up with the newest ticketing procedures. After work, instead of window-shopping designer labels, which she considered *research,* she found herself eyeing more relaxed country styles. She caught up with friends for dinner, and enjoyed her apartment in the evenings, taking in New York news. How different from Manitoulin, where nighttime comedy and crime shows on television could not compete with fresh air and the evening sky.

"Computer dating's dull and too much work, shopping for a guy! I haven't met a good man in four months," Alexis complained at the end of a busy day. They'd booked eighty rooms and airline tickets for another business conference, each client with different travel plans.

"I miss Will and the farmhouse," Lily said.

"Lily, we're partners and best friends, but it's October. Work's heating up. We can hire a temporary associate if you're not going to be here. If we can get Susie Foote, we'll be lucky."

Will called that night. "I'm glad to know you're making money, Lily, but when are you coming back?"

"It's busy season," Lily explained. "I've already booked some families to Manitoulin next summer. I'll be another two weeks here at least. I won't abandon my clients, and Alexis can't do both our jobs."

CHAPTER ELEVEN

THIS TIME, WHEN LILY FLEW INTO SUDBURY, she wore old clothes, a heavy jacket and her shiny black boots. "Those are New York boots. They'll get ruined here," said Will, not bothering to hide his smile or the gleam in his eyes.

"I like them," said Lily serenely. "Tell me what I've missed."

"Raccoons in the apple trees, bears in the compost. I won't feed the birds until we get a good snowfall."

"Bears!"

Will chuckled. "They're more interested in the garden than in you."

At the farmhouse, she went straight to the piano, and then stopped. "What did you do?"

"I took it to Sudbury to have it retuned and refurbished."

"When?" She looked at him.

"Three days after you left. It was a big job."

"Thank you!" She hugged him. It was a true gift, mellow and strong.

Two days later, Lily and Will finally got out of bed. After breakfast, she climbed into Will's second vehicle, a small, ancient pickup truck. It was perfect for her, an automatic with good brakes. She liked driving down the steep hill into the hamlet, always the view of Mudge Bay startling her with its breadth of bay and sky, and the La Cloche Mountains beyond. She picked up the mail from Ollie and headed back up the steep hill to Bridal Veil Esso for gas. A green car came barreling down the hill, seemingly aimed right at her. Reacting, Lily swung her wheel hard right, side-swiping the limestone embankment. She sucked in her breath and locked eyes with Carlotta as the green car, at the last second, jerked right and sped down the hill. Shaken, numb, Lily drove up to the fire station. No one was there. She turned off the engine, and sat silently until her heart rate slowed. On this lonely hill, a collision would have mangled the car and the pickup. Whose fault would it have been? Shakily, she got out to inspect the damage. The passenger side showed a few fresh scrapes on the door, but the truck was old. Will called this his deer-hitting pickup. The deer sprang out of the ditches in the evenings, a constant hazard. He might not even notice. She sighed as she climbed back in behind the wheel. This was a Manitoulin Island lesson she couldn't share with anyone.

Lily arrived at the farmhouse in time for lunch. Will wanted to drive the diesel to Mindemoya. "Don't worry about dinner," he said, kissing her. "I've got it covered." He was happy she was home. "I've put in a turkey to roast. Enjoy your afternoon. I'm going to pick up some parts for the truck."

Restless, Lily put on her coat and boots, and wandered out to revisit the farm. She ambled down the path to the river, reconnecting with her favourite view of the clouds reflecting on the water. This was what she had loved from the summer, but the water lilies were gone now in late October. The grasses were brown, though the trees remained glorious patches of red and yellow. This was all hers to share with Will. She breathed deeply, allowing the space and peace to invade her soul, smelling the spicy air of autumn, feeling gratitude. She'd avoided an accident. There was no end to the good things and good times coming for them. She walked behind the farmhouse and stopped under the apple tree to pluck a late red apple, happy to bite into the sweet taste of autumn, and then headed to the road, intending to stretch out her legs and lungs in a longer walk.

Turning onto the road, Lily walked along the pasture east towards the corner of the two stop signs in Kagawong, stopped in at Bridal Veil Esso for newspapers, and headed back to the farmhouse. She'd heard about Ontario's Adopt-A-Highway system the past summer, a program where people kept stretches of the roadways, shoulders and ditches clear of rubbish. When she walked along Highway 540 in front of the farmhouse, she'd gotten into the habit of carrying a plastic bag to pick up bottles, cans and other garbage strewn in the ditches. She pulled a crumpled plastic bag out of her coat pocket. In New York City, people carelessly, constantly threw their used gum and lit cigarettes to the curb and streets. Manitoulin was still relatively pristine. This was a better grade of garbage, she mused, picking up a pop can. Since tourist season was over, there was less in the ditches. She walked up the driveway toward the farmhouse. Movement drew her eyes, past the working barn toward the compost heap.

She narrowed her gaze. What was the stranger doing, sauntering toward her across the late autumn grass? Her eyes widened. She dropped the bag of garbage and stepped back, feeling a scream rise in her throat. She tore back to the farmhouse, breathless, wrenching open the screen door. She stopped and looked back.

The bear snuffled around the bag of garbage and then, uninterested, dropped it.

The bear looked at her. Will had told her that if the summer was dry, bears didn't get their blueberries and they came searching around houses for food. Lily let the screen door bang shut and slammed the front door. Bounding upstairs, she ran to peer out the window. Should she phone someone? There was no building super to call, no building guard, any of those men who protected her life in New York City. Where the hell was Will? On all fours, the bear sauntered past her truck. Lily couldn't see it. The roof of the porch blocked her view, but she imagined each step. She heard movement approaching the porch, where the window closest to the front door was almost always wide open. Suddenly she smelled Will's roasting turkey! He had put it in the oven before he went to Mindemoya. Who wouldn't be hungry for anything Will cooked?

Sprinting back down the narrow steps, Lily spun through the kitchen to the living room door, just in time to see the bear's paws pushing through the open window. The ancient wired screen collapsed before its claws, and a huge wet nose followed. In cartoons, bears were supple and friendly; the eyes, teeth and nose on this one made her clutch the doorway. She heard a whimpering sound, and realized that it was her. The bear's head swung her way. She imagined its eyes filled with disdain.

She looked around wildly, and saw the old straw broom leaning against the kitchen wall. She grabbed it and screamed, "Get out! You've got all of Manitoulin! I'm not a stranger who doesn't belong here! Don't you test me! Go, go, go-go-go!" Swinging the broom in a circular motion, she rushed at the bear, and smacked it across the snout with all of her strength. "Out, out, out," she yelled. The black head retreated out the window. She heard it move on the porch, and then silence … and a honking horn!

Had it left? She stood shaking, mouth open, clutching the broom, trying to breathe. She heard the sound of a truck in the yard, its horn blaring again. She ran to the kitchen door, yanked it open. The truck had Hydro One on the side. A man in an orange vest jumped out. Behind the truck she caught sight of the bear loping away.

Lily was rooted in the doorway. He looked at her. She stared back at him, clutching the broom.

"You okay?" His words came from a long way.

"Do I know you?" Lily asked, shaking.

"I'm Jordy. Carlotta's husband. I was passing by, saw the bear up on the porch. Then I realized that it was half in the house. When it leapt back, I hit the horn."

"Thank you," she said. "I was so scared! I bopped that bear on the nose!"

"You're Will's New Yorker," Jordy said, with a grin, his eyes going to the broom still clutched in her white fingers. "I'd heard you were unstoppable."

She allowed a small smile. She breathed more slowly. Will's truck pulled into the driveway, stopping short and sudden next to Jordy's truck. He stepped out. "Lily?" His voice was tentative, his eyes on her.

"Will, it was coming in the window," she told him. She could hear her voice shake.

"It was a bear," Jordy explained. "I saw it up on the porch from the road."

"I bopped it on the nose," Lily said, half-laughing, but feeling her eyes sting. "I think it smelled your turkey, Will."

"You smacked a bear? Lily, you're lucky it didn't come after you!"

"Too bad she didn't go for the shotgun, Will," Jordy said, still grinning. "Nothing like fresh bear meat. I never thought of baiting one with a roast turkey."

"My hothouse flower," Will said, sighing. "We're going to need more survival lessons."

Inside, Lily poured three glasses of straight scotch. They downed it and she poured again, sudden warmth and comfort. They all drank.

"Will," Jordy toasted, smiling, "I admire your bravery. A woman who can outface a bear with a broom is not for a weak man!"

"You watch it, or I'll shoo you out the door!"

Jordy stayed for dinner and helped Will tape the window. Late in the night, Lily woke up and got a drink of water. The ridiculous thought came that maybe she should go home to safe New York City. But it was live and let live, one for the bear and one for Lily.

She woke to sheeting rain, the grumble of thunder so loud her eyes sprang open to see lightning crackle in front of the window. Still stunned by her encounter with the bear, Lily added Northern Ontario thunderstorms to her list, pulling the blanket back over her head.

"Microbursts, part of life in Northern Ontario," Will yelled from downstairs. "Four trees are already down."

When the storm had passed, she got up, dressed, and they put on boots, walked in puddles. Trees had fallen, white bark and roots showing, smelling of fresh sap. Bushes and hay in front of the house lay flat on the ground. The air tingled with freshness, sunlight a shock. Will got busy with his chainsaw. Inside, Lily turned on CBC Radio to hear that a swath of fury had cut through from Tobacco Lake north to Gore Bay and east across the island to Sheguiandah. Hundreds of trees down, barns damaged, lowlands flooded. Kagawong had been lucky.

The following day, fields were greener, the only evidence other than Will's pile of fresh wood of the frightening power of weather. Grouchy over the loss of his trees, he told her, "You put too much soap in the washing machine."

Tiredness seeping though her, she phoned Alexis that night. "Manhattan and Manitoulin couldn't be more different." She told Alexis about hitting the bear on the nose with a broom.

"You are brave, Lily, and if you're asking if I need you? Nope," Alexis said.

"Can I get you to visit?"

"I don't 'do' rural anything," Alexis reminded her. "You okay, Lily?"

"I'm learning Northern Ontario. I just wanted to hear your voice."

By late afternoon, another New York voice had called, higher pitched than Alexis. Sartorious reported, "Business is so good, the whole world's gay. Do you have any cute things about Kuk-O-Wuk to tell me?"

"Alexis loves her new Hermes bag. That was nice of you."

"I've one for you. I've got your ultimate kitsch: to blend in on Manitoulin, you must be dowdy. Shall I fly to Sudbury for a few days for local colour? I'm dying to see that farmhouse. I can redo it in hunter's plaid for you. Must run, my gorgeous new man, Jacques, is waiting."

She hung up with the ring of Sarty's laughter in her ears, and went outside to join her quiet, Ontario woodsman, who sat in the Muskoka chair with a drink in his hand. It was dusk, the sky turning from pink to mauve and purple beyond the distant hill. She sat next to him, and Will reached out to hold her hand. "Kids growing up on Manitoulin don't understand Manitoulin is heaven. They're anxious, like I was, to see the world, Sudbury, Toronto, go west. Here, I hunted, fished, skated. Always had a boat. Then I crossed the swing bridge to attend college in Toronto, started my business, got married, and raised Laura. I forgot what I had lost here. I see so much of what I've missed. These fields, the lake, no time wasted making choices."

Used to Will's conversational pauses, she basked in his rhythms when he was happy. When he was distressed, she tolerated the silences. Lily had completed her second chapter about the three Boston sisters, using new parts of her creative brain. On her last trip home, more old letters with postmarks from New York and Paris in the twenties and thirties had been packed into her suitcase. Reading these letters smelling of ancient perfume and secrets, she had begun to forge her own characters, three sisters who loved one another, who grew up in a three-storey Beacon Hill home, privileged by family and cultural background, and would go on to live their very different lives.

Great-aunt Evelyn, the writer in Paris, had lived on the Left Bank and taken lovers. In the writing room, Lily enjoyed silvery solitary hours reading Evelyn's letters to her sister Emma and dreaming about their daring. Great-aunt Emma, studious, had infuriated her stern father by attending Portia Law School. The patriarch had tried to insist that her place was to play society lady and dispense charitable funds, but she had moved to Greenwich Village to take up a position in a law firm. Pictures of her, tucked among the letters, showed a pretty woman in a stylish hat and an arctic fox fur coat, meeting the camera with an uncompromising gaze. Lily had based her characters on these aunts, Evelyn and Emma, and given them a more traditional sister, Amanda.

She found writing by hand fulfilling; the story and the words moved through her. Rather than a life of doing—Lily never stopped in New York City—her time here was different. She looked out the window. The Kagawong River called to her and she must inspect the water lilies. Lily wasn't losing time because she wasn't in her New York office; she was gaining ground, rounding out her life as she walked to the river.

❧

Lily was learning to cook and wanted to show off a new dish for Anna. "I'd like to invite some girlfriends to dinner here on Wednesday. I'll cook your recipe for fish. Is that okay with you?"

He surprised her. "No women in this house after 6 p.m., other than you! I like to sit, have a drink, watch my TV programs or rent a movie."

"On the sailboat, people visited. What's the difference? There's a TV upstairs."

"In my marriage, I was often dismissed to go upstairs. I like my living room. I'll end up talking to Anna and she'll never go home."

"Of course, women find you irresistible," she teased him. "I do."

"Have dinner in Gore Bay. I'll pay." He was implacable, and she realized that Will was sovereign in his Vintage Farm Castle on the Kagawong.

The next morning, after a good breakfast and three cups of coffee, Lily gathered her Broadway sheet music and the tin can with gravel in it, and walked across Highway 540 to the pasture. She stood just inside the gate. No long distance whining to Dahlia. Singing was excellent therapy to exorcize feelings of rejection. Farmer Grey's cattle had had permission to graze on Will's back forty in exchange for fresh perch for an entire season; the deal had run for years. Cows were supposed to be docile. She stood silently, watching the herd munch and flick their tails. Maybe she needed cows as friends?

"Ladies," she shouted. "I'm living with a man I'm crazy about. Today I don't like him and I'm desperate to get rid of sadness. I can't sing my favourite Broadway love songs, because I want to throttle him! I'll do scales for you: do-re-mi-fa-sooooo!"

Twenty lumbering cows lifted their heads at the new sound and approached her, chewing. In college, Lily's singing teacher had assigned her "Sempre libera" from the opera *La Traviata*. Violetta, the heroine, sang this as she fell in love with Alfredo. While Violetta sang, Alfredo beguiled her into a duet.

Lily announced to the cows, "This is exclusively for you!"

Her second song, "I'm Gonna Wash That Man Right Outa My Hair" was from *South Pacific*, followed by songs from *My Fair Lady*, *Oklahoma* and *Carousel*. She warmed to higher notes, opened up her heart, her voice and breath, raising her arms. Lily noticed ears twitching. Were they entertained? She must learn more about cows, along with the other inhabitants of this island, if she wanted to stay. On the song, "I Could Have Danced All Night," she reached for E above high C, and held it. Nostrils flared. Twenty rumps presented themselves to her, trotting far away to the other side of the field.

Lily enjoyed a belly laugh, feeling airy and whole. They *had* stayed for ten songs. Lily slipped through the wooden gate, crossed the highway and went back to the farmhouse. She could wait for what was next.

That afternoon, Will leaned against the door of her writing room, tilting one large shoulder and one hip in a way she found hard to resist. "Still angry at me?" Not waiting for an answer, he shrugged. "I had to get it out."

"You've a right to say and be who you are, even if I don't like it."

"If you try to change me, the less happy we'll both be. Figure out if you can manage to get along with me. Meet your friends outside the house. I'll pick up the cheque if you want. Just don't try to change me."

"So why are you trying to change me?"

"You're eager to learn, Lily. Let's give ourselves more time."

Sartorius's squeaky voice over the phone was getting on her nerves, but she needed his Manhattan talk. She laughed when Sarty asked, "Enjoying your folksy, woodsy rusticating in Kuk-oh-wuk? How's that salubrious Canadian air?" Sarty took a deep breath: "That cute French boy left me. Congratulate me. I, who dabbled at the feet of Truman Capote, signed a new tie design deal with a French manufacturer. I commute to Paris. At the end of November, I've two orchestra seats at the Met, *La Traviata*. Why don't you fly in?"

"Thanks, Sarty, I'll join you for another opening. I need to be here." Even to herself, Lily sounded a little forlorn.

"I suppose there's always more for you to learn in cow land?"

"It's beautiful here…"

"Don't fib to a queen. Are you baking cute maple tarts? While I like Alexis, she's not you. Aren't you afraid of giving up your career? What about your apartment?"

"I made tomato soup with roasted squash. I'm walking the back forty, canoeing with Will, and working on my book. I'm getting to know all the shopkeepers."

"Don't you turn into a Canadian country housewife! If you do, I want your apartment."

CHAPTER TWELVE

DRIZZLING RAIN NEVER LET UP. Lily put on a bright red turtleneck
and jeans to lift her spirit. Her Boston sisters, each following her life's
dream, were having new difficulties in their lives, and Lily couldn't fix
any of it. She needed new inspiration. In the morning, she made the
coffee too strong, eggs runny, and burned the toast twice. The cheerful
voice of Markus Schwabe on CBC Morning North couldn't raise her
spirits. Will sat across the table reading the *Manitoulin West Recorder*
and the *Manitoulin Expositor.* Lily yearned for the *New York Times.*
Swap life in Manhattan for this slow, soggy Canadian countryside?

"You look bored. How's the writing? I know I'm not as entertain-
ing as New York."

"I'll go have lunch with Anna."

"You've got to have your socializing," he said agreeably. "I like
having you here. Life's tidier, happier. I'll make parsnip soup tonight.
We'll stick to the roots."

"Would you teach me how to preserve? I can learn something new."

"I've got lots put by. What's bothering you?"

"It's time for me to leave"—she looked down at the table—"next week, back to New York, where I belong."

"What? So soon? I thought we might see if this could work…"

"I'm not even sure what this is." She said it quietly.

"I'm a dolt." He touched her hand. "I thought you were happy, learning, finding something you needed. You said the book was going well."

"I think I am. It is. But I'm just a visitor, Will. It's clear you're sovereign here, and…" She hesitated. "I'm not sure where that leaves me."

"I need to feel comfortable in my own house and my barns."

"Will, I accept you exactly the way you are. I accept our differences. But is there any space here for me? Do I and can I fit into your life?"

"Put on your jacket and boots. I've something to show you in the rhubarb patch."

"It's raining."

"It's clearing."

They walked though the tall, wet grass as the clouds swept by and the sun began to lighten up the ancient rhubarb patch on the small hill that overlooked the river. Lily regarded the original rows of rhubarb, somewhat tilled, amazed at how large the leaves were in their autumn slump. His vegetable garden had only been able to flourish with a high wire fence to keep the deer away. She had enjoyed picking tomatoes, cucumbers and cabbage in the summer. All gone now. But Will had brought the squash into the root cellar before the first frost. Half-green tomatoes were ripening on the shelves downstairs.

"You haven't fallen into any more rhubarb since swatting the bear," Will said.

"That metaphor's really tired," Lily said, putting her hands in her pockets against the cold. "Rhubarb's just celery with high blood pressure."

"That's not like you."

"I've had enough."

"Of what? I'll do a roast beef. Invite Anna and Chris for dinner?"

"You'd do that now, since I'm leaving for New York?"

"I need to learn, too, Lily, about your friends…"

"They'd be yours, if you'd let them."

Each stood, looking in different directions. It was cold, their breath coming out in small puffs. She gazed down the lovely path to the river. She'd sorely miss this island. "I've been more than an agreeable guest in your farmhouse. But you're a deeply introverted Manitoulin mammal," she continued, shuffling in the grass.

"We are complicated," he told her. "And let's both keep trying, Lily."

Though the sun came out, she shivered, wondering how many flights a day there were from Sudbury to Toronto. She wouldn't be going through any winter here. It was good she hadn't given up her business. Alexis would show her how to date on the internet. Her foot found a small rock. She kicked it toward the river.

Will handed her a small box.

"What's this," she asked. Her eyes narrowed. She opened it, a knee-buckling moment.

"It's a ruby, representing the sunrise and sunset, a Manitoulin Smoothie."

Her eyes burned into his face. She could kill him. Or she could love him.

"A ring honouring a drink?"

"Lily, we needed a fight or two. You're still here."

"Is this why we're standing in the damn rhubarb patch?"

"Think you can live here, not go back to Manhattan?"

"I'll always return to Manhattan. And I love Manitoulin. Talk to me!"

"You've many talents. You get along with everybody. I don't. My first marriage was torture when we split," he said, kicking at a stalk of rhubarb on the edge of the patch. "Rhubarb's flat and frozen, but it'll come back in the spring."

"Will, look at me. I'm not rhubarb."

"I think better in the rhubarb."

She held the open box. "You're offering me a ring and rhubarb?" she asked. "You're going to the Caribbean in two months."

"I was afraid the silence and people here would swallow you whole, but they haven't. We can go south together."

"You're inviting me for the winter? Talk to me! You're a Canadian who reads Heidegger, talk to me!" She gazed at the stunning ruby, diamonds on either side, dazzling in the sudden morning sunlight.

"The ring's yours to keep."

"It's either an engagement ring or it's not."

"You do accept that I live a deeper, more muted existence than you do."

"Yes, Will. We're different. Do *you* accept that?"

"I do know you, Lily Gardner, and I love you. This could be an engagement ring."

She didn't know whether to laugh, or cry. She stayed silent in the immensity of his words. He concentrated getting the ring out of the box. She allowed him to slip it on her finger. "This ring's perfect, for a bright lady willing to accept me as I am, willing to cross the swing bridge and live with me."

The moment, the morning, the sky, the wet rhubarb, his warm hands, turned brilliant for her. Will loved her. If she could let herself be, listening more, talk less, move slower, and let him be, Will and Manitoulin could be divine. She had Anna, Chris, Muddy and Sophia, her new friends, shops and restaurants around the island, a canoe and a pickup truck. She had Ollie, Aunt Molly and Uncle Mudge for anchors. She gazed at the exquisite ring on her left hand.

"Let's keep this to ourselves for a while," Will said. "I have to get used to it."

She laughed so loud the breezes carried her sound to a beaver that lifted his head, slapped its tail and slid underwater. Will reached down and kissed her, their mouths sweet and firm, a declaration in the rhubarb patch. She felt Will's energy change to relief. His eyes squinted, crinkling at the corners as he smiled.

The sun appeared through the clouds for a moment as they walked back toward the house. She gazed up at Will, loving his full face. She danced in a circle. Creatures in the grass scuffled away. "You can quit your job in New York, and learn to cook," Will teased.

"Not likely," she murmured, but the flush of excitement and happiness coursed so strongly through Lily she held on to him. She was going to live on Manitoulin with Will, and sail with him in the Caribbean this winter.

Sitting by the fireplace that evening, Lily gazed at her ruby and diamond engagement ring. "I will need to go to New York for my doctors, dentists and haircuts…"

"You're not in prison," he said. "And there are doctors in Espanola and Sudbury. Even hairdressers. Lily, let it happen. Lose that New York imperative!" He was making Manitoulin Smoothies. "While I was in Gore Bay this afternoon to get the tires on the truck changed, I had a beer with Jack at Whiskey Corner. I know who has hemorrhoids this week. All you need to do is stay quiet and you'll hear everything."

"The fir-tree-and-moccasin telegraph. Tell me more!"

Will laughed. "I've already told you more than I heard."

❧

"Engaged!" Violet shouted. "I hope you know what you're doing."

"Mom, what does that mean? You *like* Will."

"Yes, dear, but you've waited so long—and Manitoulin's so far away. Will is not a man who'll leave his home. You will be leaving New York. I suppose it's a good time, though. I called because I need you here, desperately! A young couple knocked on the door. I showed the house. I sold it to them."

Lily felt her stomach drop. "You did this without consulting me and Dahlia?"

"It's my house, Lily. They offered more money than it's worth. Come and empty the attic!"

"And the basement. I've got to wrap my mind around this."

"Wrap quickly," the General commanded. "I need your energy and focus."

"Yes sir, General."

Will drove her to the airport. As she got out of the truck, he asked, "How do I know you'll come back?"

"Come to Long Island with me?"

"Not a chance."

"Do we need any really good furniture?"

"No," he said. "Just you."

❧

The attic in the big white colonial house on Maple Drive held thousands of old books collected over sixty years. Dolls, possibly collectors' items, rested on attic shelves. Violet was certain the entire closet of vintage clothes would fetch a fortune. Everywhere memories bubbled up. Lily's mother found a full sterling silver tea set hidden and forgotten. "So that's where that went!"

Lily sorted paintings, blankets, lace, suitcases, records, furniture, and linens from Portugal. She dispensed, discarded, and made bundles for charities.

"I feel giddy with new freedom in letting go, all the physical things of the past," Violet said, surrounded by piles in the living room.

Photographs revealed Lily's glamorous mother in mink, standing with her beloved Freddy on the streets of capitals all over the world. Each designer suit, dress, coat and hat had a story. The owner of Vintage Treasures came to call. Her eyes turned cat green. She clamped her mouth immediately. "They aren't interesting, those Gucci dresses. I'll take them off your hands." Sweeping away what Violet allowed, the lady left a cheque for $20,000. Each felt victorious.

Buyers from auction galleries, one snoot after another, paid a visit to the house, appraised furniture, paintings, silver and china. "Mrs. Gardner, we know what people will pay for that. But we have our costs, too. We buy low and sell high."

"Lily, come down from the attic. Your sister's on the phone."

Dahlia asked, "Is Mom letting go easy, or is it torture?

"Nothing seems right," Lily muttered, feeling as if she were losing her self one antique at a time. "Can you come for a week?"

"I'll be there," Dahlia answered.

"Girls, we mustn't make the mistake of measuring the value of our home or our memories on any monetary scale. When we finish, this will open new psychic space for us."

The community garbage truck lumbered into their driveway. In the driver's seat was Rugged Louie, so courtly and genial by day that they were positive he was Mafia by night.

"Louie, coffee?"

"Sure, Mrs. Gardner," said Louie, entering the house. "You're softening me up. I counted 37 bags of garbage and 200 old *National Geographic* magazines."

"Take them and sell them. Come to the basement," Violet commanded.

"I'm a grown man, and I'm afraid." He peered into the basement, and then lumbered down the steps. Ten tables were filled: Farber cookware, four broken Tiffany lamps, original Fiesta ceramic plate sets, dull silver pots and pans, old-fashioned kitchen utensils, three ancient typewriters, Monopoly games, Parcheesi, and four rusty green filing cabinets. A Mah Jong set with ivory pieces waited with three pairs of ice skates, roller skates, and eight badminton racquets.

"No one wants that 78 recording of Caruso. Not even my Uncle Lonzi."

Police Chief O'Neill warned Violet, "No yard sale. People addicted to estate sales line up at dawn. You'll need protection by the police. We stop fistfights over antiques."

While Lily and Dahlia sorted, Lily told her, "We went to auctions on Manitoulin this summer. The locals mingle with visitors. The auctioneer weaves people through laughter and buying. It's as much entertainment as commerce."

"Lily, you're on Maple Drive, not Manitoulin." Dahlia's voice was tired. "Do you want to take these things? I have no space for them." She gestured toward the living room, where they'd placed family treasures: the marble-topped antique dresser from France, the large oil painting of a green valley by a New Zealand artist and two heavily brocaded Queen Anne chairs.

They grew wearier through the afternoons, sniping at each other. "You don't need more stuff. You're becoming a vulture,"

Dahlia accused Lily when she refused to add a box of forty-year-old costume jewelry to the pile waiting for the antique dealers.

"These are family heirlooms," Lily said. "I remember Great-aunt Emma wearing these earrings at New Year's. I'm sorry to offend you by saving things."

"I guess it's easy to take it out on you. It does hurt to let go."

"Mom can't make all the decisions."

"But why do you want them? Where would you wear them?"

"It's a way of seeing where we come from. You know those letters of Mom's from her three aunts in Boston that I've kept all these years? Well, at the farmhouse, I've had time to think and write. I've begun working on a story based on the sisters and their lives. I love Will, and there are many things I can do in Manitoulin that I've thought about doing for years, and somehow never found the time."

"You're writing, Lily?" her mother asked, overhearing her. "Finally! You've written for those travel magazines for years, but I know there's more in you. You will use those letters wisely, though." It was not a question, in that voice. "You have responsibility for what you say about our family. I want to see what you write."

"Of course, Mom," Lily answered. "But it's not exactly family history, the way it's turning out. Right now it's bits of fiction, inspired by the times and their lives, way back when. I don't even know if it's going anywhere."

"You didn't know that *you* were going anywhere, six months ago," Dahlia said, looking at Lily as if she were suddenly a stranger. "You're leaving Manhattan, and your glamorous job. And now— my sister's becoming a novelist, living abroad!"

"A hundred miles from a decent bagel," her mother added. "Dahlia, you haven't seen that farmhouse! It's not bad. I know you love Will, but I only hope you can adapt, Lily—winter is coming!"

"Yes," Lily grinned. "And we'll be in the Caribbean, sailing from Virgin Gorda!"

"Point," said Dahlia. "If you and Will are truly serious, are you going to sell your apartment or rent it out? And what are you going to do for money?"

"I'll never sell the apartment. I'll rent to friends and keep my sleeping-on-the-couch privileges. As for work—I'm half-owner, Dahlia, and I'm not selling out. For this first year, we'll pay an employee with my share of the profits. I'll come in for a few weeks or a month when it's busy, to keep my professional rating. As for money, well, Manitoulin is not New York. I have savings and stocks, and Will isn't charging rent. But anyway," Lily said, shaking her head, "it's too soon to think about this."

"I can't imagine you playing wife in the middle of nowhere. You speak of Manitoulin Island with such reverence, but a woman needs her own money!"

"I thought I might commute across the old swing bridge," Lily said, dreamily. "Two months on Manitoulin, one in Manhattan."

"Marriage means commitment," said Dahlia. "If you're serious about this, you'll have to leave New York City behind."

Lily looked at her sister. "I don't have all the answers yet. Let's get back to this kind of sorting out."

Dahlia let her change the subject, but as they turned to the next box from the attic, Lily saw her mother's frown.

The days passed in a blur as the artifacts and family treasures of seven decades flew out the door. It was easy to ridicule Violet's 150 purses. They sold forty; donated eighty to Good Will, and Violet refused to relinquish the rest. "We're sending you to Bag Rehab," Dahlia laughed. "You must attend Bags Anonymous meetings once a week."

"It's my one lapse from perfection," said the General haughtily, as the three drooped wearily over the Queen Anne dining-room chairs on the fifth day. "Have mercy on me, girls. With all this space, I never had to throw anything out."

"Let's sit outside." They carried out mugs of green tea to soothe their frantic souls. Sitting at the curb of their quiet street under the maple trees, the sisters looked up at the empty branches, and at the lawn strewn with yellow and brown leaves. "Dahlia, remember making angels in the snow here?"

"Catching fireflies in the summer," Dahlia remembered. She added softly, "It was a good place to grow up."

"Hard to say goodbye," Lily agreed. "I can give up a lot of this stuff, Mom. But the baby grand piano's a problem for me. Remember Dad telling us that he got a job playing piano in a townhouse on Winter Street in Boston? He returned the first night telling his mother the ladies tickled him, wearing few clothes."

"Grandma wouldn't let him go back."

They took Dahlia to the airport a few days later. "We're nearly done here," Lily told her. "You have work and family to look after."

"I feel like we're leaving you behind, Lily," said her sister. "You're the last of us in New York. But I guess you're leaving, soon, too."

Lily felt a pang. "Not right away. We're pretty busy at the office, so I'm staying for a few weeks."

➷

Over the next few days, Lily commuted to Manhattan, spending evenings in Great Neck with her mother. They catalogued sheet music ranging from the thirties to the eighties, page corners creased and dog-eared. When her father had died, they'd mourned in the too-silent house. Lily sat over the piano, playing through old favourites, late into the night. She played as if she could still summon her father in from another room.

"You've played that song six times! Time for bed!" called the General from upstairs.

The next afternoon, Violet stood by the piano in the living room. Twenty photographs had rested on that piano, but her voice was firm. "In Florida, I won't have room for it."

"I want it," Lily stated.

"It would be a black ghost in your living room," Violet said, looking away. "You'd have to take out all of your furniture. No living in the past. We can't let possessions possess us."

"I *play* the piano," Lily reminded her mother. "I'm the one who took lessons! The only reason there isn't one in my apartment already is that I was always traveling."

"But you have a little piano at the farmhouse," Violet said.

"Mom, it's not the same. This belongs with me in New York."

A surly, obnoxious dealer came to inspect the piano. When he gloated, saying "Aha, the sound board's cracked, but I'll buy it," Lily stood there, seething. She had checked with the Baldwin people, who offered five times his price. "Call me when you're ready," the dealer said smugly. "Your mother won't be able to refuse my offer."

Lily tore his card into little pieces. "I'll buy it, Mom."

"I'd never accept money from you."

"Why are you so reluctant for me to have it?"

"You have a future with Will in Canada. I don't want you living in the past."

Morose, Lily took the train from Great Neck to Manhattan, and put the key into her apartment door. She stood amidst her clutter. She was as guilty as her mother. She knew now why Will loved his barns. What if the General relented, and the piano didn't fit in the apartment elevator?

Finally, every room in the house on Maple Drive was empty. Only Violet's bed and TV upstairs, and the piano were left. Four days to closing. "I'm sorry I called you a vulture," Dahlia told her that evening from Florida.

"I'm sorry, too," sighed Lily.

"Two more piano dealers are coming in tomorrow," said Mom.

Lily phoned Aunt Molly on Manitoulin. "I understand your dilemma of piano love so well," said Molly. "Our mom sold our piano while I was at school. I've never gotten over it. Your soul is in your piano. The instrument's made of wood, strings, and steel, but your own piano resonates with laughter and family."

"Mom's sure the piano won't fit into my apartment. She's determined to sell it."

Uncle Mudge had good advice. "It looks like a loss to you, but be patient and gentle with your mother. She has memories in that piano, too. Allow her the time to grieve over that, and to see that the piano isn't just memories to you, but also part of who you want to be now."

Lily called the Salvation Army to donate her own living room furniture. When the men arrived, she handed each twenty bucks to take it all. Here was sunshine and space for the small couch, two antique chairs, and a cherished Baldwin baby grand piano.

"If you sell this piano to me, I'll find a nice fiberglass piano for your daughter. An apartment model will be much more appropriate," said a nasty potential piano buyer to Violet. Lily was sick with outrage.

"Trade Baby Grand in for plastic?"

She drove to the Tinkling Ivories Factory in Manhasset, a dark mausoleum made more dismal on a rainy day housing a cadre of orphan pianos. All brands and types waited in cruel silence, beckoning to be taken away. Moving along a row of 40 pianos, Lily plunked away. She couldn't bear the tinny sound, the unfamiliar tones. You fell in love with a certain man, and the certain sound of a certain piano.

Piano buyers left messages. A bidding war began. Lily couldn't stand it another minute. She stood in front of her mother. "I declare the piano to be mine, a legacy from my father. I'm the only one who plays it. My living room is empty, waiting for the piano. I will have it."

"Dear, I'm protecting you. You idolized your father as a little girl. Now you've chosen Will to love, and he's totally opposite. I don't want you carrying the ghost of your father into this new marriage."

"There's a difference between carrying ghosts and having an identity, Mom. Will would never leave that old farmhouse. All I want is one piano."

"Lily," Violet said, wilting. "I can't fight you. If you want it this badly, it's yours."

"You mean it?" Afraid her mother would change her mind, Lily rushed out to make arrangements with piano movers.

"Will! Baby Grand is mine!" she told him triumphantly on the phone that night.

"I'm glad it's working out, Lily. It's an important link to your musical roots. You understand now why I have old family stuff here."

"Mom didn't understand why it's so important. She thinks I'm hanging onto the past."

"You are, but that's not a mistake," he told her. "Are you going to bring it to Manitoulin?"

"There's no room for it in your house," she said, regretfully. "We'll be in Virgin Gorda for most of the winter anyway. I'll keep it here in my apartment until spring. I've sold a lot of my furniture to make room."

The piano handlers took off the lyre and legs, wrapped Baby Grand in blankets, and placed it on a mover's dolly. They pushed it slowly down the front walk to the truck. "That'll be cold cash, Miss Gardner," said the teamster.

She waited at the front door of her building. Baby was swaddled in cloth and wheeled into the vestibule. Clenched in Lily's hand were five one-hundred dollar bills to go to the men after the piano was installed and reassembled. The men were roughly dressed, but they moved the piano so gently, and the foreman gave her a toothy grin of success as he and it fitted exactly into the elevator. He held in his stomach, and draped himself over the piano.

She bounded up five flights of stairs, hovering there until the elevator doors opened. Baby was carefully extricated and sailed into the living room. A clean space waited against the wall. The men put the legs and lyre back on.

She paid the foreman, his smoky breath in her face. He spit on his finger, counting to five. When they left, Lily cleaned Baby's ivory keys and sat down to play scales. The sound resonated warmly, rich in her small living room. She slid into "Embraceable You," and raised her voice, her father's tenor in her memory, and joyful that the piano was in its next home. Hers.

Two days later, Violet locked the back door of her empty home for the last time.

"Today is our graduation, on to the new. We're free, Lily!"

Autumn leaves crunched underfoot as Lily crossed the front lawn. A dog barked in the distance. They met with the lawyer, signed the contract of sale, accepted the cheque, and drove to the bank. Lily had arranged Violet's flight to Fort Lauderdale. At the curb at LaGuardia, her mother stood as the skycap took her luggage. "Being with you and Dahlia has been a celebration. Thank you, darling!" She kissed Lily one more time. "Enjoy your wonderful new life on Manitoulin!"

Back in their Manhattan office, Alexis eyed Lily's engagement ring. "I still don't believe it," she said. Lily worked until Alexis deemed booking and ticketing complete for their next mega-business conference. Phones rang nonstop, computer keys clacked and invoices churned out of the printer. The bulk of ticketing finished, Lily phoned Will at the farmhouse on December 1st.

"Business is crazy," she told Will. "I'll need another week."

"I keep coming in to tell you something, and you're not here. We had snow today."

"*SNOW?*" Lily choked down a scream.

"It melted right away," Will assured her, his voice touched with amusement. "But winter's definitely coming. Come home and keep me warm."

"Susie will stay permanently, but our Christmas season is here."

"She can't come, Will!" Alexis shouted from across the office. "We're too busy! I'm chaining her to the desk!"

"The good news," Lily told Will, "is that we make excellent money. The bad is our clients expect perfection. Alexis has all she can do to handle the corporate work. I can't just leave now if I'm going to be away for most of the winter. We're booking the Caribbean, winter vacations, sailing for Christmas and into February and March."

There were three beats of silence at the other end of the line.

"Are you having second thoughts?" Will asked calmly.

"NO!"

"Then do what you have to do," he said firmly. "I'll have the boat prepared in Virgin Gorda and get the house ready for winter without us. When you get here," his voice deepened, "you'll be all mine."

"You must stay until Christmas," Alexis told her firmly once she'd hung up. "Business is booming, and if you're leaving me with Susie, please mentor her through her first Christmas rush." It wasn't a question. She knew Lily cared as deeply as she. They had worked long and diligently together to build the business.

"We'll be fine then, 'til spring, and you can write our newsletter from anywhere." The agency newsletter had been Lily's project from the start, and they both believed it had gone a long way to building the business and creating a sense of community among their clients.

"Your last Manhattan Christmas!" Sarty said to Lily over dinner late Friday evening. "You're abandoning everything tinsel, elegant and shiny, with parties galore. For northern snow!"

"I'm abandoning you for Will," Lily told him, her eyes dancing. "Northern snow is an added bonus!"

"You are a cruel woman."

"Heartless," she agreed. "I'm thrilled to tell you my niece is moving to New York and will be taking over my apartment."

❧

Saturday night she called Will again, hesitant to mention her delay. He was full of anticipation.

"Remember Doris? She worked at the Bridal Veil Esso this summer?'

"Yes."

"Angie, her sister, cleans for a living. She came by to get the house ready for you."

"What?" Will hadn't seemed aware of the state of the house when she'd visited in the summer. Perhaps, she thought with amusement, the General had had a cleansing effect.

"How soon can you come?"

"Well… Mom's settled in Florida," she told him. "And Susie knows what she's doing. But Will"—she forced herself to continue—"the sheer number of bookings is going to keep me here a bit longer."

"Aw, Lily," Will said, disappointment deep in his voice. "You're not going to make it for Christmas, are you? Can you at least be home with me for New Year's Eve?"

"Anyone who isn't booked by then won't be booked by me, Will," she promised, her heart in her throat. He had said it.

Home with me.

Chapter Thirteen

Lily's arrival on Manitoulin was hot, happy and laughing with Will, but frigid with a cold front following the early winter storm that had dropped six inches of snow on the island. She called it Severe Manitoulin Winter. She felt the chill deeply, especially when the temperature was announced in Celsius on CBC. The day after she arrived, they drove into Gore Bay and she bought long johns from Webb Brothers.

Her niece Amy called from her Manhattan apartment that evening to say she had successfully moved in, taking half of Lily's closets as agreed. Lily was thrilled to have her home—and Baby Grand—in safe hands. Amy had grown up in Boston, but already loved Manhattan. And Susie Foote, according to Alexis, had established herself at Lily's desk. Lily didn't mind at all. She'd even given Susie her coffee cup that said *Good Morning, Gorgeous.*

"It helps when a client yells in your ear," Lily had told Susie. "I keep that coffee cup filled, and Advil on hand for tumultuous travel days."

Each morning, Will and Lily drank fresh coffee in easy chairs in the mudroom, watching the light on the field in front of the house. If the sun made the frigid morning seem warm, they put on heavy walking boots and did the back forty. A narrow path led past "her" cows munching hay, and back past the silent swamp, frozen hard beneath their feet. The wide expanse of sky gave her sunlight on snow. Crows flew overhead. They looked for deer and wolf tracks, the winter signs of Manitoulin. Here she could think, or not think, breathe deeply and swing her arms, loving her sense of well-being and watching Will's flannelled figure in front of her.

Then Will repaired to one barn or another, while she climbed the narrow steps to her writing room. Most winter mornings were sunny. The farmhouse was warm, and Lily loved the feel of the old house wrapped around her. Drawing on her great-aunts' letters for historical detail and language, she had begun to craft new characters for her book: Sarah, the ambitious law student determined to have her own practice, and her sister Vivian, a rebellious and sensual sculptor who followed love to Paris and saw the world through stone. She would draw from Great-aunt Evelyn's letters to evoke bohemian Paris in the twenties. Their older sister Amanda, although more socially conventional in ambition, was equally determined to succeed.

Lily's clothes hung in the bedroom closet to the left of Will's, her shoes in a row on the floor below. Will took her suitcases down to the basement. She smiled at the room he was making for her, allowing her to sweetly settle in.

She began, quietly, to build an independent, engaged, self-reliant life, unlike her busy, buzzy Manhattan existence. She did not use the telephone, and found herself sleeping soundly. TV and radio informed her about the world, and she emailed friends. She relied on the two island newspapers for local news: a church supper they might attend, and the upcoming winter fair. The *New York Times* online kept her in touch with city news and the wider world. She drove into Gore Bay for tea with Anna. Once, they went to Providence Bay and dragged Sophia out for lunch at their favourite garden restaurant in Tehkummah.

Will had her book their flight to Virgin Gorda for the third week in January.

"Since we're this late anyway, I want you to have a few weeks of Manitoulin winter," he told her.

She loved her desk, customized for her height, with its straight-backed, comfortable chair. A voracious reader, Will dropped a completed paperback or history book on the bookshelf to the left of her desk nearly every day.

"If you have time," he would tell her. "That one's pretty good."

At the end of the first week, they drove into Gore Bay for groceries. She wheeled her cart around the store, and exchanged pleasantries with the woman at the deli counter. Before picking her up, Will stopped at the gas station on the corner to gas up, return wine bottles, and get his fill of town conversation. This was all so new, this routine. When they turned back into their driveway at the end of the day, and with the engagement ring on her finger, Lily felt eager and happy.

She'd brought five songbooks from Manhattan, looking forward to playing the little piano now that its rich notes were in tune. She'd arranged them at the piano the second she'd arrived, unable to resist picking out a few bars before she even took off her coat.

Each day passed rapidly. She couldn't say what she accomplished, but she had time in her writing room, time at the newly tuned piano, time hiking outdoors with Will, time by herself to walk down to the Kagawong River. The snow was not yet so deep as to require snowshoes, though she eyed with some trepidation the pair that had appeared for her in the mudroom. Will prepared their dinners, always delicious. Then, he relaxed in the living room with cognac and his current book while she did dishes. The television was never on in the evenings, but slow, sweet jazz records cast a spell. Within two weeks, Lily felt comfortable, as if the farmhouse were becoming home. The routine was punctuated by Will's cooking for Aunt Molly and Uncle Mudge or Muddy every few days, and on the second Saturday they were invited for dinner at Whiskey Hill. Staying exercised and lean was forcing her to think about her mother's two favourite words: *portion control*!

Lily learned to bundle up in layers, with long johns under jeans and the three layers of tank, t-shirt and sweater. She developed a fondness for mittens, scarves and hats. On a blue-skied cold day, she bundled up and went out to watch Will split wood. Shortly, she was piling the split wood onto the woodpile against the barn.

"Wood makes you warm twice," Will told her, swinging the axe down with a crack that split a 16-inch piece of poplar in two. "Once when you cut it, and once when you burn it."

"I see three times," she told him. "Once when you pile it."

He sent her in for coffee, and she came back with a thermos and two deck chairs. She sat and watched his arms and shoulders move, slowly in rhythm with the feathery clouds' sweep across the sky. She just might *not* miss the hustle of crowds at street corners waiting for the light to change, or the constant sirens, or the rush of clients asking for ticket changes. She imagined herself as a slow-talking woman of dignity, of new distinction, a woman becoming a writer. She was newborn here in Kagawong. This completely different life, and the old farmhouse and its ancient fixtures, was becoming hers.

At the beginning of the third week, dark clouds began to pile in the morning sky, and the world beyond her windows turned white, the road hidden by the falling snow. They spent the next two days watching the snow fall, the world muffled beyond the house.

"This is your first real Canadian snowstorm," Will said on the second evening, when he went to shovel the snow from the door to his truck. It was as high as her waist. If she'd ventured out she would have been lost.

"It'll be over by morning." He was right. Every bare branch was lined with white, but the sky was light as the sun finally rose.

"The roads aren't too bad, but be careful, Lily," Will told her. Looking out the living room window, she couldn't see any border between road and ditch.

"I'm eager to see Aunt Molly. I think I can make it over to have tea with her."

He nodded. "I put new winter tires on the pickup before Christmas." She'd never been allowed to drive his diesel three-quarter ton, a man's truck for hauling and shipping, but she felt at ease in the little pickup. She and Molly sat over tea in the winter living room, the fire blazing and the late afternoon grey-white beyond the broad windows.

"I was hoping you two would commit," Molly admitted, after they'd talked about all the family and community news. "Have you set a date for the wedding?"

"We haven't talked about it," said Lily. "In a few weeks, we'll be sailing out of Virgin Gorda. Then back here in the spring to redo the house, buy new furniture and plant a garden."

"It's about time," Molly said. "Will loves that land, but that old farmhouse needs a woman's touch. I've some family pieces for you, once you start. It's too late to see them today. It gets dark early this time of year—and the snow is settling in for another round."

Lily glanced out the window. The winter afternoon was an appreciably deeper grey.

"You'd better head home," Molly told her. "Manitoulin in snow is a completely different world."

᠀

Driving around the curve of Mudge Bay, Lily peered out at the endless snow. The road was slippery, and she felt the truck shimmy as she pressed on the brake. The back end swung towards the ditch, and she turned the wheel to stay in her lane. The pickup had other ideas. It slid sideways, and then whirled around in a circle. Suddenly, she couldn't see the ditch or the road. The wheel jerked out of her hands. She braced for a crash as the truck slid entirely off the road.

Dead silence.

The wind had stopped. Imprisoned, Lily sat staring through her windshield as she hung sideways in her seatbelt. She couldn't see up or out. She shut the engine off and squirmed sideways, stretching below for her purse and cell phone, both taunting her from six inches beyond her reach.

She turned to her left, and tried to push open the heavy truck door, straight up into the falling snow. Taking a deep breath, she braced her feet and unhooked her seatbelt, while slowly pushing the door up against gravity. The tilt of the truck thankfully allowed the door to rest open. She climbed up and out, struggling, wet, over the snowbank. Snow fell on the silent truck. Lily stood alone on the road in an endless expanse of wind and white. The snow melted on her hair, and she realized she wasn't wearing gloves. No way she could or would go back into that ditch.

She looked both ways, feeling a chill that had nothing to do with the weather. No houses in sight. Could she walk to Muddy's down the road? Or back up to Aunt Molly? Whiskey Hill was too far away; she'd freeze to death. Will would find her in the morning, a statue. She looked at a patch of frozen rhubarb at the side of the road. Ha, finally in the rhubarb. Not smiling, she walked carefully towards Muddy's, afraid to run and risk falling into another ditch. Pushing her hands deep into her jacket pockets, she turned in the direction she'd been going and slogged slowly, head down, toward Muddy's house. She arrived breathless and shivering, and banged on his door.

"Hold yer damn knickers, I'm coming," Muddy growled, opening the door in long, wooly underwear, his stomach sticking out.

"Muddy, I drove into a ditch, or something!" She was shaking with cold and fear.

"I hope you didn't wreck it. Will went to five dealers to find that pickup."

"I could have died out there!"

Muddy snickered. "It's just a bit of snow, New York. Good thing I brought home the tow truck. Phone Will. I'll need help."

"I'm afraid to phone him! Can we do it?"

"You want the pickup to freeze in the ditch? I'll throw on some clothes."

Muddy fired up the tow truck and she hopped up into the passenger seat. As they parked back at the curve of Mudge Bay, a car had already stopped to survey the damage. "Slid right off, did ya?" a fellow from Kagawong laughed.

"Next time, hope it ain't you," Muddy shouted back.

"Everybody does a winter ditch dive," said the next driver, through an open window. The Kagawong crowd passed by, slowing to gawk, to sneer, to cheer, to laugh, and be glad it wasn't them.

"Everybody's got something to say," Muddy said, as he manoeuvered the tow truck on level ground behind the pickup. Three inches of snow had already covered it. Will arrived and parked.

"At least it's not my diesel," he muttered, shaking his head. He turned, "You okay?"

Lily couldn't look at Will. She nodded, and twisted toward the frozen bay. He patted her shoulder. Said nothing. She heard the gawking onlookers drive on as the men got to work.

She turned back to watch. Standing by the truck, Will pulled a lever, allowing the cable to freewheel from the winch. He then pulled the cable to the pickup, hooking it under the rear bumper. Muddy turned the motor on. Will stood at the side of the tow truck, operating the controls that engaged the winch. It creaked and groaned as it began to pull out the little pickup. The winch turned, slowly, grinding, inch by hard, tough inch.

Suddenly the cable sprang back like a whip, snapping at Will's right leg. He dropped to the ground. Lily screamed, seeing blood and something white protruding. Will lay deadly still, the cable curved beside him. Blood pooled slowly from his leg onto the dirty ice. Muddy jumped out of the truck, rushed to Will's side, and applied pressure.

"Lily, he's breathing. Get over here! Keep steady pressure on his leg. I've got a radio in my truck. I'm calling Mindemoya for an ambulance. Don't move him!"

Will's face was grey, drained of colour. Lily lowered her head to hear him breathe. Everything was knocked out of him. She wanted these moments back so she could change them.

"Lily, put the pressure on with all your might," shouted Muddy, already talking on his radio, smart and fast. The ambulance from the Manitoulin Health Centre in Mindemoya was on the way. "I hope he don't bleed out. Let me take over," Muddy said, pushing Lily aside.

It was a twenty-minute drive from Mindemoya to Kagawong. They heard the siren coming off the Billings Stretch. The ambulance arrived in twelve. Muddy kept pressure on Will's leg, while Lily babbled at Will, apologizing, telling him to fight, though she knew he was unconscious. Two strong-looking EMTs jumped out of the ambulance. One knelt down by Muddy while the other opened the back doors of the unit.

"Jake, get the backboard. We'll immobilize him," said the driver. "Muddy, don't help. We've got it."

Jake and the driver, in concert, lifted Will onto the stretcher and slid it slowly into the ambulance. "Miss, get in quick if you want to go." She jumped in. In the back, Jake administered oxygen and made sure the bleeding was controlled. She looked at Will, breathing laboured, under the mask. The bandaging was doing its job. The bleeding had stopped.

"I saw his bone stick out," Lily said, shaking with fear. "He won't die, will he?"

"He's breathing, ma'am. We're doing our best," Jake said, adjusting the bandage to re-evaluate the injury. "Stay quiet, okay? We're pretty good at this."

The driver radioed ahead: "ETA ten minutes. Transporting a white male, fifty years old, unresponsive, compound fracture to his right femur."

The ambulance pulled up with a lurch, and the doors flew open as people ran towards it. Lily had never paid attention to the little country hospital as she drove by, never thought she'd need it. The people in the building might be responsible for Will's life. She thought of New York University Hospital, looming over First Avenue, as they lowered Will out of the ambulance.

"You're in luck," said one of the men as they rolled the gurney into the ER. "Dr. Mac just walked in. He's the orthopedic surgeon on island this week." He directed them into an examining room.

"Miss, you must wait outside," he said, kindly, and she realized he was a nurse. But she cowered in the corner, watching Dr. Mac survey the swollen, broken skin with the bone coming through the wound. The doctor cut Will's pants, exposing his entire leg. He had Jake grab hold of Will's ankle and apply traction. "Hold tight," he commanded, realigning the two ends of the bone. "We don't have the equipment to properly treat him. He needs to be transported to Sudbury General. I'll stop the bleeding, apply a traction splint, and sedate him."

Within forty minutes, they heard the whomp-whomp-whomp of the Ontario Air Ambulance. With deafening noise, a Bell 212 landed on the helipad. A flight medic rushed into the ER with his equipment to prepare Will for the flight to Sudbury. Jake and his partner placed the stretcher near the gurney. "May I go with him?" she begged, crying.

The flight medic looked at her. "You are…?"

"His fiancée."

"We're not supposed to, but if you promise to be still." The medic turned to the nurse, "Don, it's pretty bad. Come with us." Mindemoya was seventy-six air miles from the hospital in Sudbury. The flight took forty-five minutes. Lily huddled in her seat, watching the lights of sprawling Sudbury rise up. Don adjusted the IV drip. The medical team was waiting, ready to take Will into the operating room.

"Please go to the waiting room," a nurse said, giving her a pillow and a blanket. It was bleak and empty. She phoned Muddy in Kagawong. Aunt Molly and Uncle Mudge knew all about it. "Great Spirit," she prayed, "I'll never care if he runs to the barn, has silent days, or is never social again."

She curled up on a bench, but couldn't sleep. It was forever before the doctor came out. "He's stable. He'll need therapy and rehab. Lucky he's in good shape. We'll keep him in intensive care overnight."

"May I see him?"

"Miss Gardner, he's sedated, sleeping."

Lily phoned Winsome, crying, and told her about the accident. "Lily, my Verne come to pick you up. We have a spare bedroom. He on de way."

Within fifteen minutes, Verne arrived in his truck, wearing his pajamas under his heavy coat. "We glad to have you, Lily. Winsome's anxious for your company. I take you back in the morning."

At Winsome and Verne's home, they sat at the kitchen table, Winsome wanting to feed her supper, a Virgin Gorda dish of lamb and rice. "You got to be starving. What's this I see, a ring on your hand?"

"We're engaged. I'm back from New York," said Lily. "And I almost killed him!"

"So soon," said Winsome. "I make you chicken soup. You need a massive dose."

At 3 a.m., Lily went to Winsome's kitchen, seeking hot chocolate. The rhubarb ditch extraction kept playing, the dark blood on the ice, the whir of the helicopter, the operating room, and her stupidity.

"I told everyone in town that you didn't try to kill him," Anna said, when Lily phoned her in Gore Bay the next morning. "I said you have your own money. You've now become part of island fabric."

Lily laughed weakly. The fir-tree-and-moccasin telegraph was alive and active. "Just tell everyone he's here and okay."

"The break was low on the femur. He'll need lots of therapy, but he's stable," said Don the next morning. "They put pins in to stabilize the fracture." Don, it turned out, was the head nurse in Mindemoya. He had stayed the night. Will lay in bed with a huge metal contraption holding his right leg eight inches up off the bed. Heavily medicated, he smiled goofily at her. She kissed his warm cheek.

"The good news is I'm on drugs. Only broke one leg. Sex'll be fascinating!"

"Whatever you want, Will. You're alive," she said.

His voice was weak. "Where there's a will, there's a way, and I'm Will. Where's a will, there's a waaaaaay…" His voice faded and his eyes drifted shut. Lily turned as Muddy slouched in the door, looking as if he hadn't slept.

"We got the pickup out. I replaced the two front tires this morning."

"Muddy, you're my hero!"

"That cable was too old. My own damn fault!"

"No," said Lily quietly. "If I hadn't slid into the ditch…"

"Shoulda woulda coulda, stop it, you two," said Will, surfacing again to lift his head. "The drugs they're giving me are terrific. But no sailing this winter." He gazed out the hospital window, and then chuckled weakly. "And now you're engaged to a gimp with a broken leg!"

"You two got engaged?" Muddy's jaw dropped. All of Manitoulin would soon know. One stop at the gas station in Gore Bay would do it: the American came from the city, trapped him, got a ring and tried to knock him off. Definitely wants the farmland. Muddy would have to counter-attack.

A perky nurse entered the room. "Will Mudge, you've got to remember me—Barb Slade? You took me to the Senior Prom."

Lily flashed her engagement ring, pre-emptive action. He was wounded, but he was hers.

The attending doctor appeared an hour later. "Mr. Mudge, your medical protocol is bed rest and traction, we hope for only four weeks. You'll be transferred to the rehab centre. You'll need a lot of bed rest to allow the bone to knit. You'll limp if you don't do the physical therapy. The pins in your leg may come out in three weeks, prior to going to rehab."

"Can I get out earlier?"

"You don't want to. You'll have a walker, then a cane," the doctor said. "You're lucky, Mr. Mudge. The femur broke exactly in the middle. Not too close to the ligaments and knee joint, or to the hip socket."

"I'm here to help, Will," said Nurse Barb, smiling, leaning over to smooth his sheets.

Lily stayed with Winsome and played with the baby. In two weeks, Will's first cast had come off, his leg weak and sore. He'd lost muscle mass from being immobilized. "He's some cranky, having to use stool softeners," Muddy told her.

"They say I'm a candidate for blood clots and embolisms," Will said, gloomily. "Sweetheart, beer's a laxative. Sneak me in a few bottles."

Lily shook her head no, but knew she'd do it. When she arrived for lunch the next day, two bottles of Muskoka microbrew lay at the bottom of her bag, snuggled up against some ice in a waterproof plastic bag.

"There's nothing for you to do here in Sudbury," Will told her, glaring at his leg, still elevated in traction. "You could go back to New York for a few weeks while I'm tied to this jeezely bed. Too many people are fussing over me." He was propped up on his pillows, the next thick cast around his thigh and part of his hip. Nurses fluttered around him. "No pun, Lily, but this might be a good break for you—winter will be long once we move back to the island, and I won't be mobile. I'm listing *Northern Loon* with a charter company. Bart's agreed to captain. We may as well get revenue, and Bart stays employed. In the spring, we'll fly down. If I let you go to New York, promise to come back? I'm damaged goods."

"No, you aren't. I brought lunch," she said. She opened a bag of hot chicken wings and with one eye on the door poured the beer into two cups.

"You," Will told her after a healthy sip, "are the light of my life. All the people I don't want to see are going to be bringing me baked cookies. I'll get fat as a pig lying here."

Muddy brought her passport and purse from Kagawong. "You're sure, Will?"

"I know you love me. Bring back bagels!"

She kissed Will goodbye. As she stepped out the front door of the hospital, she froze to see Carlotta.

"Everybody's heard about the accident, the pickup you ditched." Carlotta's voice dripped with venom. "I'm in Sudbury today. I brought Will his favourite chicken wings."

"Carlotta, he'll like that. He'll be glad to see you. Thanks for coming."

Carlotta's face showed disbelief. Her eyes narrowed at Lily.

"You're his friend, and we need your energy, Carlotta." Lily ran away down the steps. Always use sugar, never vinegar.

❧

Sarty and Lily giggled at dinner the next night in Greenwich Village, so glad to see each other. "Well, I don't care if he is an Ontario backwoodsman," Sartorious declared, holding her hand up so that her engagement ring caught the light. "He has excellent taste."

"I can't disagree, Sarty," Lily said merrily.

"I want him to be good for you, making you happy. I wish I could imagine you seriously enjoying life so far away from everything."

"Sarty, there's part of me that doesn't exist here in New York," Lily told him. "I'm writing—seriously writing, for the first time.

I'm at the beginning, but I'm starting to see the shape of the book, and it's more fun than I can tell you."

"I'll start designing your dress for the Booker Prize!"

"Not so fast. Laugh if you want," Lily said, serious for a moment. "But sometimes my Boston sisters seem more real than anyone I knew in my whole life in Manhattan. Alexis and Susie have things under control at the office, so I'll head up to Boston for research early next week. And if you want to be useful, design a 1920s coming-out gown. I'll use it in my book!"

"Ah! The age of glamour! You've got it!"

➤

"Hospital life sucks," Will decreed. He had done well in rehab. They were sending him home early, with a long and complex exercise regimen to strengthen the healing leg under the supervision of Mindemoya. Muddy would pick him up.

"My research is done here," Lily told him. "I'll be on the next plane! He can pick me up too."

Will was waiting, hunched over crutches by the arrivals door as she walked in from the plane. His face lit up. "I didn't think you'd really come back!"

Lily rode in the front, sandwiched between the two men, with the back seat filled with Will's crutches, luggage, and exercise equipment. Lily was in control of the music all the way to the old swing bridge.

"These CDs are for you from my girlfriends, all coming to Manitoulin. They'll be staying with us in the farmhouse," she teased. "Who's boss now?"

"Will," Muddy shot back, "you've created a monster."

"She's my monster," Will said. His voice was weary, but satisfied. Lily looked out the front window as they crossed the bridge, feeling her own sense of satisfaction. This crossing was for *real*.

Manitoulin was her home. Manhattan would be just a place she visited. She took care of hundreds of clients. Taking care of one person named Will for a few months wouldn't be hard.

Will's hand folded over hers. How many careful ways could they have sex, snowed into the snug farmhouse for a long winter?

CHAPTER FOURTEEN

WILL ADMITTED THAT HER DINNERS RANGED from experimental to, well, palatable. Ensconced in his favourite chair in the living room, he was at ease, leg up and healing. In lieu of his sailboat in Virgin Gorda, a Manitoulin Sunset, sweet with rum and island flavours, rested on the table beside a pile of the latest books. He hated when the phone rang, disturbing his peace.

"Daddy, I'm driving up to see you and Lily," said Laura. "I need to know that you're okay. I'm so glad we've moved back to Toronto."

"Get ready for Laura," Will warned Lily. "She'll take over the kitchen."

"Maybe she'll teach me to make a few dishes," Lily said cheerfully. "Or not."

The large SUV honked five times entering the driveway and parked in front of the farmhouse door. "Daddy, it's so long since I've seen you," Laura squealed, stepping down from the truck.

She was covered in a full-length tweed coat, opening to a blue cashmere sweater over Escada jeans. Her faux alligator boots sank into the snow. Lily blinked at Laura's sophisticated Toronto fashion.

"Hello, Daddy! Lily! Tim says hello! I brought two cases of wine, steaks, and new country music," she said, her face shining. "Do you hurt, Daddy?"

Will hugged her from his crutches. "I'm okay, Laura, now that you're here."

What did a daughter have that a fiancée did not?

"Daddy, are you still living in the 1800s with your crummy kitchen?"

"Don't pick on your old man," Will said. "Let's get everything in the house."

The farmhouse buzzed with new vitality. Lily was thrilled by the diversion. Laura expressed her opinions freely. "I should have bought that cook top stove. For God's sake, Daddy—it's not just you in this house now. Lily deserves an upgrade. I invited six friends for dinner tonight. I'm cooking perch! Lily, do you mind?"

"Thrilled to maintain my status as dishwasher," Lily said. It was true. This week would be full of noise, laughter and activity that might distract her from writing, but Laura knew the farmhouse. It was her childhood summer home. Lily had never really constructed her sense of self around domesticity. Will had made her a writing room; he and Laura could keep the kitchen, and he could spend the week cooking with his daughter.

Lily was happy to meet Laura's friends, the younger working generation on Manitoulin. She liked them all, from the young fisherman to the musician who brought her guitar and filled the farmhouse with music. Will was gregarious as friends stopped in and rum bottles dwindled to empty.

In bed, Lily gently chided Will, "How come you don't mind Laura inviting most of Manitoulin here?"

"I know 'em all. And it's only a week. I'm a curmudgeon, Lily."

"It stings a bit, that you have different rules for Laura and me."

A week later, Will stood with one arm around Lily and waved with the other from the front door as Laura blew kisses from behind the wheel and swept out of the driveway. Will said, "At last, they're all gone."

"Admit it," Lily teased. "You enjoyed all those people."

"I enjoy alone better." It was, Lily had come to realize, true.

The bright days of March were punctuated by Will's therapy and exercise. He was able to drive the snowmobile, skimming across the frozen expanse of Mudge Bay when the ice was hard and slick. Lily sat behind Will, her arms around his waist, her belly snuggled tight against his back.

"Lily," he shouted over the engine, "You could be slaving away in your high-rise office, arranging life for others. Aren't you glad you're here? We're coming up on Clapperton Island, there on the right. Want to know the secret of winter on Manitoulin? If you can't stand being on island in the winter, you walk off!"

"You can walk off Manitoulin to the mainland?"

"Winter, solid ice!" he yelled. She laughed.

"Will, when Laura was here, you never once hid in the barn."

"She'd just drag me back to the house. She never lets me hide."

Three days later, Jordy knocked on the door. Lily smiled and opened the door quickly.

"You're just in time for lunch!" She reached up, impulsively hugging the man, and hurriedly stepped back. "Don't mind me hugging you. I'll never forget that you saved my life."

"Bear was already running, Lily," Jordy answered, embarrassed. He turned and went into the living room where Will was sitting, his leg up, reading the *Expositor*. "Will, we sure have our challenges, eh?"

"Take a load off. Want a beer?"

"Nah, working. I came to check on you and the Mighty Huntress here."

Lily stood at the door. "I still dream about that bear coming in the living room window."

Jordy pulled an envelope out of his pocket and handed it to Lily.

"Brought you these."

Lily opened it and tilted its contents out into her palm. "Claws!" Three curved, dangerous bear claws sat in her hand. She looked into Jordy's eyes, surprised to see admiration.

"My cousin took a bear in the fall hunt," Jordy told her. "I told her about you and the broom. She sent those to you. She said to tell you, bear claws represent courage. It's a thing to know, about yourself."

She went back to the kitchen, preparing sandwiches and calling Will and Jordy to the dining table. Male banter ensued, while she thought of the bear and the broom. In her memory, it had been a farce, and frightening.

After lunch, she drove to Gore Bay. Back at the farmhouse, she laid out the prescribed groceries on the kitchen table, washed her hands, and opened the cookbook to study her self-designated new cooking assignment.

"Heat the pan, and braise the meat," she read.

"I'll take over, sweetie." Will made a show of it, laying his crutches against the sideboard. His big burly hands, that held her so lovingly, also caressed the potatoes and fondled a roast beef into succulence.

"Let's write Uncle Burley's Cookbook. I'll publish it!"

"Don't be over-ambitious. Food's about making and eating, not writing and publishing. I'm in recovery mode."

"My sister is an inspired cook."

"Maybe I chose the wrong sister," Will shot her a sideways glance. He grinned down at the food in preparation. "Maybe not. Bet she's never faced a bear."

Will often chatted on the phone with Dahlia.

"We've never competed, Will," Lily told him. "She loves teaching, Stuart's great at business and they have two good kids. I used to tease them about being suburban, and now I'm backwoods Canadian country."

As the weeks passed, Lily struggled to stay still and contained in the farmhouse. She worked on her book about the Boston sisters, one of whom was now discovering Manitoulin sixty summers earlier. This had not been part of Lily's plan, but she was delighted by the way the character of Amanda, the society wife and art patron, seemed to have a mind of her own. In defense, Lily haunted the library in Gore Bay and studied the accounts of early Manitoulin settlers, delighting in their epic tales of adaptation. The quest was, she thought, to appreciate the journey and move slowly. Lily did her exercises and stretches every morning and walked two miles daily to the post office, the air smelling green and wet as March became April. She and Will were both seeking something, she felt, but the process was not one of reaching mutual conclusions, but in being together for the journey. Her hands weren't empty. She filled them, writing about a woman of her great-aunt's generation in Manitoulin, cooking, getting out when she could to have lunch with her friends. She loved hearing stories about how people came to Manitoulin, and stayed. She wondered at the way that Will seemed to own serenity and loneliness at the same time.

Coached by telephone, Lily prepared Molly's ratatouille with eggplant and tomatoes, stewed with garlic, thyme and rosemary. As she drew it out of the oven, she slid in an apple tart, the product of an afternoon's lesson from Anna. Will inhaled appreciatively from across the kitchen. "You've definitely mastered the art of slow simmer."

"And lots of cuddling." Lily smiled at him.

Headlights flared against the windows. A car door slammed and the door rattled frantically. Carlotta did not wait, but burst in. Her face was swollen with tears, her hair a mess. "The boys are with my mother. Will, I'm pleading for refuge."

"You have a house!"

Lily knew she was invisible, but got up, filled a glass of water and handed it to Carlotta. The distraught woman shrank into a chair and laid her head on the table. Lily looked at the half-finished casserole, their interrupted dinner. After wrenching sobs, Carlotta pulled her head up, embarrassed, stood and took a tissue from a drawer in the breakfront. She knew where everything was in the farmhouse. "My mother won't talk to me."

There was silence in the kitchen. It would be a long night.

Then Carlotta got up abruptly. "You don't want me here. Walk me to the car, Will?"

"With his crutches?" Lily protested. Carlotta's eyes stabbed into hers.

He turned helplessly toward Lily. "I'll be back in a few minutes."

When he returned, Lily asked him, "What happened?"

"What's past is prologue. Forget about her. Where were we?"

"The apple tart is burnt," Lily said.

❧

Spring on Manitoulin was snow to mud, ice melting in the bay, days tart with warmth over cold, brilliant sun or damp and grey.

Lily had a new life with old fixtures, a water pump, maple trees, cows in the pasture, and Mudge Bay. Curtailed by Will's accident, their schedule was slow, with evenings of reading, cooking, listening to music and occasional TV.

Writing had become more difficult as winter waned. The sculptor Vivian, after a final break with her father, was on her own in Paris with little money. Amanda, despite her happy marriage to a Boston businessman whom she loved, had somehow also become summertime smitten with a Manitoulin fur trader and trapper, attracted to his broad shoulders and tales of winter life among the Ojibwe. Lily was deeply annoyed, and found herself stalking away from her desk in high dudgeon at her character's poor judgement. She went downstairs to Will, who was equally discontented.

"I'm not healing fast enough," he said. "I'm going stir-crazy."

"If you're restless, let's take a drive around the island."

"I know Manitoulin too well," he said. "I'll go to the barn. See what I can find."

He'd begun to spend more and more time in the barn, and Lily, having lost all patience with the eldest Boston sister's foolishness, began writing short comic sketches about her own experiences on Manitoulin.

"I'll make a picnic for us to eat on the bluff. We'll be out of the wind," she offered one day after a morning's visit with Molly, leaning against the barn door and watching Will putter at his workbench.

"No thanks, I'll exercise inside the barn," he said. "You're always moving."

"Sometimes I have to move to be still inside," she said.

"I wish you could learn to be more tranquil," he said, not acknowledging her point.

"I don't stew about our differences. You hide from people. I go to them.

"I keep myself for pondering," Will looked at her.

"You and I see the world so differently."

"You gulp everything!"

"We New Yorkers surely do gulp," she said brightly. "Let's take an easy walk while the sun's shining."

"I don't feel like walking. You always want to exercise. Or talk to people, or learn something."

"Why are you picking at me, Will? What's wrong with exercising, learning, working for the future?" Lily leaned back against the door.

"When we concern ourselves with the future, we destroy the present."

"You can have both! The challenge is to balance it all." She held her hands open, imploring him to listen.

"You miss what's happening now, Lily," Will said. His counter was strewn with papers, pliers, and an open can of beer. "You're so busy. I hate it when you don't understand."

"Only a person from the biggest of cities can appreciate the smallest of details on Manitoulin." Her voice rose to a shout.

"I have things to do," he said. "I'll get my own sandwich. Shut the door, please."

"Okay, I'm walking one Manitoulin mile by myself."

Chapter Fifteen

"Ollie, would you look at my stories about Manitoulin?"

In the post office, Ollie sat down to read a piece she'd written about the inability to resist downing butter tarts in the Canadian winter for ballast and warmth. He looked up. "Not too bad. Why don't you try sending these to the newspaper?"

The managing editor of the local paper was encouraging. "You're a travel writer from New York, wintering on Manitoulin? That's already funny," he said. "Send me a few columns."

Lily emailed the butter tart story and one about falling off the Kagawong dock. The phone rang two days later.

"Can you provide twelve more columns?"

"I'm making every mistake a city slicker can. I've got plenty of material."

"I can see you trust your readers' intelligence, Lily," he said. "Your columns build a bridge halfway. Your readers will do the other half."

Lily dashed out to the front yard. Baby raccoons peeked out from under the porch. A full moon rose in the east, while the sun set red and orange. She felt the world around her. Lily danced, part ballet, part joy, and part cheerleading.

"They want twelve columns! I have permission to ask obvious and stupid questions, so I can listen and learn how people grow in Northern Ontario."

Will watched her from the door of the working barn. "I knew you could do it!"

As April passed, Manitoulin began to clear away winter. The summer people would soon arrive. Lily's life on Manitoulin grew larger. She studied Big Red, the Manitoulin phone book, and found the number of the pilot house at the swing bridge. Walter Jones answered, "Sure, come by. Be careful. Hold tight on the steps. When winds get high, the pilot house shakes."

She looked over the North Channel from inside the 20 x 20 foot pilot house. "I'm the engineer on duty," her host said as he operated the bridge.

"It's an impressive operation," Lily said, intrigued by this unaccustomed view.

"This bridge took a whole year to construct. It was built by the Algoma Eastern Railroad to give Manitoulin rail access. They finished in 1913, and it was named a Heritage Bridge in 1988. At first, cars had to be ferried across the channel, because the bridge was used only for the train. In 1945 it was opened to cars. The bridge clearance is 14 feet wide and 22 feet high. Total length is 574 feet."

"How does it work?" Lily asked, peering through the scratched windows at the bridge below.

"You just watch. The bridge runs smooth but it's noisy, so we've got to wear ear protection gear. We swing the bridge with gas engines and three levers. First, of course, we stop traffic. Then we pull the bridge wedges and engage a clutch, just like to a car; give the motor some gas and it swings out into the channel. It takes about eight minutes to go wide open. When the water traffic has gone through and we're clear, we swing it closed, and it's the cars' turn. Cars on the island side always come off first."

"Thank you," Lily said, imagining Boston society lady Amanda's first journey across the bridge. "There's something magical about a bridge, but one that swings out over the open water seems even more romantic."

"This is one of the few swing bridges left in Canada," Walter told Lily as she turned to leave. "Hold tight down those steps, now. We don't want you swimming in the North Channel. Current's fast and cold."

Will was almost completely well now, but they hadn't talked about whether they would return to Virgin Gorda for the spring, or remain on Manitoulin and put in a summer garden. He split wood sometimes in the evening, and loaded it onto the woodpile against the barn while Lily watched from the deck chair and sipped at a before-dinner drink. Feathery clouds swept across the sky. "Two people stopped me in town this morning," he said. "They liked your column about the swing bridge."

Lily had learned to say "Mmmm-Chee-ging" instead of West Bay. Jessie Eagle called her. "I like what you write. I've arranged for you to meet an Anishnaabe artist tomorrow at his house. Danakii Makowin has a show in Sudbury next week.

➙

She drove to a modest home overlooking Lake Mindemoya. A tall man with a smooth face, bright eyes, straight nose, firm jaw, and a thick braid down his back opened the screen door, not happily.

"Forgot you were coming," he said, beckoning her in. The walls of his living room were bright blue, with canvasses depicting figures outlined in black, bold and beautiful. Reds, oranges, greens, yellows—the canvasses vibrated with colour, each begging for her attention. "Is day-old coffee okay?"

"You bet." Her eyes moved to the blue-green view of Lake Mindemoya through a broad window. She took a deep breath. On the easel was a painting of an Anishinaabe woman in profile, leaning into her child, deep pink moving into crimson and soft yellows. Every line bespoke gentleness and warmth.

"It's for my sister, her first child," he said quietly, the rhythms of Anishnaabe underlying his speech. Lily knew the Native people she chatted with, at first, were put off by the way she spoke, a tiny freight train, bubbling between enthusiasm and questions. Then they would smile, amused. She tried to be calm. She accepted a large mug of coffee, heat warming her hands.

"Thanks, Mr. Makowin. May I take notes?"

"Call me Dan," he said, nodding. "Danakii means homeland." He pointed to an old chair that stood before a paint-splattered wooden desk. She sat and took out her notebook. Dan answered her questions in short sentences. "My goal is to depict Anishnaabe teachings. We tell stories," he paused, "that have been handed down through our oral tradition. My art is for people to learn, to appreciate what we have and what we are on this earth."

As he spoke, his voice warmed. He spoke of the beauty and power of spirit, of learning and sharing. It was her work as well, she thought at one point, although she produced nothing like the beauty of his canvasses.

It had been two hours. "You are a good listener," he said.

"There's much to be learned on this island," Lily answered. "My readers will be grateful to hear what you have to say. Can I email you a draft before I send it to the paper, to make sure I've made no mistakes?"

Dan nodded. "That's a good idea, but I can tell you will write well about this," he said, "and then—" He broke off with a laugh as Lily's stomach growled.

"I don't come to M'Chigeeng often," she confided, smiling. "I've promised myself a hot turkey sandwich at the local restaurant. May I treat you, please?"

"My stomach is telling me to go with you," he agreed. "I want to hear about New York."

The M'Chigeeng restaurant was a hub of activity. Dan and Lily sat at a table by the window, devouring hot turkey sandwiches, heavy with gravy, and fries.

"You two are quite the cozy pair," Carlotta said, stopping at their table.

Dan stood. "Carlotta, I haven't seen you in a while."

"I don't want to interrupt," Carlotta said, as if she deserved an explanation. None came. They watched her walk away to sit at a table with three other women. Despite the lunchtime hubbub, her voice carried. "Some New Yorkers think they have original experiences here. She's becoming an Anishnaabe wannabe."

Pretending not to hear, Lily paid the bill, and they left the restaurant and got into her pickup. The engine started but the little pickup couldn't move.

"Tire's flat," Dan said, his face clouded. "Have a spare?"

Fifteen minutes later, he had fixed it. Lily dropped him off at his house. "Thanks for lunch," he said. "I want good spirits for you."

"I saw Carlotta at the post office this afternoon," Will said. "She saw you with that young artist at the Seasons."

"He's invited us to his opening in Sudbury."

"You go. Count me out."

So she did, driving by herself to Sudbury, attending the art opening and staying overnight with Winsome, her husband, and

Sunshine, their new baby daughter. The baby was beautiful and bright. Lily loved playing with her. Winsome had clearly taken to Northern Ontario and had started her own custom tailoring business while her husband was a chef.

As Lily's newspaper columns appeared, she began to receive positive feedback. "Our readers enjoy your struggles," her editor said. "We've heard a lot back about the red squirrel, and when you got poison ivy. Your appeal lies in the encounter between Manitoulin and your sense of humour. Keep getting into trouble, Lily."

Her Canadian bank account grew with small steady checks. "You've got guts, Lily, to make your mistakes public," Will said. He sounded approving.

"I enjoy writing these," she admitted. "I'm putting down roots, Will, writing myself into the island, even if I'm just a new gal."

"Why don't we stay in on Saturday instead of going to dinner? You've done enough this week. Let's roast that pork."

"We've been invited by the Millertons," Lily objected. "We'd planned to cook the roast on Sunday."

"You want to write about their maple sugar shack," Will said, sounding resigned.

"I'll cancel," she said, answering the tone of his voice rather than his words. She'd seen the sugar shack in full production earlier when the sap was running, but now she thought she could write a piece that also talked about marketing the syrup to tourists. She could visit the Millertons another time alone. Will seemed to be in hibernation mode even while the rest of the island opened into spring, but Lily was determined to make herself a friend of silence if that was what he needed. Cook the pork roast they did, slow simmering with sautéed apples and onions.

"This was tasty, Lily. I like slow cooking, another blessing here on Manitoulin."

"Are you upset with me? My writing?"

"Nope," he said, getting up to watch TV in the living room while she collected the dirty dishes. "I admit I'm sometimes a bit tired of your enthusiasm."

"You said I make you see new things, feel new emotions."

"Yet when I tell you I save myself for myself, I mean it."

"You watch other people and observe their actions."

"You have continual ambition. You seem to need to be accepted and known on the island, but you've already got that—here, from me, already a beautiful woman in my eyes."

"I do struggle to achieve balance," she said, thoughtfully.

"I hope you'll keep growing into Manitoulin mellowness," he told her, his eyes warm. "This is a good place, but if you need New York bustle, you won't be happy here."

"Will. Of course I'm happy."

"You've become busy tracking stories, or driving to South Baymouth for the day. You meet Muddy for lunch at Twin Bluffs."

"He's coming for dinner tomorrow."

With rum and cokes in their bellies, Muddy and Will got expansive and raucous about Canadian politics. Lily was happy to cook, serve and clean up. She went up to bed quietly.

A week later, visiting Whiskey Hill, Lily was surprised when Molly asked, "What's going on?"

Lily paused. "Will's...restless, reticent. He's easily irritated when I talk. I like this new life—time to write, time to cook, time to just think and be, time to get to know Manitoulin—but to him I still seem to be 'New York busy.' He spends a lot of time in the barns," Lily admitted.

"Maybe his investments aren't good. It may be a rough patch. He's a brooder. And you know he hated being laid up and inactive."

"The better I feel on Manitoulin, the more I feel I'm losing him."

"You do depict a livelier sense of Manitoulin than we locals tend to see," Aunt Molly said. "The ladies in my quilting club like your columns. They say now we have to live up to it. It would be shame to let the joy of your discoveries pass you by."

"It's the column, isn't it?"

"Will's bigger than that."

"He's looking at me differently."

"You may be too focused on what's happening around the island and not on Will."

"Maybe."

Malcolm Jones, a beekeeper in Honora Bay, summoned her in the middle of May. "I've a story about bees and being for you." Sitting in his comfortable home, she could feel nonetheless a tremendous underlying anger. She suffered for thirty minutes listening about bees and honey. "Mr. Jones, have I done something to offend you?"

"You're a fine writer. But sweetness and light don't always help. I've got terminal cancer," he blurted. "I thought you could help me. I thought you could listen."

Shocked, she nodded and clamped her mouth shut.

"When my first wife left, nothing meant anything. I sold my business. I came here on a whim. Manitoulin has a way of clearing out city mentality. Within four days I bought this house. I've always wanted to keep bees. I met my wife Jane and we had our child, Amelia. I'll be in hospital soon, dying. You came from a city to a new life on Manitoulin," he said. Tears, all the sorrow of his life gathered into his voice. "You search, like me. You want to tell the best about people. Tell this."

She wrote the first column about the beekeeper, the hives, and the bees. The second, what Malcolm wanted people to know, was about being. This was not the kind of writing she'd been doing, an easy escape from the novel that refused to obey her wishes. This was a trust, even more than Danakii Makowin's work had been.

A few days later, Malcolm opened his door to Lily. She sat and waited, terrified while he read her column. Making one correction, he looked up, and gave her his first smile. "Yes. You're a promising gardener of other people's souls."

She handed him a jar of Will's rhubarb preserves. He gave her a jar of Manitoulin honey.

His friends gathered around him. When she phoned to bring ice cream, two weeks later, his wife answered. He'd been rushed to Sudbury, and would never come back. Lily sobbed for Malcolm Jones, who had been a kind teacher, in the end. She felt she had to seize the springtime, the very essence of now. Cherish every moment to nurture Will and learn to love him the way he wanted to be loved.

Chapter Sixteen

Rhubarb leaves sprouted, wrinkled and green, from the wet, dark earth. The stalks pushed upwards, inches longer each day, and asparagus rose at the same rate from the ground warmed by the May sun. Within a few days, Will and Lily were bringing in armloads of red rhubarb stalks, shorn of their leaves, and beginning to chop and cook and jam and bag rhubarb for the bottomless freezer in the basement. The days alternated between sun and rain with May mud and black flies. Lily took garlic pills against the black flies. Her column about learning to thrive on Manitoulin was widely read. "The Winds of Manitoulin," reported on a highly satisfying farmhouse dinner she and Will had attended, celebrating burps and farts as magnificent applause. She never used those words; all was suggested. People stopped her in Gore Bay and Little Current to laugh and chat. Having new faith in herself as an interviewer and writer, she felt a growing exuberance.

When Lily drove away from the farmhouse, she would glance at the little apple tree in the front yard, happy to see green leaves again. She often told herself she lived in a Garden of Eden with Will. She felt her confidence grow along with the leaves on the little tree. Heading off to an interview, she would leave Will with the counters piled high with rhubarb, and return at the end of the day to a dinner of asparagus, leek soup, baked salmon and rhubarb pie. Will still said nothing about the boat waiting in Virgin Gorda, and Lily was happy for that, loving Manitoulin in springtime.

"Will, I went to Little Current today and interviewed the commodore of the Little Current Yacht Club. He's charming, a retired academic and a skipper in the summer. He and his wife will be taking their sailboat to the Caribbean this autumn. You have so much in common. We're invited to dinner with them next week, when I finish the interview," she said with excitement, wanting to draw Will into this expanded life of hers. Will took a sip of wine and continued his dinner silently as she told him about letters from her readers and her next interview. Finally, he asked, "How's your book coming about the Boston sisters? You're not home very much."

"Manitoulin people and their work here are interesting. I'll get back to the book."

When Lily rose from the dinner table to put their empty dinner plates in the sink, Will stopped her.

"I've got to tell you, Lily, I find myself drained around you. When you're so busy, nobody gets to have you."

"I'm trying to be what you want!"

"You still insist on dragging me along."

"You mean I'm not living up to your expectations? Aren't we struggling in the process of accepting each other as we are? And as we're becoming?"

"I'm struggling mightily, Lily." He turned away from her.

"You have your own time, Will. Especially your inner places that you hold away from me."

"You disrupt my flow. That's why I go to the barn!"

"You go to three barns and I can never find you!" Her chest tightened. "No one forces you! You tell me funny stories and drink a gallon of rum. What do I take away from you?"

Neither spoke. Lily continued to clear the table. She had read recently about the character of Lilith, Adam's first wife. When Adam tried to dominate her, she uttered God's secret name and resolutely left the Garden of Eden. Scholars contemplated whether Lilith was ultimately an autonomous woman. Lily thought she was learning not to resent Will's silences. Wasn't she learning equilibrium? She did not belong exclusively to Will. Why couldn't their polarities be sustained here, in balance? Was Lily's energy and desire to prove herself introducing her own garter snake into their Manitoulin paradise? She hated it when Will held himself away from her. Was she doing the same? Lily had grown an immense appetite for this life in Manitoulin.

"When I want to move closer to you," Will said, after a while, "you're off interested in something or someone else. I love Manitoulin because being here feels eternal. You leech that away from me in your rushing."

"Have I grown to be more creative than you want? I listen to you," she said, beseechingly, as her heart plummeted. "I have such gratitude in finding you and loving you, Will." She was careful to keep her voice even. She wasn't begging. She hated this discussion. There's always a deal, Anna had told her one afternoon over tea. Often lovers don't know the deal entering into a relationship. Had Will finished rescuing her from Manhattan?

"When you came, I thought I wouldn't be so alone. We began well. But you've discovered the rest of Manitoulin," he said. "You're devouring it. Anyway, I thought I'd retired to be a silent partner, but the business isn't going well and my partners have asked me to go back to Toronto for a while. Why don't you think of going back to New York?"

"What?" Her eyes flew to his.

He didn't mean just for a visit.

She sat down before she fell down. "Will, I adore you and I love it here. We can resolve this! I can keep changing!"

He shook his head. "I've taught you all I can about Manitoulin." His eyes were on the table where he sat. "But you'll never be content with me, here. You don't settle."

"I'll always come back to you."

"There'll be a time when you won't." That blend of serene temperament and quiet self-assurance burned away before her eyes.

"That's so patronizing," she said.

Will shook his head. "I'll remember everything sweet with you. You've done brilliantly here."

"But not with you."

"You need a bigger life than I can give you, Lily. You belong in New York City."

"You do self-doubt too well," she said quietly. "You've tried to give me what I needed, and I tried and wanted to give those gifts back to you." How had she missed all this?

He stood up, a heavy, silent presence. Nothing she could say now would make any difference. Lily wanted to scream so loud the cows in the field would break though the fence. "You're abandoning me, and you're going back to Toronto and replacing me with a dog!"

"I never said that!" Will said, transfixed.

"I saw Ollie in the post office in Kagawong today," she said, almost blankly, and then she half laughed. "He said to tell you that the puppies were weaned, and you could pick up yours next week."

A giggle escaped her. It grew bigger inside her, so funny and stupid—a dog would be at his side whenever he whistled. She realized and accepted it instantly.

She took the dishes to the counter, and stared out the open screen door towards the west, where the sun shone low in the sky, its evening light touching vibrant spring green with gold. She looked down at her empty hands. Her heart felt shaken from her. Will, standing near the table, reached his hand out to her. She stepped back.

"Okay, then. I'll leave sometime next week." She looked around the kitchen. It was no longer hers—no longer home. In the absurdity, she said, "I'm being thrown off Manitoulin and replaced by a dog."

"You may have a better deal than me, Lily. You're able to handle this."

"I used to be a sheepdog, herding my clients, and I thought I got slower here, with you. Guess not." Why was she going for pathetic humour when her life was being crushed this minute? She had bared her soul. She had had Will and her readers laughing as she parlayed her clumsiness into adventure. People told her they recognized themselves where remorse and laughter met. What a lousy joke. She went to the mud room, put on her boots and grabbed a jacket. She walked down the driveway, past the apple tree, out to the road toward Bridal Veil Falls, one foot in front of the other. There were no cars parked. Feeling despair and revulsion, she sprinted to the steps overlooking the falls. Her head ached and she felt empty.

Thundering water fell from the majestic rocky ridge, down into the half circle of the wide pool below. Where she had swum in the summer, hiked in the fall, and stood in the winter, the spring waters tumbled down. Despite the glowing sunset, everything in front of her turned grey, her Kagawong home yanked from under her. Exiled. Out of Eden. She stood, gasping in a rush of tears. She fumbled for a tissue, found one of Uncle Mudge's linen handkerchiefs in her pocket, and wiped her nose. She dashed down the steps to the bottom.

If she yelled, not a soul, a deer or a fish could hear her in the din of rushing water. "Will's a coward! I don't want to leave! I love him! I love Manitoulin!" If she was begging, nothing was listening. Lily's Manhattan self wanted her to stop this rant. She had betrayed Will by doing too much on the island. He needed attention that she wasn't capable of giving. In a new puddle of self-hatred, she thought she could feel her spirit pounded, drowning, into the depths of the water.

In Virgin Gorda, Captain Mal had told her she needed a cold island. She had found one. She felt suddenly jealous of Winsome, who had her husband, her baby and a loving home in Sudbury. How could she have lost so much in one evening? As she stood by the plunge pool, the thundering waters seemed oblivious to her agony. She had fallen for romantic illusion, she suddenly felt, almost ashamed of her pathetic drama in the face of nature's power. Her girlfriends in Manhattan each had been angry or sodden over lost loves, and all had recovered. Would her mother be relieved? Lily backed away from the pool and picked up a piece of pink shale and threw it fiercely into the ravine. She picked up four stones and put them in her pocket. She'd take pieces of Manitoulin with her. Bridal Veil was indifferent, neither a sign from the spirit of Manitoulin nor a flying bird to lift her spirit. She sighed, turned and walked along the wooded path toward the North Channel. The stream bubbled as she nimbly passed the rocks and trees she loved. She thought, "The bridge between Will and me has collapsed…"

The landscape of Bridal Veil Falls had grown into her through each season, so her steps felt sure along the path. It was the universe that felt uncertain. Will would not, could not provide further support. Her boots slipped on the wet spring ground. Dirt and mud splattered. She tried to imagine herself a warrior in a strong painting, finding her way through unexpected terror. She uttered "courage and boobs up" and made her way toward the little bridge by the Old Mill. She searched for a place to sit, to stare, to have relief, but the last of the sun was sinking into the westerly expanse of Mudge Bay, and the water was cold and black. There had to be another life waiting for her.

She passed the town dock, jogged along the curve and up the hill to Molly's house, and banged on the screen door. Molly met her at the door, alarmed. "What's wrong?"

"Will's broken up with me! What he first loved about me has driven him away."

Lily crumbled to her knees and buried her face in Molly's lap; Molly's warm hands caressed her shoulders. "He's asked me to leave. Back to Manhattan. It's over. I'm such a failure."

"You're no failure, whatever Will has decided he wants," Molly said. "Your time here has been important." Lily sobbed, anchored by Molly's competent hands. Molly simply held her.

"You've made a lot of friends here," she said, after a while. "If you're rejected by Will, you have an ability to make others laugh. You haven't lost yourself! Here's a hanky." Lily took the pressed linen handkerchief and blew her nose.

"These are strong linen hankies," Lily sighed, half laughing through her tears. "I seem to have two." She held the new hankie in one hand and drew Uncle Mudge's sodden handkerchief out of her pocket. She went to the kitchen and brought back two glasses of water, handing one to Molly. "Water, the falls, the bay, the faucet, and my tears…"

"Think of your writing as maple syrup," Molly advised. "You and Will are both richer for the time you've shared, but, Lily, I'm not surprised that he doesn't want to—or can't—keep up with you. That's not *your* fault. Will's got a different style and history."

"Molly, I'm reaching for perspective here!"

"That's what I'm giving you." Molly's eyes were steady. "Lily, I know you love him."

"Dumped! And am I ever hurting!"

"I know," Molly's voice softened with compassion. "And Ev and I will miss you if you go back to New York. But don't let go of the tree of life even if Will doesn't want to be under the same leaves. Others do. Everett wouldn't give you a hard time if he didn't care deeply for you. This gives you a new way of seeing what you already have."

"What'll I do back in Manhattan? Repeat everything I've done?"

"Who says you have to go back right away?"

"I can't stay here. I'm a reject!" She sniveled, blew her nose and laughed ruefully.

"Not to us, you're not. You've become family."

Uncle Mudge appeared in the doorway. Seeing Lily's tears, his eyes widened, and he slipped away.

Beneath a half moon, Lily walked back around the curve of the bay, past the ditch she'd driven into, by Hunt's General Store, past the double chairs outside, past the Sailor's Church and the Kagawong Park Centre, to the farmhouse. She stood in the driveway and looked at the house with renewed eyes. Its eaves drooped, and plants still sprouted through the cracks in the walls. The porch slumped. She was seeing it again as an outsider. It had grown so dear to her, but she knew that her love for it was love for what it could have become, remodeled as she and Will had discussed, planning newly painted brick and a rebuilt porch. She didn't love it the way it was, and she wouldn't miss the ancient plumbing and mice. She did love Will. He didn't want her. No plans, no future.

Silently, she entered the house.

"Lily?" Will's voice came from the living room, where he sat in the darkening room. He half rose from his chair, and she raised her hand as she paused in the doorway.

"It's all right, Will," she said, quietly. "It's all right."

Alone, she went upstairs to bed.

Chapter Seventeen

Leaving Manitoulin was a week-long ordeal. The weather turned cold and dank, and although Lily revisited every beloved spot on the farm, the natural world seemed to have turned away in rejection. Over the week, as she said her goodbyes, she met friends and readers everywhere, but it only compounded her loss.

She called her editor at the newspaper. "I'm moving back to New York. I still have ten stories in the works. May I email them?"

"Are we losing you?"

"Not unless you want to." Her voice became stronger as she realized the truth.

"File your columns by email. Use the digital highway to do your interviews."

She bought another suitcase in Gore Bay and packed her things for shipping. Over afternoon tea, Sophia gave her a scarf from her new spring line. "Remember us in New York," she bade gently, as Lily ran the soft, textured silk through her fingers.

Lily met Uncle Mudge on the Kagawong dock, two days before her departure. Spring winds threatened to blow them off their bench. "Each time I found something you wrote that was wrong, it made my day. Who calls Manitoulin a paradise, anyway?"

"You did," she pointed out, comforted by his irascibility.

"Stop making me the authority—and stop sniveling!"

Watching the whitecaps, Lily said, "You've been a good friend. I value your mentorship."

"Get off the pity pot. This gives you a chance to look at your life clearly. You don't want to spin away from what you know has become fact."

Walking from the dock, they encountered Carlotta in the parking lot. "Word has it you're going back to New York City," Carlotta said, entitlement blooming in her voice.

"Don't be surly, young lady," said Uncle Mudge.

"You think you're the greatest, don't you, Mr. Mudge!"

"Smart enough to still think you're a lady," he said, walking past her. Uncle Mudge took Lily around to the passenger side of his station wagon and opened the door for her. They drove up Whiskey Hill to his home.

Lily burst into tears. "How the hell does she know?"

"Stop that caterwauling. When you're settled back home, you'll be telling me how lucky you were." His mouth clamped shut as he turned off the ignition and opened the truck door. "Molly will have lunch on the table."

That evening in Gore Bay, Anna Brooks poured tea. "There'll always be more for you on this island."

"I'm going back to hot islands. I'm done with Manitoulin."

"You're not. You simply need distance to treat your soul. Carry on growing. It'll be different, of course. It wasn't easy being with Will. He's a good man, but he withholds. It's in your nature to be crisp and open. The more stories you tell, Lily, the more connected you'll get. When you write about life on Manitoulin, it becomes more for us," Anna said. The clock chimed. "You're not done with us, and we're not done with you, Lily Gardner."

❧

Back in New York, Alexis was exhilarated. "Wow, am I glad you're back, and I hope for good! Get to your desk immediately. Susie's taking a week off, and then we're moving her into her own office across from reception."

Lily hadn't planned to leap back into work—or to take Susie's job. She wasn't sure *what* she wanted next. She felt raw, recovering from the deepest blow. He did not want her. The noise of the Manhattan traffic grated on her ears as she walked along Madison Avenue.

"Business never calmed down after the winter rush," Alexis told her. "Weren't you paying attention to the numbers I sent? Good thing you're back, because I was going to have to hire someone." They'd had more hiring disasters than successes.

"I thought we were in a recession!"

"Not our clientele. Susie started working the social media. But, Lily, you've got to get rid of the 'eh' thing!" Alexis' grin was teasing.

Lily hesitated, then let herself giggle, drinking again that strong black coffee from the office pot. "I wait for the lights to change at the corners," she confessed. "I blink at the shop windows, all the new shows and even using elevators, Alexis. I've only been back two days. I'd forgotten there are so many people in Manhattan!"

"Susie wants to become a partner. We have to be fair to her."

"I understand, Alexis. It feels like I'm been away a long time."

"We've more than enough work for all of us," Alexis said.

"I see that," Lily said, looking at her old desk piled with new travel reservations.

➤

"Miss Lily, Mr. Sartorius asks that you dress to kill tomorrow for *La Traviata*. He'll pick you up in a limo," the secretary told Lily. Lily would be hearing "Sempre libera," her favourite. The heroine, Violetta, sang, "Ever Free!" as she fell in love with Alfredo, who beguiled her into a duet. Lily smiled, remembering her concert for Farmer Grey's cows. "If twenty rumps retreated, the aria needed more practice," she told Sarty in the limousine.

"Forget those damn cows," Sartorius said. "Those black suede gloves are perfect with your vintage Dior. At least you didn't lose your looks in the backwoods! Do you like my tux?"

"You're a magnificent man!" They arrived in front of the Metropolitan Opera House and the procession of limousines slowed. When they stopped, the chauffeur opened the door. Entrances were made.

"Hold your head high, Lily," commanded Sarty. Festivity permeated the night with display and pomp. Chagall murals greeted them over the grand lobby as they were swept along the red-carpeted steps. "Look at the millions spent in jewels and gowns tonight. Lily, up, up!"

The beautiful people watched each other. Sartorius knew the fashion crowd. "Look at the floozies in their rubies!" he murmured, and they laughed. They found their seats in the centre of the orchestra. In the display of wealth and beauty, it was a grand New York City night, full of extravagant fashion and competitive creativity. The conductor played *The Star Spangled Banner*. All in the hall rose as one, and then the curtain rose. Lily swayed to every nuance in the opera's tone, breath, and cadence. When Violetta sang "Forever free," Lily felt herself in the field, with her cows. Sarty placed an arm around her.

After the first act, he took her to the Opera Guild Room. They sat at his reserved table, and drinks appeared.

"Here's your usual, Sir, Mesimarja arctic brambleberry liqueur, on the rocks, with a curl of kumquat, and one for the lady."

"I taught him to say that," Sartorius said, slipping his favourite waiter a twenty. Lily's giggle was a crescendo of optimism. Yes, six months ago, she'd been singing in the back forty; tonight she was at the Metropolitan Opera.

Back at her apartment, there was a message from Will with his number in Toronto. She wrote it down and pushed the paper to the back of her dresser drawer.

There was more news Monday morning at the office: "Our Susie's been hired by another agency! Lily, may we return to our original partnership agreement?" Alexis raised her eyebrows at Lily expectantly.

Lily nodded, "You bet, Alexis," and felt an inner pang. Too soon, she was sliding back into her Manhattan life as if Manitoulin had never happened.

"It's a deal. The mayor wants Little Dix Bay. Get the newest suite." Alexis handed her the file. Back to work.

Her niece Amy had been cast in a new play in London, England, so Lily's apartment was vacant. In the evenings, she remembered Will sitting at a dining-room chair drinking coffee, she all the while wondering if his weight would break through the delicate caning. Lily swore she heard an owl outside her fifth floor window one night. She remembered the sound of the wind from the field, and the road from Gore Bay to Providence Bay, so relaxing and you only had to watch for deer at dusk. She had pictures in her kitchen of the Kagawong harbour, of her friends.

Even the coffee she drank tasted wrong, lacking the subtle aroma of wood smoke. A store window filled with fishing apparel made her think of the docks. She had become a foreigner in her own city, learning Manhattan anew.

Lily kept writing columns. She interviewed guitar virtuoso Arturo Cárdenas on Manitoulin by webcam. Born in South America, Arturo found the island a welcoming place to spend a year composing. He gave concerts at Café in the Woods, his Bossa Nova rhythms enchanting summer people and Haweaters alike.

"Of course I miss Argentina," he told Lily when she asked about his homeland. "Life is full of loss, Lily, because our feelings are real. I have moments of pleasure, excitement performing my music, but pain when I finish a concert, knowing the moments are gone. But like love, music can be felt and heard again. We may long for one person, or a place, like my home. We also long for the peaceful end of a relationship, the cessation of pain."

"My engagement ended a few months ago," she confessed.

"I do hear sadness in your voice. You've been given the painful moments of parting, the precious gift of loneliness. Your American writer, Thomas Wolfe, wrote that 'loneliness is the central and inevitable experience of every man.' Loneliness is what we experience, and then we can move on. You don't want to skip it. It's an important part of being an artist, of growing."

Lily's newspaper column continued to resonate. She subscribed to the *Expositor* and the *Recorder*, keeping current with plans for Summerfest and Haweater Weekend.

"I read your column every week," Anna Brooks told her when she called to ask about the Gore Bay summer festival. "It's almost like having you here."

"I'm learning to work on the digital highway, Anna. People are eager to share what's happening," she said.

Her mother called from Florida in mid-July. "Molly's been clipping your columns for me, and she just sent the latest batch. Are you still working on your book?" Her mother had been sympathetic and understanding about the break-up with Will, but unrelentingly optimistic about the future. "No one who knows you could picture you in that rural backwoods farmhouse forever, Lily," she'd said practically. "The entire island of Manitoulin might have held your energies; that old farmhouse never could."

Lily spent a busy summer in New York, sailing with friends on Long Island, attending open-air art shows and occasionally visiting the Hamptons. She began to date casually again. She tried a computer dating service, but gave up. Stillness was a struggle in New York.

"I'm calling to say hello from Kagawong, checking on the old pipes in the farmhouse," Will said on the phone. "Laura gave me a German Sheppard puppy. I'm calling her Lola."

"Is there a reason you called, Will?"

"I've been reading some of your columns. Aunt Molly sends them. I wanted to wish you a happy summer…"

"Thanks Will. Enjoy your new dog."

Gradually time began to move faster. Alexis and Lily planned a business conference in San Diego, and they were immediately invited to plan another for Fairbanks, Alaska. They caught up on all the Broadway plays, delighted to have many clients among the actors and actresses. But even walking home in the summer night after a Broadway musical, her head full of songs, Lily felt restless.

At home, she reread her manuscript about the Boston sisters, getting nowhere. She put it back into the drawer.

"Lily, you're working and playing too hard. I do know how much you hurt over Will," Alexis declared late one afternoon.

"Wrong assessment, Alexis," Lily said. "I'm just enjoying all New York has to offer."

Lily continued to talk to people on Manitoulin and write her columns, but the island grew slowly more distant. When she returned a phone message from Anna in Gore Bay, Lily was happy to find Anna out and to leave a message herself in return. Aunt Molly wrote her a letter with a fancy Canadian stamp, asking why she wrote so seldom. Did Lily need an infusion of maple syrup to make life sweeter? There weren't any real conversations, no fir-tree-and-moccasin telegraph gossip, no dock talk. In the evenings, Lily thought of the sweet light on the Kagawong River, when the sun set after nine o'clock and shadows lengthened, turning the evenings into gold, pink, and deep red. She kept busy at the exercise club, met friends for dinner or went to the movies.

Soon it was Labour Day, and Lily wrote of fish fries, sailing, clothing designers, the *Chi-Cheemaun* ferry and vacations on Manitoulin. The eight-week summer was over.

One cool morning in late September, Lily woke to the sound of rain and a heavy feeling behind her eyes. She looked up at the clock and let her head fall. Even the fine view of the courtyard below couldn't raise her spirits. During sunny days, light filled the apartment, and she was grateful for the fine space she inhabited in Manhattan. What was on her list today? For a moment, she could think of nothing, her mind frantically scrambling through clients and itineraries, unable to remember who had left and who was still to book. She turned her face back into the pillow. It was all the same thing anyway—only the details changed. She pushed herself out of bed, and sneezed violently.

Manhattan's morning taxi, bus and pedestrian rush grated down the back of her neck on the way to the office, and Lily slouched over her largest mug of coffee as she waited for the computer to boot up. She sighed when an email from the BVI tourist office opened, displaying an intensely sun-drenched red sailboat in the Virgin Gorda harbour. She remembered swimming off the boat at anchor there, she and Will climbing back aboard to dry off and make love. Her mind filled with too much memory. She put her hands over her eyes, uncomfortable and grieving, and shook her head. Was she homesick for Virgin Gorda or Manitoulin or herself?

She punched keys to bring up the day's first client. Yet another fall tour was in store, booking Little Dix Bay and swanky charter sailing trips. She had been asked to lead another familiarization tour to the BVI, with new properties, managers and fresh funny travel stories to tell. Yet this new felt like more of the old routine. Winsome had emailed: they were expecting a second baby. The morning passed in a blur of phone calls and bookings, and a frantic search for lost Louis Vuitton luggage that had not followed its owner to Beijing. Like Lily herself, it had not gone where she had planned.

At lunch, Alexis looked into Lily's office door, and then shook her head as Lily sneezed four times. Loud. "Go home, girlfriend. What you've got, no one here wants."

Over the next two days, September rain continued to fall on Manhattan, and Lily developed the kind of sniffling-coughing-sneezing cold that TV commercials enthused over. A soothing, rich pot of Dahlia's dill chicken soup bubbled on her stove, and she pulled out last winter's blue flannel nightgown, purchased in Gore Bay. She paid no attention to time, sipped her sister's chicken soup and fell asleep watching old movies.

Her mother and Dahlia phoned her daily.

Her doctor said, "You've got the '100-Day Cold!' Rest and fluids—and make an appointment for your annual physical! I haven't seen you for two years!"

Two days became a week, and Lily slouched around her apartment in flannels. Alexis remained relentlessly cheerful and refused to allow her in the office until she stopped sniffling. The skies remained grey and low. By the end of the week, at the nadir of boredom, she wrapped a blanket around her shoulders and pulled out a box she'd packed that spring and never opened. She piled books to give away, put books on her own shelves, and began to sort through files. There were notes on Manitoulin history, background for chapters on the Boston sisters, a few unfinished columns, and Aunt Molly's recipe for sour cream rhubarb cake. Lily put the recipe aside to try later, and began rereading notes about Great-aunt Evelyn, marching among the suffragettes as a girl with her mother. This was the beginning of the right to vote for American women. The childhood experience must have given Evelyn the strength to resist parental pressure and social convention, when she chose writing and Paris over Beacon Hill.

She began to scribble in the margins, and only when she stood to go to the computer did she realize that the apartment had grown dark around her. Chilled and stiff, she gathered up her cold mug of tea, the blanket, and the papers, and moved to the kitchen to put on the kettle. It was well past suppertime as she turned on lights and heated soup, but she pulled out her laptop and began to type between spoonfuls.

CHAPTER EIGHTEEN

IN OCTOBER, ANNA AND CHRIS BROOKS CAME to visit. They settled in at her apartment. Chris opened the window to see five tall trees and their barren branches shifting in the wind at fifth floor height. "I didn't picture trees in Manhattan."

"Your apartment is comfy and crisp," Anna said. "Bravo, you're healing away from Will. We want to go to Radio City Music Hall, and plays on Broadway."

"You are my gifts. You've brought yourselves from Manitoulin."

They stayed for a week, and Lily found her Manitoulin memories resurfacing. When they left, she began weekly phone calls to Molly and Anna, reconnecting as New York drifted into the cold weather of November.

"Lily, come with me to an art opening on Bleecker Street," Sartorious invited. "I'll have the car pick up you up at the office."

"Not tonight, Sarty, I've research to do. Maybe next week?"

Lily found herself, these days, rushing home from the office to write about her Boston sisters' struggles for identity and fulfillment. She'd drawn upon Evelyn's childhood memories to create for her character Sarah, the lawyer, a passion for social justice.

In late November, Lily checked in with her doctor. "I'm sending you for a mammogram," he told her. "You're that age."

"I remember you!" the technician laughed. "'Boobs up!' Two years ago! You know how many Sarah Bernhards I get a day complaining about their breasts being pressed? Stay still!"

In thirty minutes, the technician, her face guarded, returned to the waiting room. "The doctor says we'll need a needle biopsy of your left breast."

Three days later, Lily was lying on the table in Dr. Hilton's office.

"You have stage one breast cancer."

"I do not. I have a broken heart."

"You're not listening. You have two options. We can do a lumpectomy, and follow up with radiation, and possibly chemotherapy, to be sure we get it all. Or you can have a mastectomy, complete removal of the breast." Lily inhaled sharply.

Dr. Hilton met her eyes. "I know, it sounds extreme. However, we have a better chance of removing all the cancer, and usually no radiation or chemotherapy is necessary. We can do the breast reconstruction in the same surgery: remove the breast and insert a saline implant at the same time. You have a little time to think about this, but not much. We need to begin treatment soon."

"Doctor, can heartache bring on cancer?"

"Early detection is a gift, Ms. Gardner. One out of eight women in North America is diagnosed each year. When we catch it too late, there's not much we can do. The nurse will give you the next steps. Your prognosis is good."

Lily was glad she was lying down on the table when he told her. *Breast cancer.* Betrayed by her own heart. Betrayed by her own breasts. She sat up and stared down at her toes. "Don't you start," she told them. In a daze, she dressed and accepted an envelope of instructions from the nurse.

She walked out onto Fifth Avenue. She must attend exercise class and do laundry. She walked slowly toward her office before the news sank in. She stopped in the middle of the sidewalk.

She had received a great gift while she stood crying below Bridal Veil Falls.

Will had sent her home.

It might have taken another year before she'd found a Canadian doctor and gotten a physical, much less a mammogram. Stunned, she sat down on a bench on Fifth Avenue and began to cry. What a gift! And now her challenge was to concentrate on wellness. This was her next experience, her new destination.

>

"Sweetie, most of the women I know have had breast cancer. It's an excuse to get great big implants. It'll improve your social life," Sarty said, trying to make her laugh.

But Lily was shaken. Dahlia took her to her appointment with a breast surgeon. Lily's briefcase was filled with pathology slides, mammogram reports, and strategies. The doctor peered at Lily's pathology slide.

"The diagnosis of breast cancer compounds every emotion that I feel about death. I've accomplished nothing in my life except to plan travel for other people!"

"Cut the crap, sister," Dahlia said. "We'll get through this."

"I need to go back to Manitoulin," Lily said.

"Why would you want to go there? You got your life back from Will and he doesn't care. Mom's coming back for Christmas."

In her apartment, Lily played the piano, all the old songs she had sung with her father. Melancholy blues and irreverent jazz. You had to live each day to the fullest, the cliché said. Her father had died so young—smart, funny and generous to his family, and then gone. She did not tell Alexis or anyone on Manitoulin about the diagnosis until she made hospital arrangements. Settling deeply into her work allowed her occasionally to forget that she had breast cancer. It felt private. She only needed the love and support of her mother, her sister and her piano.

Her mother was worried by her silence. "I can tell you're not out to dinner with Sarty. Are you working late at the office?"

"Mom, I go directly home. I'm thinking what medical treatment to choose, and I've been writing about the Boston sisters' disastrous relationships. I am," Lily said reflectively, "taking perverse pleasure in someone else's misery."

"Lily, that's not like you," her mother said. "You've the best doctors to choose from in New York. This will all be over and you'll be fine again. You caught it early, honey."

At home, Lily watched the clouds pass by her window. She knew life was fair and difficult. There was limited time. She wasn't only her body, she knew that. Would she choose a lumpectomy? Or a mastectomy? The loss of a body part, her breast, would not make her less lovable, but she had felt unlovable anyway, these past months. Disease was the loss of health. Anger could be healthy. But at who? Will? Lily suddenly wept, pulling out Uncle Mudge's hankie, which she'd been carrying like a talisman since Manitoulin. She lay in the middle of her sovereign bed in her sovereign apartment, thinking of beekeeper Malcolm Jones with deep understanding.

"Legend had it that Amazon women, prized archers, chose to cut off a breast in order to shoot their arrows with more power,"

Lily said to Dahlia, practicing what she would write. Her Manitoulin column had been picked up by the *Sudbury Star*. She had a wider readership, but she hadn't yet written about her cancer.

She knew coincidence was God's way of being invisible. A letter written by her father for her eighteenth birthday surfaced in a file among her family papers: "Welcome to the ranks of women, my beloved daughter. May you become the best of them, clear in your thinking, vigorous in your action, and successful in your own right, helpful to mankind. Good health to you, darling daughter, and long, ripe, full years. With love, your adoring father."

Lily kept exercising, eating well, and amazingly, she improved on the piano. She couldn't move the tumultuous Boston sisters along. It was herself she was moving.

The morning of the operation, her mother and her sister walked her into New York University Hospital. Deeply sedated, Lily swore she saw big cow eyes gazing at her, munching, flicking. The mastectomy and implant were successfully completed. No radiation or chemo.

"Your pathology report's clear," said Dr. Hilton. "You're cured. The reconstruction has begun well. In a few weeks, we'll start to stretch the skin over the new implant. Do your arm exercises several times a day. You'll have two matching breasts in no time."

"Our Lily Blooms with a New Challenge" was the headline her editor had written in the newspaper. "After two years' columns, Lily is in our hearts. Now she faces a new challenge, one of an entirely different nature."

"You touched the innermost part of my fear. I was able to go through my own process more easily," one reader wrote.

Recovering at home, Lily was healing. She was getting used to the new way her body felt and looked, and was eager for the implant to match her right breast. She dreamed of Bridal Veil Falls as winter snow fell on Manhattan. She felt well, and playing the playing the piano helped her strength. She had all four of Arthur Schaller's songs about Manitoulin and played every one.

Spring brought new shocks: Alexis was in love! Ben was a charming professor, shaggy, gentle, courtly, and tall. Alexis told Lily, "I'll wait until he discovers that he's in love with me! I'll keep dating 'til he comes around."

Lily's own future felt new and fragile. Grief continued to surface, a whisper she pushed aside, determined to embrace this life she was building. Concentrating on her new identity as a breast cancer survivor, and yet again a city gal, she resolved to discover New York City museums. She visited the Statue of Liberty one afternoon, and she swore Lady Liberty winked at her. At work, she paid greater attention to Canadian tour and travel companies, sending her clients to such destinations as Vancouver, Winnipeg, Ottawa and Halifax. She booked clients to Sudbury and Manitoulin, remembering the open fields and late sunsets, riding with Will in the boat—or was it simply the island she missed?

In April, the director of the Circle of Hope Breast Cancer Support Program in Sudbury phoned her. "Everyone knows you from your columns. Would you address our meeting at Cambrian College?"

Lily talked to Anna in Gore Bay. "Do the talk, and come to Gore Bay," Anna said. "Make this spring a fine celebratory time for yourself. He's not here."

At the Cambrian College auditorium in Sudbury, 200 women gathered to hear Lily speak about her experience of breast cancer. Lily felt as if she were in the centre of a powerful, healing group of women. After the talk, a woman from Copper Cliff said, "The difficult experience of cancer shook my belief that I'd be around until ninety, like generations of my family before me. I've less time than I thought to do what I want." Another woman told her, "I find time for rewarding volunteer work now. Despair constitutes growth through the turmoil of crisis, as I find my way toward a new appreciation of life."

"Your room's ready," Anna said, when Lily phoned her from Sudbury the next afternoon. She was staying with Winsome and her husband. Winsome's two-year old, Sunshine, was chubby and cuddly, and the new baby turned out to be twin boys. They talked about the people they knew in Virgin Gorda, which warmed Lily's soul with Caribbean sunshine.

"Anna, I'm not coming! I'll use the digital highway! I'm not crossing that swing bridge."

"Don't let the memory of Will run you off the island! Pass by that old farmhouse. You're a naturally open woman. He was a naturally closed man. You got in there, and he withheld," Anna said. "I need to tell you things. Time to come back, dear friend!"

Chapter Nineteen

Lily bought the most expensive anti-ditch and anti-deer car insurance when she picked up her rental car at the Sudbury airport. She passed Nairn and crossed the bridge to Espanola, driving up the winding roads of the La Cloche Mountains. The signs greeted her like old friends. She passed Sunshine Alley and Birch Island. She noticed the road had been widened in the last year. The traffic light was green as she approached the bridge. The day was sunny, and the waters of the North Channel cobalt blue. Bumpety-bump her heart thumped with the wheels on the bridge. Off the bridge, she passed the ice cream shop and went into Little Current to the local restaurant on the corner to have whitefish over salad. She dropped into Turner's and her bank, greeted with shrieks of "Lily, you're back!" She was *glad* to be here and still a little proud of the monies she had earned writing about Manitoulin. Pulling out of Little Current, she drove around the curve on Highway 540.

McLean Mountain rose above to her left, and on the right, familiar fields sloped toward the North Channel. She felt her spirits lift.

Following Highway 540 past M'Chigeeng and the Billings Stretch, her heart quickened at the green sign, KAGAWONG. A bit nervous, she stopped at Bridal Veil Esso for gas, and then parked at the falls. *Unencumbered* was her new word, a new journey, being herself. Learning, as she knew, didn't have to stop because she no longer lived there. She stood for a few moments listening and looking at the water fall. What had been tears now seemed like clean water, washing away some of the past. She was thinner, fitter, her hair shorter. Her breast implant had been filled and she felt balanced. Optimistic. She would see Manitoulin in a new light. She drove into Kagawong, and at the top of the hill Mudge Bay opened before her with whitecaps. The Canadian flag snapped in the wind. She dashed up the wide cement steps to the Kagawong post office. Without losing a beat, behind the counter, Ollie grinned, asking, "How are we?"

She wasn't due in Gore Bay until late afternoon, so after chatting with Ollie, she wandered down to the Sailor's Church, sitting for a few minutes, thinking of the last year, amazingly with gratitude. Then she walked to the dock where she'd once fallen in. The late April breeze filled her lungs with the air of the North Channel, and she felt something open up in her chest. She giggled about her amazing chest, with one natural breast and the other a wonder of modern medicine. She returned to the car and continued towards Gore Bay. As she drove past Will's farmhouse, she glanced briefly up at the second storey. The windows were boarded up tight. No looking back in the rearview mirror, she told herself, feeling only a light tug of sadness. Lily passed the Billings dump, where she had not been allowed to shop, and the trailer park on the left. She knew these open spaces, the hay fields, and followed the curve overlooking Ice Lake. The lake was serene, weeds growing straight up. She pulled into the Brooks' driveway as the evening sun ducked behind spring clouds.

"Come in and freshen up quick!" Anna said. "We're due at the potluck dinner at Gordon Township this evening. I've made my famous turkey hash." She pulled Lily's suitcase toward the guestroom at the back of the house, and in a few minutes they were driving through the twilight to Gordon Hall for the Women's Institute's annual potluck.

"It'll be a good feed on tonight," Chris said to Lily. "You're much too skinny."

People greeted her happily, as they all helped themselves and found seats in the hall. There were bowls of baked beans, mashed potatoes, noodles, beef, a platter of whitefish, salads, rolls and butter. There was beer, wine and apple juice. Lily sat next to Chris and Anna, and watched a thin young farmhand go back six times to heap up his plate.

"Fresh Manitoulin air and hard work will do that," Anna observed. And then the homemade pies, chocolate and vanilla ice cream, butter tarts and merriment. It was real.

"Good to see you, Lily," were the greetings. "How's life in the big city?" Lily kept smiling and nodding. They didn't roll home until midnight.

The days passed in a whirl of visiting. Anna and Lily bought fleece jackets and wore them to a Lion's Club fish dinner. They attended a pancake breakfast at the Missionary Church in Mindemoya, and drove to Providence Bay for fish and chips. Lily stopped in every store to see what was new. One day, Lily and Anna drove out to Meldrum Bay for lunch at the local inn and walked on the dock. At an auction in Silver Water, Lily bought a tattered pink quilt for twelve dollars. No self-respecting Manitoulin woman would keep such a frayed thing. Anna bid on an antique typewriter, getting it for six. When they returned home, Anna turned on her sewing machine, tidying edges of the quilt, and Lily hunkered over the old typewriter to clean and lubricate the keys for Anna. It worked.

The next morning, Lily sat down at Anna's kitchen table to write about coming home to Manitoulin. During the days that followed, she traveled to Spring Bay to interview the quilt lady, to Jack Seabrook's Farm Museum in Mindemoya, and to Providence Bay to inspect the trailer park. She drove to South Baymouth to talk to the local artists about their work. She visited Sophia at Dominion Bay as often as she could, vowing not to buy any more clothes. She found herself glad it was spring and too early for swimming. She wasn't ready to face her body in a swimsuit yet. Even with good sleep at the Brooks' home, she realized that she was still fragile, feeling new in many ways on Manitoulin, still healing, but not at all over everything.

She called on Aunt Molly and Uncle Mudge. She'd brought him shirts from Sartorius' New York—designed, upcountry clothes—which Uncle Mudge swooped up immediately while they chuckled. Molly and Uncle Mudge were tentative, reluctant to bring up old memories that began in laughter and trailed off in unfinished sentences. They understood why she only paid them one visit this trip.

In slants of sunlight, Lily found herself expecting Will to appear around a corner, but she kept on keeping on and listened and wrote stories for her column. She didn't touch the Boston sisters' manuscript, which remained among the papers in her briefcase. She had not anticipated the intensity of recognition and belonging she felt on her return to Manitoulin. She had no home on the island, no family. Yet she knew that this cold island had become one of the homes of her heart.

Back in Manhattan at her check-up, her doctor reported that her breast reconstruction was healed. Lily had gotten used to it. She was glad to be home. She had Baby Grand tuned and spent evenings at the piano. She had missed her own home cooking and doing laundry, and yes, dusting. An occasional rat would find its way through the pipes in her old building, but they would flee her kitchen when she brandished the broom. The few weeks on Manitoulin still amazed her. She had plenty to write about, and she was glad to be home.

Dahlia bubbled with news one night on the phone: "We've sold the business and our house in Darien. We're buying a home in Florida. It's on a golf course! We'll be near Mom's condo, so we can keep an eye on her. I'm heading to Florida to work on the house."

Alexis was dating her shaggy professor, over the moon in love. "Ben's funny and smart, and he loves to travel. My God, I might be getting a life outside this office," Alexis dished with Lily. "He listens to me, Lily. And, oh, did we go to bed! I've invited him on a cruise."

"Oh, good. I like him too," Lily told her friend.

Alexis and Ben returned the following week, with suntans and non-stop smiles. Alexis floated into the office. As early summer bloomed in Manhattan parks, everyone seemed to be in love. Lily's mother called from Florida.

"Uncle Mudge invited himself to visit you?" Lily's voice rose.

"He didn't just invite himself—he's here, Lily." Her mother was laughing. "He doesn't tell you everything. He's played golf with Stuart, cribbage with Dahlia and swims with me. We're laughing all the time." For a moment, Lily felt left out.

"I don't want him to love Dahlia more than me," she told her mother.

"Honey, you and Dahlia do not compete," Violet decreed. "Why don't you come visit?"

Lily found Uncle Mudge happily fixing Violet's patio screen door. Lily secretly inspected to see if they were staying in separate bedrooms. She was ashamed of herself.

"I'm hosting lunch at the golf club in honour of my visitor from Manitoulin. Come along," ordered Violet. "You'll meet my friends."

A boisterous buffet lunch began, the nonagenarians discussing daily aches, pains, and physical losses. "Leo, don't eat that third piece of cake. It makes you sneeze. I'll hear about it all night. What do I do with him," Leo's elegant wife Blanche, in Giorgio Armani and Prada heels, rolled her eyes. As they proceeded to the coffee stage, plans for the afternoon floated in the air.

"Let's hit a few golf balls after lunch. I feel strong," said Leo.

"Not today," Ev said. "We can play nine holes tomorrow."

"I may not be alive tomorrow," said Leo.

"Leo, where are your hearing aids? They're not in your ears!"

"They're in my pocket. My shirt pocket hears everything."

"Are we hitting balls this afternoon?"

"I said yes fifteen minutes ago, I think," Ev said.

"I only asked you five minutes ago, I think. Or was it yesterday?" Leo asked.

Lily held a napkin over her mouth. She must report this to Molly.

"By the way," Uncle Mudge told Lily as they prepared to leave, "Will bought a small townhouse, three floors, in Cabbagetown. Laura made him buy the latest stove and refrigerator."

"This has nothing to do with me, Uncle Mudge."

She returned to New York feeling that her family was getting along quite well without her. Work was waiting. She sent clients to Italy and England, to the Greek Islands, on African safaris and many to Sudbury, where they rented cars and traveled Northern Ontario. If she couldn't be there, she could book her clients there. Lily spoke to people in Sudbury and Manitoulin to arrange fishing expeditions, trips with the Great Spirit Circle, and visits to pow-wows and agricultural fairs for her clients.

In the evenings, she pulled out the draft columns and notes she'd collected during her visit with Anna and Chris, and polished biweekly columns for the newspaper. The editor called and asked if she would like to put her columns into a paperback book for summer readers.

"I'll think about it," she said. She ought to spend time on the Boston sisters, she knew, but she wasn't ready to pick it up yet. She was focused on her own life, remembering how lucky she was to be back in New York City for that life-changing diagnosis.

Through summer days of sun-drenched heat, while the denizens of Manhattan withdrew to air-conditioned offices, Lily leapt at the chance to lead a tour of Tortola and Virgin Gorda. The summer sea breezes were heavenly and the visitor traffic light. She returned to Manhattan happy, feeling good again about her life's work, revealing new places to people and taking care of them. She began swimming in the pool at the exercise club; it smelled of so much chlorine that no one wore good bathing suits.

As August beat down on Manhattan, Lily flew north to attend Haweater Weekend, the Wikwemikong Annual Cultural Festival and powwow, and the Manitoulin Country Fest, hosted by the Little Current radio station. For these events, so central to Manitoulin culture, second-hand reports would not suffice. She spent ten days on Manitoulin in a frenzied rush of farmer's markets and festivals. She kayaked on the Kagawong River, the water lilies shining up from the surface as they always had. The farmhouse was still boarded up, black-eyed susans growing wild in the tall grass. She came back with material to write biweekly columns well into fall.

With September, the rhythms of the season took over at the office. Lily and Alexis sent travelers to Turkey, Italy, Hong Kong, and Australia. She spent evenings crafting her old columns into stories, and as the weeks passed, her book *Simply Manitoulin* began to take shape. She sent the manuscript to her publisher.

"Lily, it's a love affair with the island," he said over the phone a week later. "We'll send a few suggestions for revisions. We'll publish for the spring season."

By spring, *Simply Manitoulin* was off the press. Lily phoned Will in Toronto to say that some of her newspaper columns had been published as a book. "I'm bringing Violet. The Manitoulin Tourist Association is hosting a book launch and reception. We'll stay with Molly."

"Stay in the farmhouse," he insisted. "There's a bed on the first floor. I'll put the hydro on. Don't shoot the raccoons under the front steps."

"The raccoons are still there? Will, I'm bringing my *mother*..."

"Nothing scares the General. There's perch in the freezer—just help yourself, Lily."

"Why are you inviting me? Our relationship is over."

"Hey, we're friends. You always took good care of the place. I know you'll vacuum up the flies..." Will chuckled. "Really, Lily—it'll give you your own space to have people over. You know you'll be seeing everyone. Business here takes too much of my time. I'll feel better if I know you're in the place, if only for a few weeks. I'll tell Muddy to look in on you—he'll help if you run into any problems." Lily hesitated.

"Please, Lily. I'd like to think of you and friends there, the dining room full of light."

She could picture it herself, and the idea of feasting all her Manitoulin friends in the farmhouse caught her imagination.

"If you're sure, Will, then, yes. And thank you."

CHAPTER TWENTY

VIOLET ELECTED TO USE A WHEELCHAIR to get through Security, Customs and Immigration at the Toronto Airport. "I feel lousy with rheumatoid arthritis, but I want one more trip to the island," she said. "Ev and I have a date at the Kagawong dock." At the Sudbury airport, they chose a large rental car, and stopped in at the printer's to check on the book. The manager told Lily, "Staff's sneaking reads of the galleys. That's a good sign."

Chapters hosted a book launch. The local television station sent a TV crew. CBC Radio hosted an interview. "The book is based on my encounters with Manitoulin," she told the radio show's host, "I hope the readers will fall in love with the island as I did. But the common theme is how each of us can blunder through life and new experiences, make mistakes, and learn to laugh at and love ourselves. We may disappoint one another. Yet we keep growing. It's about learning how to find home where you are." When she said the words, Lily felt something settle inside. This *was* what she'd learned: that home was where she was.

In Kagawong the next day, Lily unlocked the farmhouse door. Electricity went on at the first snap. Lily opened windows, letting in the smell of freshly cut hay. Early yellow daylilies fluttered against the windows. She looked around at the clean kitchen, strangely thrilled that Will wasn't there. Molly had urged them to stay with her and Uncle Mudge, but Lily wanted some leisurely, quiet time with Violet in this summer of her mother's life, possibly the last Violet could travel. Lily peeked into the dining room to see her friend, the old piano. Nostalgia and joy washed over her. It was in tune. Violet came to listen in the doorway.

"Your father would be thrilled to hear you play," she said, as Lily picked out the final notes of "Long Ago and Far Away."

Lily got up. "Mom, I'll put on the kettle. If you make tea, I'll put chairs out on the porch and you can enjoy the lilies while I get us settled in."

Lily made the bed downstairs, catching, as she spread the sheets, the lingering scent of soft cotton dried on the line. Molly must have dropped by with fresh laundry, for Muddy never would have thought of this. She put the groceries away, and unpacked Violet's suitcase.

"It's too cool inside. Join me in the sun," her mother ordered, and Lily poured herself tea and settled beside her. "Honey, this farmhouse is five years older than I am."

Lily smiled. "If it's still cold in the house when you want to lie down, I'll fill hot water bottles! I'm glad you're here."

"I never believed you'd stay here in these backwoods, Lily," Violet said. "But you must have missed your namesakes, these bright yellow lilies, when you left."

"There's a lot I've missed," Lily admitted. Her gaze settled on the expanse of green pasture in front of them, the fir trees to the left. Her gaze went straight to her much-beloved hills to the west. She and Will had lived with this view over coffee in every season. The lilies waved in the breeze. She took a deep breath and smiled at her mother.

A car drove in and Molly stepped out with a picnic hamper. Lily hugged her and went to find another chair. "Violet, I've been counting the days and here you are! You must be tired from your trip. Since you just got here, I cooked an easy dinner for you, fresh fish, sweet potatoes and a salad. All you have to do is heat the fish up. And Sophia has invited us to visit her at Dominion Bay in a few days. She has new styles!"

"Thank you, Molly," Violet said, receiving a hug from her friend. Lily took the hamper.

"I wish you'd stay with us."

Another car pulled into the driveway. Out stepped Ev Mudge, pressed and clean. "I came right away to greet dear Violet," he said, smelling of aftershave.

"Ev, we agreed I'd see Violet first," Molly said. "Go fishing or something!"

"No nap today, Lily," Violet whispered to her daughter.

Everett waited impatiently on the porch, tapping his newly shined shoes. He planted a kiss on Violet's cheek. "It's been too long since my visit in Florida." He sniffed her perfume, "Ah, the smell of French civilization. Tomorrow, I'll take you ladies to dinner."

"Ev, tomorrow's the launch. Never mind. I'm grocery shopping in Gore Bay," Molly said, getting up, shaking her head. "Too much competition here. I'll see you tomorrow, Lily, at the book launch. And call me if you need anything!"

"Let me move our chairs further into the sun, Violet," Everett said, helping her up and slowly moving both wooden chairs to the edge of the lawn. Their heads were close together. Lily's mother laughed. Lily brought out fresh tea, cheese and crackers, and retreated to the house to vacuum and dust. Five minutes later, she glanced out the upstairs window and met her mother's eyes. Violet motioned for her daughter to come outside, now!

Uncle Mudge took Violet's hand for a brief moment.

"I must take a nap, Ev," she said, taking her hand back. Watching her mother and Uncle Mudge, Lily felt a sad tenderness. What did they know about friendship and acceptance that she did not?

Violet awakened early in the evening and sorted her pills and vitamins. "I'm your old Rolls Royce! I wake up, turn on the key, stretch slowly, warm up, and get going. I've got silver in my hair, gold in my teeth, gas in my stomach and lead in my feet."

"Where do you find these jokes?"

"In the *Reader's Digest.*"

The next day, cartons of the new book were delivered to the Kagawong Park Centre. They were laid out on a table, on a red cloth with fresh flowers in a bowl. When Lily drove into the parking lot, it was full. Ollie Hill stood outside, waiting for her. "Hurry, three hundred people are here!"

There were faces Lily knew and those she'd never seen before, talking and laughing, selecting scrumptious appetizers catered by the Anchor Inn. Lily got Violet seated, took a deep breath, and stepped onto the stage in front of the microphone. "Thank you all for showing up!"

Lily read from her book: the part about falling off the dock at Kagawong, and another about her mother's first visit. People lined up immediately to buy their own signed copies.

"I'm Jean Ryan from Providence Bay. It's my husband Jack's birthday next Sunday—I need a signed copy for him, as well. And will you come to the party? Please? He would be thrilled."

Lily hesitated, then thought, why not? They exchanged numbers. Through the afternoon, Lily signed books while Violet sat at another table. She was so clearly the General, an elegant old lioness, that people lined up to talk to her, too.

"Dang right about yer ma," whispered Farmer Lem Tompkins to Lily through missing teeth. "I'd like to talk to her about my golf swing, but I'm plain scared of her."

"Mom, this is Lemuel Tompkins, a golfer. He loves the golf stories about you."

Speechless, Lem bowed to Violet.

"Lemuel, let me see your swing," she ordered. Lem assumed his golf stance, to the delight of people waiting in line. The General gave Lem a golf lesson right there. Soon there was a line-up. Violet received five invitations to play golf.

The reception concluded after six pm, talkers still standing in the parking lot because the Park Centre was locked up. Lily and her mother drove to Whiskey Hill for a celebratory dinner. Violet and Aunt Molly were busy in the kitchen, while Lily, exhausted, plunked into one of the four wooden chairs on the porch. She stared at the expanse of blue water and clouds, the round white quartzite La Cloche Mountains shimmering far off. The world seemed full of light this bright June evening. Lily subsided into a weary sense of exultation at the unexpected success of the launch. She had had no idea how many books had sold. People had waited in line for hours to have her sign the book.

The screen door of the stone house squeaked. Uncle Mudge grunted as he slowly lowered himself down into the chair next to her. There was an ominous feel to his silence. He cleared his throat.

She shifted uneasily. "You paint Manitoulin as a mosaic of stunning richness. You celebrate the hidden pleasures, the unappreciated lore and adventures to be found in life here." He paused. "I read your damn book last night. You even show how love can cross time and countries, but you didn't write about failure."

"People want happy endings, even you!"

"Don't use humour to cover your hurt," he said sternly.

"You're awfully harsh on my launch day."

"It's well written, Lily, I'll give you that."

"Will didn't want me. I can't change that."

"You avoid my point," he growled. "You know I'm not talking about Will. You make huge efforts, spending time and money to come here. Every time you cross the bridge, you share how worlds change. You make everything nice and pretty."

"Make up?" She jumped up and crossed her arms. "Not fair!"

"Who said anything about being fair? Fiction's your rival life. You do it charmingly, making fun of yourself, but you hide. Tell the goddamn truth, Lily."

"When I was diagnosed with breast cancer, I learned there's nothing to hide."

"Bullshit."

"Damned if I'll whine about being kicked out of Paradise."

"Not having Will may be the biggest gift in your life. You've got everything but guts, Lily, everything but backbone."

"We all want to live and play artfully. Why are you being so hard on me?"

"Blunders about rhubarb? How about writing something real, a story that grapples with pain and heartbreak?"

Violet was poised at the screen door. "Ready for our walk, Ev?"

"Saved by your mother," he replied, softening his voice. "Lily Gardner, I cheerfully remain your severest critic. You have more in you than sunshine and shining hills." He gestured contemptuously at the view before them. "You have the talent to write something real, Lily. If you'll dig deep enough…"

He went to the screen door, his voice different. "Violet, my dear, the evening is young and you're so beautiful. That's a song I used to like."

Lily felt like she had been hit in the stomach. She took a deep breath. She had sold all the books they'd brought today.

Uncle Mudge had seen through her. She had fought those feelings with the distraction of work, exercise classes and local colour stories. She must pay attention to that inner companion, the whisper of sadness that had been living with her since Will had left her. She still had work to do.

She felt tears on her cheeks, and the chair held her as she sank deeper into it. She was tired from the afternoon, stunned by Uncle Mudge's challenge. In her rush and ebb, convulsive tears, she felt totally alone. She was glad no one had come out to the porch. Sadness was a hard and terrible gift. Looking down, she saw one of Uncle Mudge's linen handkerchiefs next to her, and she let the tears flow.

Chapter Twenty One

Over the next several days, Lily and Violet traveled around the island, stopping in at gift shops and museums to talk about Lily's book, but taking time to play tourist. They parked the car and Violet looked at the scenery while Lily collected fossils in ancient stones along the North Channel. They dined al fresco on lobster pizza at a restaurant overlooking the Gore Bay Harbour, shopped, and then had dinner with Anna and Chris.

In Kagawong, Lily walked her mother through the small Saint John the Evangelist Anglican Church, telling her the story of the pulpit, which had been made from the bow of a boat that had wrecked in a storm decades earlier. Islanders had later salvaged the wreckage and refinished it, incorporating it into the pulpit of the 'Sailor's Church' serving as a reminder of the uncertainty and reclaimed beauty of life. The next Sunday, Lily and Violet attended a church service with Ollie.

On Saturday, they drove to Providence Bay, past the hardware store, and turned at the Ryan family's narrow gravel road. Lily parked by the side of a sprawling, timber-frame log cottage, beyond which they could see the wide curve of sandy beach. Water sparkled and flat grey rocks framed the bay. A small sailboat approached the dock. People in bathing suits sauntered along the beach, while others swam. A pretty blonde with merry blue eyes bounded out of the house. "Glad you could make it! I'm Maureen. You met my mom at the launch in Kagawong, welcome! Come meet my dad, Jack, the Grand Patriarch. Today's his birthday."

"Your Grand Patriarch meets my General," Lily whispered to Maureen. Jack sat at the dining table, which offered a panoramic view of the bay. With a grin, he stood up to welcome them, sprigs of his silver grey hair jumped out, like Albert Einstein's mane.

"Welcome to my party!" Jack said. "Sit by me, Violet, and enjoy the view. It's the reason we're here." Jack introduced them around the family as Maureen stepped out on the porch and the lunch bell reverberated to the beach. Family, friends, dogs and cats wandered up. In the kitchen, Maureen's husband served their guests. "Bill's a professor at Laurentian University," Maureen said. "He knows the complete chemistry of the ideal taco spread."

While Violet fixed her plate, Jean took Lily aside. "Do you see the guy pulling in our sailboat? He's my second cousin—staying at the campground for the month. He's from Manitoulin, but got a job in Maine. Comes here all the time. He bought your book yesterday. Wants to meet you."

Lily watched the tall, broad-shouldered figure at the dock. His tanned shoulders gleamed in the sun as he drew the small boat up upon the sand. She joined the others at the table and assembled her lunch plate. Violet and Jean were in deep discussion.

"I came here with Jack just after the war," Jean told Violet. "He was stationed in Halifax at the naval base and so dashing in his uniform! We were married the week after VE day."

"I grew up on a farm ten miles north of here," Jack's eyes met Jean's across the table. "I knew the moment I saw Jean that she was the one." He laughed. "It took me three weeks to find the courage to ask her to dance!"

Lily regarded Jean as an authentic frontier heroine, coming to live on Manitoulin at the end of World War II.

"What courage did it take to leave Nova Scotia, marry Jack and travel, sight unseen, to live in the wilderness of Manitoulin, not knowing a soul?"

"It wasn't exactly the nineteenth century, dear," Jean said "I was in love with Jack. My parents liked him. He told wonderful stories about the farm in Spring Bay. When I got here, I was scared to meet his family. We were married and already expecting Maureen. I spent my first Christmas on Manitoulin in labour."

"It was hard to find work here after the war," Jack said. "So we pulled up roots and moved to Toronto. I got an engineering job. But we missed the island, and after the first winter, Jean laid down the law: we moved back as soon as we could, and I opened my own construction company."

"Once I'd spent that first year here," Jean smiled, "nowhere else would ever really be home. We winter at the Spring Bay farm; our summers are always here, at Providence Bay."

Warm laughter flew in the afternoon sun among the Ryans' extended family. The man from the small sailboat was now in the kitchen quietly selecting taco toppings. He had dark brown hair and an athletic body, his shoulders and chest well displayed in a blue tank. The big table had no room, so he ambled down to sit around a stone table on the lawn.

Her tacos built, Lily settled into an empty spot next to the stranger, balancing her taco-filled plate on her lap. He smiled at her.

"Hello, I'm Joel. I'm Jean's cousin, visiting for the summer. I read your book."

His black hair, a trifle too long, curled around his neck. His eyes were blue above a straight nose and sculpted chin. His long legs showed dark hair on his thighs. He was barefoot. Despite his smile, his eyes held a deeper gravity.

"Hello, Joel," she said with her own smile, interested. "It's good to meet you." She held out her hand. He wiped the taco sauce off his hand with a paper napkin, and took hers. Sparks. She asked, "Are you on holidays?"

"I took early retirement. Every day's a holiday, now."

"You're a lucky guy."

"No, I'm not," he said slowly. "Two years ago my wife died of cancer. We were going to travel. I promised her I'd go to the places we wanted to see." Silently, he looked out to the bay. "She loved visiting my family here."

"I'm so sorry for your loss," Lily said, thinking of her own ordeal. "Sometimes it's hard to keep going after a loss."

"We'd always intended to drive across Canada, so I bought an RV and started in Newfoundland this spring. I've camped on the Avalon Peninsula, swum naked in the ocean off Prince Edward Island, and driven through Montréal in rush hour!"

"The North Atlantic in June? Daring and cold," she said, laughing, picturing him naked and blue in the surf.

"I came back to spend a month here. I plan on driving the TransCanada to the Pacific Rim on Vancouver Island. I've time now. I'm staying nearby at the trailer park."

They concentrated on devouring the delicious, dripping tacos. He handed her a paper napkin.

She giggled, saying, "Thanks, I say that genius is never tidy."

"And these tacos are genius," Joel agreed. They finished their tacos in silence. "Let's take a walk to the beach," he suggested.

"Your book's so funny," he told her as they walked down to the water. "Perceptive writing for a New Yorker trying to learn island ways, 'falling into the rhubarb,' as you put it, so many times. I could hardly wait to see what would happen next. Do you have any other books?"

"No, I'm actually a travel agent. Alexis, my partner, covers for me while I'm up here. I started writing for our company newsletter, and it just," she gestured widely, "grew."

"Do you book many people to this region?"

"My specialty's the Caribbean, but Ontario's great for summer camping, some fishing and hiking," Lily said. "Last year, I rented cottages for young families on Manitoulin. This year it's a dozen already, as well as sailors who charter from NYC and want to sail the North Channel. Every client I send has a great time."

"Tourists return again and again to the island," he agreed. "My wife and I loved vacations here, visiting family. This summer it's been good to be here, remembering my childhood. Jean found a cabin in Prov she wants me to buy, but I like the flexibility of the motor home. Do you stay in the farmhouse you write about in your book?"

"Yes. Though my fiancé and I broke up, we're friends. He lives in Toronto. Are you traveling alone?"

"With my bike, guitar, golf clubs, and scuba gear. I plan to do freshwater diving off Tobermory on the Bruce Peninsula. Would you sail around the bay with me this lovely afternoon, Lily?"

"Yes, I'd love to. I've sailed around the British Virgin Islands, but not off Manitoulin."

Pushing the boat into the water, he said, "I've dived most all the Caribbean islands."

"I've done nothing deeper than simple snorkeling on reefs."

"There's nothing like it," he assured her. "Hop in." She moved nimbly to the bow of the *Debra Ann*. He handled the sails, catching puffs of the afternoon breeze. The hull sliced through the water. Lily watched Joel as he concentrated on the wind and sails, feeling as if she were waking up from a long slumber. He looked up and their eyes met. Blushing, she glanced towards the family gathering around the sun porch. Jack, Violet, Jean and Bill chatted, enjoying the summer afternoon.

Joel invited the Gardners to see his mobile home. Violet was immediately curious to inspect it. "Look at that marble-topped galley... and oh, my," Violet put her hand to her mouth delighted. "A washing machine and dryer, TV set... and bookshelves!"

"I knew I'd be spending a lot of time in this RV, so I made sure it would be comfortable. But I'll tell you, no matter how many DVDs I have, it gets lonely. Books are good company." He gestured at the shelves. "I'm reading a lot of Canadian writers this summer. It's a beautiful country, but you can't watch birds all the time."

"Alastair MacLeod," Lily commented, picking up *No Great Mischief* from the table.

"Do you know it?" Joel asked her. "I picked it up in Nova Scotia. The opening section is all about two maritimers traveling through Northern Ontario."

"Joel, where did you grow up?" Violet asked.

"Providence Bay. I attended university in Toronto, and was lucky to find a great career in Maine at the Hinckley boat manufacturing plant. Their work is superior, though I may be biased. I have a 40-foot yawl, one of the first fiberglass boats Hinckley made. I married and our son was born in Maine. He's studying at Columbia. You ask all the questions mothers ask," he teased. When he laughed, his dark hair drooped over his forehead.

"Simply conversation, young man," Violet said sternly.

"Violet, I know mothers," he returned drily. "Ladies, if you're in no rush, may I take you to dinner?"

"We'd be delighted," Violet said instantly.

Hungry after an afternoon on the lake, they dined on beef tenderloin with grilled tiger shrimp, Béarnaise sauce, and Savoy potatoes. "They developed this at the Savoy Hotel in London," the owner told them, stopping by their table. "But our chef adds a Manitoulin touch. It's good to see you again, Lily."

"Delicious, as always," Lily said. "I've missed this."

"I've something special for dessert," their host smiled. "Save room." As the evening waned, crème brûlée arrived at the table, and they lingered over liqueur. Joel bid them goodnight at the front door of the restaurant. "I'll walk back by the beach," he said, hugging each, lingering seconds longer when he held Lily.

Violet's arthritis magically disappeared on Manitoulin. Farmer-golfer Lem Tompkins encountered her again on Meredith Street in Gore Bay. "Violet, see the improvement in my swing!" Standing in front of the *Recorder* office didn't faze him. Almaz from the pharmacy walked by and giggled.

Uncle Mudge bustled in Violet's presence, delighting Kagawong, the hamlet so small that the fir-tree-and-moccasin telegraph buzzed and chortled. Townspeople paused at the glass windows of the general store to watch them chatting on the dock over ice-cream cones. He, butterscotch; she, chocolate. Two fishing rods leaned against his knee. "Ev put a worm on her line for her," said Shannon, a Kagawong resident. "They're so adorable, I can hardly stand it."

Ollie stood at the post office counter when Lily stopped for mail. "You think in terms of community, Lily, with your newspaper columns," Ollie said. "I know what it takes for you to cross the old swing bridge."

Back at the farmhouse, Lily teased Violet. "One of us is enjoy-ing the company of a Mudge. You're like two tea kettles whistling at each other." ·

She reported to Dahlia. "Everett's sweet on Mom. She's acting demure."

"Is he still critical of you?"

"Always, but Mom's laughing all the time. We're doing well. Red geraniums are blooming on the veranda. The book is selling *very* well."

"Thanks for taking care of her," Dahlia said. It's good you're both exercising your minds and bodies in Ontario. I bet you're shopping!"

"You knew that!"

Chapter Twenty Two

"To gather critical acclaim for your book you must give a reading at the bookstore in Owen Sound," Uncle Mudge declared. "They've sold books since 1987, concentrating on local writers and artists, a Mecca for book lovers on the lake."

"It's the other side of Lake Huron," Lily said, uncertainly.

"We'll take the *Chi-Cheemaun*," Uncle Mudge planned. "We'll drive down the Bruce peninsula, and be there by lunchtime. They make ginger juice from local apples," he told Violet. "We'll stay over."

"Your book received a nice write-up in our local paper," the owner told Lily on the phone. "An author cancelled for Friday, so you come! I'll put a sign up outside the shop."

"We'll be there."

"I'll drive," said Uncle Mudge. "I need new books. Be ready Thursday at 7 a.m. We'll make the early ferry."

Two days later, in early morning light, Lily loaded Uncle Mudge's truck with six book cartons. There might be shops along the way amenable to selling her funny summer book to tourists. At South Baymouth, Uncle Mudge parked in a designated lane at the ferry terminal. "Ladies, this is the official start of our trip. I went to school with the fathers of the captains."

"I bet you taught them everything they know, including navigation." Lily couldn't help mocking him.

"Don't argue with Ev, Lily," Violet said, cheerily. "You'll lose."

Parked, they waited and watched the stately ferry glide slowly into the South Baymouth harbour, docking perfectly. The ship's visored bow opened, jaw agape, disgorging eager passengers. Motorcycles, cars and trucks drove off, racing past the shops and restaurants and onto the ribbons of Manitoulin road. The attendant directed Uncle Mudge aboard, and he tucked the car snugly up against the preceding SUV.

"Everyone remember our section!" he directed, and Lily noted the C1 on the wall nearby. Uncle Mudge went around helping Violet slowly get out of the truck. They made their way up the steps directly into the ship's giftshop, overflowing with T-shirts and caps, jackets, jams and jellies, plates and dishes, and *Chi-Cheemaun* memorabilia. Lily had written and published cheerful newspaper columns about crossing on the *Chi-Cheemaun* the summer before. She had met the operations manager and chatted with the cabin crew, but had never taken the ferry herself.

The captain and staff gave generous permission, weather permitting, to passengers wishing to visit the bridge. They were led by the first mate to the spacious navigation deck overlooking the expanse of blue sky and the lake rolling beneath them. The helmsman steered, guided by an electronic compass. He explained an indication of a touch of 1/10th of a degree on the wheel. "Shows drift to exactitude."

The captain stepped onto the bridge. "Uncle Ev, I heard you were aboard. You're a happy sight. Dad's boasting he'll beat you at chess next week."

"Robby, he hasn't got a prayer. I coached Bobby Fischer as a teenager," said Uncle Mudge.

"Uncle Ev and dad grew up together," the young captain told Lily. "Dad was captain of the *Cheech* for 22 years. It's a family tradition. I alternate with another captain during the summer months, and in the winter, we teach area navigation and marine emergency at Georgian College." Noting Lily's fascination with the wheel, he asked. "Would you care to steer?"

Lily handled the wheel gently as the first mate stood close by. She was acutely aware of the swing, weigh and drift of the 7,000 ton ship as she glided steadily through the powerful Lake Huron waters towards Tobermory.

Later, Uncle Mudge and Violet had lunch in the cafeteria and read newspapers, while Lily patrolled the decks, noting the tourists and travelers for her next column. Mothers rested with small children snoozing in their laps in the bright summer breeze. Lovers sat close, talking softly, and two large dogs nestled at the feet of an elderly couple. Inside the vessel, children played electronic games in the amusement area. Only one read a book.

As the vessel neared Tobermory, Lily scrambled back to section C1. Violet and Uncle Mudge were already strapped into their seat belts.

"I was hoping to leave you aboard," Uncle Mudge said.

They drove south on Highway 6 down the Bruce Peninsula, through green farmland, and past busy shops and neat houses. "I reserved two rooms at the Mad Hatter Inn. It's an elegant Victorian bed and breakfast. My treat."

Their rooms were on different floors, to Everett's disappointment. The three dined quietly, said good night early, and met for a gourmet breakfast the following grey morning.

"Ready for more exploring?" asked Uncle Mudge, chipper in a snappy new brown and white plaid shirt.

That evening, Uncle Mudge dropped Lily off with a carton of books at the book store. "Mr. Mudge, no time long see," the owner said, greeting him with warmth. "Let me tell you about our new writers." Uncle Mudge piled up twenty hardcovers and gave the clerk his credit card.

"I'll buy two of Lily's book to start her off right in Owen Sound," he said, and muttered to her, "even if it's not up to your potential."

Lily tried not to feel riled. Her book was popular and she was proud of it, even if Uncle Mudge didn't see it as great literature. She'd be doing her first reading in a book store tonight. How many might attend? Owen Sound was charming, with local art galleries and a vibrant cultural scene; there had to be plenty of readers. "You two take the afternoon and evening off and go to dinner. I'll handle the book reading."

"We're here to support you, honey," said Violet.

"Let's vamoose, Violet, the kid can handle it," Uncle Mudge said.

It rained into the evening, the street in front of the shop puddled and desolate. As Lily's reading hour approached, the owner opened a bottle of Bordeaux and poured her a glass. "Don't worry. The usual suspects will stagger in to see who our latest author is."

Lily sat at the signing table, ready with a stack of books. Seven, eight, nine o'clock came and went. No one came. Embarrassed, Lily examined every title in the shop, and bought five hardcover books and two paperbacks, handing the owner her credit card. "Staying open shouldn't be a total loss for you."

"Its summer," the owner explained. "Many go directly to their camps. We'll stick it out one more hour." Suddenly, the door shot open. A tall figure in a yellow rain slicker and hood covering his face dashed in. He stood, drenched. "Have I missed the book reading for Lily Gardner?"

Lily jumped up: "What are you doing here?"

"I didn't think I'd find a parking spot," he said, breathlessly, "so I ran all the way from the hotel. Is the party over?"

"How did you know I was here?"

Catching his breath, Joel replied. "I didn't. I went diving off Tobermory. I wanted to get in all the wrecks. Today it was churned up—conditions were just too bad. People that run the operation insisted I stay for dinner. I read in the newspaper you would be here." Joel took off this slicker. His black hair curled around his ears, damp from the rain. He looked around. The shop was empty. "Looks like you might need rescuing."

"Uncle Mudge bought two books to start me off, but not a soul has come."

"I'm a soul." He walked toward her and slung one arm around her shoulders. She smelled his wet hair.

"This is Joel, a new friend from Manitoulin," Lily told the owner.

"Good to meet you. Take my card. I'll take five of her books."

"You've already read it."

"It doesn't mean I can't send 'em to friends. Start signing."

"You are being rescued," the owner laughed. "Would you like a glass of red wine?"

He nodded. "Do you have mailing envelopes? I'll address them now, and pay shipping."

Joel and Lily waited for the owner to lock up.

"I can't tell Violet or Uncle Mudge only you showed up," Lily said.

"Tell her that everyone who came into the book store tonight bought a book."

"That's pure genius! Where are you staying?"

"At a small bed and breakfast—all I could get on a summer weekend. I've a room with a queen-sized bed. Lily, I've an invitation. Will you stay with me tonight?"

Her fingers curled into his strong hand. Tired, with seven books sold and two glasses of wine, Lily felt vulnerable. She imagined his body against hers, all too aware of his warm strength. She leaned towards him, and then thought of her recovery from breast cancer. Though the implant might feel and look like a real breast, the scar wasn't insignificant. She'd thought of getting a tattoo, flowers and leaves—a reclaiming of her self—but hadn't, yet. Or wouldn't. And what would Joel think, with his own wife having died of cancer?

Under the open umbrella, outside in the rain, Joel kissed the back of her neck. She closed her eyes with pleasure; his lips were gentle and soft, his chest hard against her body. Why resist this closeness? She knew, with Joel, it would be amazing sex. He had charm and laughter. Everything about him interested her. But a kiss wasn't a promise to anyone. She wanted him but she didn't want to fall for him. She'd want more and not get it. "My mother won't sleep 'til I'm back."

"You're here with your mother?"

"And Uncle Mudge. He drove us."

"Maybe she's having a marvelous time with him, not one second thinking about you?"

"She's in her eighties and he's almost ninety!"

"And that means...?" He laughed, and took her arm. They began to walk.

"Violet grew up in Boston," she said, as if that explained anything.

"When we're back on Manitoulin, I'll take you for a moonlight paddle and serenade you with my guitar. Come back tonight with me. I want to hold you."

She found herself warm, wavering.

"I'll see you to your hotel later."

"I can't worry my mother," she said, feeling like a teenager.

"Well, then, I'll drive you back now. I can wait," he said, his dark eyes melting into hers. Had he rejected her now? They walked, and jumped over puddles. He began, "I'm singing in the rain, what a glorious feeling..." and she dissolved in delighted laughter. They found his car in the hotel parking lot and he drove her up the hill. He saw her to the front door of the Mad Hatter Inn and she kissed his cheek lightly. Her mother was fast asleep in their room, snoring lightly.

Chapter Twenty Three

Violet became addicted to summer life in Kagawong. Mornings began with the symphony of birds and breeze, a full day driving to other towns, often meeting people over coffee or lunch, and finishing their days with sunsets blushing in late dusk. Often their day's travels included a reading or book signing, as Lily left copies of her book in gift shops and museums across the island.

As June became July, Lily strolled along the river in the afternoons, counting lily pads and looking for beaver. What could she have done differently with Will? She was well over him, she thought, but her heart did not want to leave, and she kept reminding herself that this could not be home. Back at the farmhouse, Violet spent the late afternoons ensconced in a cozy lawn chair, napping with her book. This was magical time. The General had not fallen or tripped or gone bump in the night, but had settled into the downstairs bedroom at the farmhouse happily. Lily would lie in the upstairs bed each morning, contemplating the familiar view of the fields and hills beyond. Her life had taken her beyond this. Her life had sent her home to Manhattan from under the apple tree. She smiled to think she'd told the doctor she had a broken heart, not breast cancer. That was long over as well. Taking care of the farmhouse as the summer's temporary mistress was enough, an absorbing reprise on her own terms. ·

Joel moved his fifth wheel to a trailer park on the North Shore, between Kagawong and Gore Bay, to be closer to the Gardners. "It seems wrong to have Joel visiting at the farmhouse, coming for lunch," Lily fussed to her mother.

"Will has no claim on you. You're a free agent," Violet stated. "Will may have a new girlfriend by now, and it's only lunch, my darling daughter!"

So Lily enjoyed making lunch for Joel and walking with him along familiar paths around the back forty. Lily found herself squelching the occasional memory of a different set of broad shoulders, but scolded herself for her qualms, grateful that Joel was smart, inquisitive, and interested in sharing Manitoulin with her. They walked past the cows, along the edge of the swamp. Mostly, they were silent, enjoying the fresh country air and the lazy summer calls of sparrows and red-winged blackbirds.

"I like how the property leans down to the river," Joel said one afternoon, as they stood together on the bank of the Kagawong River. "These old farmhouses need enormous work to keep up, though—plumbing, wiring, and structural work."

"It's worth it, if it's your family home," Lily said, thoughtfully. "Will's deeply rooted here. It's lovely that he's asked us to stay."

"You love the island. Have you thought of buying property?"

"No," Lily answered. "I'll probably visit friends here often, but I don't feel the need to root myself in a particular piece of land, despite the fact that this island feels like home. Manhattan's equally my home, with work and roots there. Soon it'll be time to go back. This summer has completed something, for me," she said, thoughtfully.

"You haven't had that midnight paddle with me," Joel said, meeting her eyes. "This summer isn't over yet. Why don't you and Violet come for dinner tomorrow?

The next afternoon, Joel set up the grill on the sandy beach of Lake Kagawong to cook ribs and chicken from the Burt farm. Violet made a salad in "the kitchen on wheels," and they settled in enjoy the intensely hot July day. All afternoon, white clouds piled up on the horizon.

Lily stood with Joel at the grill, watching the wind on the water. He said, "You're putting me off. Why are you so self-protective?"

"I don't want to fall for you. I'm not ready for another relationship."

"You've already fallen for me, Lily. You haven't asked what smart ladies ask these days. I don't have Herpes or HIV, and I have new condoms."

"I get tested for HIV along with everything else," Lily answered. "I've been celibate a long time."

"When someone as delightful as you appears in my life, it would be sad to waste what I think we can have together," Joel said. "But I won't push. Much. Would you bring Violet to the table? After dinner, I'll see you both back to the farmhouse."

Lily and Violet settled at the picnic table. In the distance, the high-piled clouds were looming darker.

"We'd better eat fast," Joel said, glancing up as thunder rolled in across the lake.

The ribs and chicken began to disappear, appetites fueled by the drama across the lake. The clouds moved westward across the horizon. Faint flashes of lightening were occasionally visible, far in the distance, but it came no closer. They proceeded to ice cream dessert before the wind shifted and the dark clouds began to race in. The temperature dropped. The wind whipped up, tearing spray from the tops of waves and driving the water in to pound violently on the beach. The sky grew dark with grumbling thunder.

"Better get Violet up into the rig," Joel said. "I'll check the tie-downs."

Lily and Violet each grabbed dishes. "Mom, I'll take those dishes. You get back into the trailer."

"I don't like this," Violet said, looking worriedly at the oncoming storm. "Shouldn't we go back to the farmhouse?"

"We wouldn't make it in time."

Violet stumbled on the steps of the RV. Lily caught her mother and pushed her back up the steps, struggling to pull open the door against a blast of wind. They were blown inside. A gust slammed the door shut. They tumbled onto the rich, beige carpet.

"Lily, get off me, I can't breathe."

Lily rolled off her mother, sitting up. "Are you hurt?"

"No, but in this wind, will the trailer turn over?" Violet asked, her voice rising. The rain arrived with rattling drumbeats, and then settled into a steady pounding like a Black Sabbath concert on the roof. Lily peered out the window but could see nothing beyond the deluge.

"Stay on the floor, Lily. You've talked about storms barreling across the island."

A bolt of white lightning blinded them, followed by a bass-drum crash they could feel in their chests. With a terrible sound, a tree splintered close to them. Lily felt her stomach clench. Situated on the lake, they were directly in the path of the wind.

"It's so cold, I'm terrified," Violet said, shivering. Lily pulled a blanket from the couch to wrap around them. In deep shadow, they huddled together on the floor as the RV shuddered in the blasts of wind. Lightning stabbed at the windows, and almost immediately the thunder pounded, so close and loud Lily could feel it.

"Where's Joel?" cried Violet.

A thud resonated through the RV as another tree crackled and bounced against the ground. A thousand wet green leaves crashed against the living room windows. Lily screamed, "Joel, where are you?"

"Push the door open—" Joel yelled, his words cut off by heavy thunder. Sheets of water flowed down the windows.

Lily crawled to the door and pushed it open against the wind. Joel battled his way in, grunting, dripping, falling, as the door slammed against him. Breathing heavily, he lay on the floor. Lily caught a glimpse of something dark streaking the side of his face as the lightning flickered again.

"Joel dear, are you okay?" Violet asked, her voice thin.

"I'm fine, Violet." He sat up, and pulled both of them close to him. They huddled together as the RV was buffeted by the fierce winds. "These storms usually go through pretty fast. It's probably hitting the whole island."

"I hope this isn't our last night alive," Violet said, grasping Joel's hand.

"The rig's strong and so are we," Joel said, tightening his arms around the ladies.

"I'll be damned if we're going to die on Manitoulin," Lily said, and clamped her mouth shut, realizing it could happen. Raging winds were known to lift and turn over rigs. Downed electrical lines killed people. Freak accidents, floods, and drowning caused deaths everywhere. Manitoulin wasn't safe at all. She wrapped her

arms closer around her mother's small, thin frame. Life was fragile. Lightning crashed again, and she breathed in ozone and Joel's
sweat. She hadn't had the courage or guts to enjoy Joel. If they
came through this terrifying storm, how would she conduct her
life? Forget patience and prudence. Uncle Mudge was right. Her
newspaper columns were vignettes of life, rich and varied, but they
were ephemeral.

Joel looked at her and their eyes locked. The rig shuddered,
bouncing in the gusts from the lakeside, not quite lifting off the
ground. "I tightened everything underneath. We'll be good," Joel
said, as if he were holding down the rig with determination. The
windows were plastered with leaves. The world was crying.

Imperceptibly, gradually, the wind grew weaker and the noise
of the storm subsided into the distance. They were still, and then
Violet spoke. "I guess we're alive."

Slowly, Joel got up on his knees, kissed Lily's face, and helped
Violet up to the sofa. "Anything hurt, Violet?"

Violet shook her head. Joel opened the door and looked out.
"Are we ever lucky!"

"Lily, what about the farmhouse?" Violet asked, suddenly.

"It's been solid for over ninety years, Mom. Are you sure you're
okay?"

"Fine, dear." The General was back.

Other campers spilled out of their trailers and RVs into deep
mud and puddles, as lingering rain sprinkled down. Lily marveled at
the enormous fallen trees, some more than five feet across. Yanked
from hundreds of years in the island ground, the ancient, spidery
root systems were exposed to the air. Wet leaves gleamed, stuck to
every surface. But there was palpable relief; no trees had fallen on
anything of value, or on any one. The park's residents had come
through. The owner emerged from his tool house with a chain saw.

His wife, eager to help anyone who needed it, said, "These storms across the Great Lakes can cut the heart out of you!"

Lily got the General settled on the couch in the RV while Joel inspected wheels and undercarriage. She found alcohol and a band aid, and went out to swab his face. They were through the worst of it.

"Lily, my grill landed in the parking lot," he said, staring across the campground.

"Joel, you put on dry clothes," Violet ordered through the trailer's window.

"So like my mother!" Joel climbed up the steps, back into the rig, and pulled off his drenched shirt. Lily's eyes snapped to his bare chest. She felt as if the lightning had hit her. Joel met her eyes, and then went into the trailer's tiny bedroom for dry clothes. The acrid smell of burnt wood hung in the air.

"The rig held well." Joel emerged from the back, passing her a jacket. "Lily, help me wipe off some of the leaves. We'll take Violet back. And then, Lily Gardner…"

Lily helped Violet into the rental car, which seemed miraculously undamaged, and they drove back to the farmhouse. The landscape was wet and wind-tossed, but the violence of the microburst hadn't reached beyond the park. Lily was relieved to see the farmhouse snug, all windows safe. One pot of red geraniums beckoned from its new perch, on the roof. Another had flown past the working barn. A squirrel chittered at them. Inside, the farmhouse was undamaged. Turning on the lights, Lily helped Violet into her summer flannel nightgown, and put on water for tea.

The phone rang. Violet answered. "No, Molly, everything is fine here. No, no damage. I'm just settling into bed with tea," she paused. "Yes, that sounds fine. See you tomorrow. Bye, Molly."

Violet hung up the phone, and looked with steely eyes at her daughter. "I've Molly's number, dear, and I'll be fine here alone tonight. I'm going to bed now. Good night. Drive carefully." She went to her room and firmly shut the door.

🦅

Sun filtered into the bedroom of the fifth wheel the next morning, and Lily cuddled up to Joel in his 800-thread count Egyptian cotton sheets. He traced his warm finger along her cheek. "I'd hoped you wouldn't take much longer to come to me," he told her. "Who'd believe I met a lovely lady from Manhattan on Manitoulin?"

Lily quietly stretched and kissed his cheek. He hadn't said a word about her implant, only kissing her scar softly. She knew he was on a journey of grief and healing, and so, basically, was she, and it was good.

"We celebrate a perfect morning on Manitoulin," he whispered, reaching for her.

Violet asked no questions when Lily arrived back at the farmhouse, humming with relaxed joy. On the news, they heard that across the island many ancient barns had fallen as the storm had cut its terrifying swath. But no one had died. Lily went out to the apple tree. The trunk had split. A crevice, white and raw, deeply cleaved the tree, and she could smell its wrenched, raw wood. Lesser branches veered toward to the ground. Higher branches on the remaining limb stuck straight up in anguish. She wanted to put her arms around it. It stood, gnarled and small, split in half, but still alive despite its trauma.

"Manitoulin's exhausting for an old lady, but I'm not quite ready to go home," said Violet. "Let's have one more expedition to Sophia's boutique on Dominion Bay!"

"I made a special jacket for the light climate in Florida, Violet," Sophia said, ushering the ladies in. "Sold!" Violet said, trying it on. She perused the new sweaters and skirts, necklaces made of pearls and lapis lazuli. The afternoon was quiet, and Sophia made tea as Violet regaled her with their micro-burst adventure.

At a pause in the conversation, Sophia whispered to Lily, mischievously, "*Ach*, Manitoulin thunder and lightning seem to suit you!"

Lily shook her head. "Joel's on his way to Vancouver. I'm going back to Manhattan. Who knows if I'll ever see him again?"

"Anything is possible. Kurt and I found Manitoulin advertised in a German magazine in 1971, and here we are. Who knows what the future has in store?"

Once Violet had paid for her purchases, Sophia placed a silver necklace over Lily's head. "This is for you. It is of Bridal Veil Falls, flowing with the universe. Some days are dark, some are light. We cannot make judgements. We must flow like the falls, and understand later," Sophia said, "Good, *ja*? I make that up."

"You radiate joy," Lily said to Sophia, thanking her.

Sophia hugged Lily at the door. "You begin a new heart life. This can be fine for now. In life, we must take chances. This is what brought you to Manitoulin in the first place."

Joel called that evening. "We missed out on our moonlight paddle. Come hiking with me instead? I'm climbing the Cup and Saucer tomorrow."

Lily and Joel hiked breathless and laughing up the steeply inclined path of the Cup and Saucer Trail.

"I thought I was in shape!" Lily panted between giggles. "This is a major feat—and there's no bottled water at the top!"

"Yes, there is. I carried one for you," Joel said, taking a bottle out of his backpack.

They stood together at the edge, gazing across at the quartzite ' hills of La Cloche Mountains, the oldest mountains in the world, ground down to white rolling hills. Redtail hawks flew below them.

To the left, they could see the islands of the North Channel, and below, a vast carpet of pines and cedars, a rich, deep green in the sunshine. The view looked east over miles of forest towards Rockville and the green bay area of Lake Manitou. Below the cliff to the southeast was a small, dog-leg lake. A cranberry marsh lay at the base of the lower level cliff promontory.

"That's called the saucer," he said. "And just off one of the trails is a brass marker set in concrete, marking the highest point on the island. It's back from the cliff edges surrounded by trees, so there's no view there. The loop trail's about ten kilometres, with adventure trails leading off. I've been climbing here for years."

Lily reached in a pocket for her pen and paper, but they'd fallen out on the journey upward. She smiled to herself and leaned into Joel's shoulder, content to inhale the stunning view.

They paddled two kayaks along the Kagawong River one morning, and later had soup and crackers at Bridal Veil Esso. They swam under Bridal Veil Falls in the afternoon, Lily not even thinking about how her implant appeared in her swimsuit. At the end of the week, Joel drove Violet, Molly, Lily and Uncle Mudge on the long road to lunch at the Meldrum Bay Inn.

"Thanks for staying longer," Lily said to Joel. Their table looked out on the serene harbour and the boats at the dock. "I'm not ready for summer to end, yet."

Joel turned to the group. "Lily's slowing down. Amazing huh?" They walked on the dock and Joel sang to her. Uncle Mudge winked at Lily.

"You have a fine voice, Joel," Violet said. "My husband sang and played the piano."

"My wife was a concert pianist, Violet. I still have her Steinway. My son plays."

"Joel dear, I didn't mean to bring up sad memories," said Violet.

"Grief takes time to heal, Violet. These days are bright, with you. And not all memories are sad—sometimes they're just memories." Everyone was silent, each loving, longing, grieving, flowing, ebbing and letting go. Lily touched her necklace, recalling Bridal Veil Falls, that horrible day.

At the trailer park, their last night together on island, and under a waxing moon, Joel set up his new grill and fed them steaks with fresh corn and garden vegetables.

"I promised to serenade you on tranquil waters. I rented that red canoe," Joel pointed to where it lay on the shore. She got in. Joel carefully placed his guitar in the middle, and shoved off. They paddled out, stowed the paddles, and Lily turned in her seat. He took up the guitar, and grinned at her.

"There's a quotation I've always liked," he said. "The historian Pierre Berton once said, 'A Canadian is someone who knows how to make love in a canoe.'"

She giggled, feeling flirty, and his fingers began to pick out something lilting and sultry. Softly, he began to sing. The canoe drifted slowly toward shore. The lights from RVs, cabins and campfires flickered.

"Sing it again." People on shore clapped for him. Joel played a complicated bossa nova with intricate chord work, his deep tones sliding through the night like velvet. She sang a third note above him; they played with rhythm, melody and harmony. When it ended, someone yelled, "You two, in the canoe, one more song, eh?"

The world was singing with them.

Finally, their canoe nudged the sand and they stepped out, pulling it ashore together. Joel drove Violet back to the farmhouse, and returned to the RV with a litre of Farquhar's chocolate ice cream. He brought that with two spoons into the bedroom.

"Chocolate courage," Lily joked, feeling her eyes sting. "I'll miss you, Joel."

"Ice cream always helps," he teased gently. "I came to Manitoulin to get away from a habit of grief. I needed the courage to do less, very little for a while, to live more fully with myself. With you and Violet, I've been able to rest and to play. I'm glad we're both crossing the bridge tomorrow. We're headed in different directions, but we're doing it together."

The next morning, Lily locked the farmhouse door, said goodbye to the possum family and whispered thanks to the farmhouse for all the love, happiness and even deep disappointment she'd felt within its walls. She was grateful to have shared it with her mother. The little apple tree, deeply split, was rebuilding itself, and the smell of seared wood had disappeared. She stood under the tree and kissed both sides of the trunk. Violet waited in the car.

"Mom, when we closed the house on Maple Drive, you said we were free."

"It's time to move on, dear," Violet said serenely, turning her face towards the road.

Lily drove to the Bridal Veil Esso to wait for Joel. His Silverado and fifth wheel barreled around the corner, and she followed along the Billings Stretch, past M'Chigeeng, past lakes, hillocks and pastures with yellow hay bales, past the glorious blue water of the North Channel, past sailing boats bobbing along in the distance, past Sucker Creek and the Honora Bay road, around the curve to Little Current. They stopped for the red light in front of the swing bridge.

Joel stepped down from his truck. She stepped out of her car. He picked her up for a last hug. "Be careful and be safe, Lily. I hope this hug will hold you awhile. I'll always remember Manitoulin with you," he said, lowering her feet back on the ground. They lingered in a last touch. "Lily?"

She looked up at him.

"It's not the time for you to take me seriously," he said. "But this isn't goodbye."

"No," she agreed, her eyes stinging. "But our Manitoulin summer's over. I'm headed to Manhattan, and all of western Canada waits for you. No expectations, no regrets."

"Time to go," he agreed, pulling her into a last hard hug, and turned away.

Lily bolted to her car, not looking back, and slid in behind the wheel. "Let's listen to CBC Radio." Joel was still grieving, she told herself. Why didn't she have better timing, in so many things? She thought about this summer on the island, traveling and shopping with her cherished mother, driving all around the island, taking the *Cheech* to Owen Sound to talk about and sell her book, singing and paddling with Joel. No judgements. A car honked behind her. She touched the brushed silver of her flowing Bridal Veil necklace and drove slowly across the bridge.

Chapter Twenty Four

Summer in Manhattan passed into fall and winter. In the process of group ticketing and piled coffee cups, Alexis made a stunning announcement: "Ben asked me to marry him!" She showed Lily her stunning diamond ring. Ten minutes later, she booked the owner's suite on a Caribbean cruise for the following week. They were married at city hall on Friday and left Saturday on a ten-day cruise.

"I don't waste time," Alexis hooted.

Ben grinned into Lily's laughing eyes. "I wasn't going to let her come to her senses, once she said yes."

For two weeks Lily was a space jockey at the computer, keeping prices low, managing two assistants. They were so busy that Lily rented a triple room at the Berkshire Hotel and they camped out, working late and ordering up room service. When the honeymooners returned, Lily and Alexis traveled to Jakarta to handle the daily changes for a United Nations Conference they had planned six months ago.

Somewhere, Lily found time to play piano and keep writing. Her column flourished. Joel had driven across Canada, his progress punctuated by postcards arriving at Lily's Manhattan apartment as fall became winter: postcards came from Winnipeg, Banff, Whistler, Vancouver and Victoria, lighthearted and friendly.

Then, suddenly, it was the merry month of May again, and Lily was giving herself a gift, a trip to Northern Ontario. She drove from the airport to Manitoulin, directly to Sophia's on Dominion Bay. Sophia greeted her, bright with affection. "We go to the garden, *ja?*"

Walking through the vegetable garden, Lily smelled the earth warmed by the early May sun. The sun touched on tiny green lettuce leaves, the red-veined springs of beets, and stalwart, upright young onions. Sophia bent to pluck an offending weed. "This year I've planted alliums: onions, leeks, chives, garlic, and shallots. The garden teaches me patience. All things have a season. There's no loneliness among growing things."

"It's good to be back," Lily said. "Manhattan's such a different pace." They walked companionably back to the house.

The phone rang. "*Ach*, you are here? You need lumber from Kurt?" Sophia looked at Lily, her eyes wide. "You never guess who stands in my kitchen!" Sophia handed her the phone.

"I didn't know you were here! Where are you staying?"

"With Anna and Chris in Gore Bay. How's your leg?"

"Back to normal," Will said. "I thought you'd be guiding in the Virgin Islands..."

"Manitoulin has my heart," she said, and then added, immediately, afraid he'd take it the wrong way. "I've missed Molly and Uncle Mudge, Anna, Chris and Sophia, and I've columns to research."

Cradling Sophia's phone on her shoulder in the shop with brightly coloured jackets and scarves, Lily thought of thread, threading a carefully worked exchange. Lily loved metaphor, and hated it, this unexpected new needling and backstitch.

"Lily, stop by tomorrow. I'll cook salmon and rhubarb crisp. I never thought you'd cross the swing bridge by yourself."

Sophia hovered anxiously trying to hear both sides.

"I've interviews tomorrow."

"It would be great to see you. Bring your hiking boots," Will said. "Wait, your hiking boots are here. I'm cooking anyway."

She hung up, met Sophia's eyes, and shrugged. "He told me to go. Now he wants to cook for me."

"There's always more to learn. You don't need him to be on Manitoulin."

Lily dressed carefully the next morning for her interview with an island painter. She wore an azure shirt, designed by Sophia. Her skinny jeans fitted perfectly; she loved her brown boots—not Prada, but a carefully stylish choice from L.L. Bean.

"You look nice," Anna said over breakfast the next morning. "Just for this interview?"

"Nothing special, Anna," Lily said.

Anna stirred her coffee, and lifted sober eyes to meet Lily's. "What are you up to, Lily Gardner? I know you'll be in Kagawong." Without waiting, she asked, "Heard from Joel?"

"He's on his own journey. Manitoulin's mine, Anna, finally mine. I'm independent here, with friends like you."

"Why meet Will, then?"

"It's time to complete something. See you later," Lily said, kissing the top of Anna's head.

She enjoyed two hours of chat with the painter, talking about his collages and paintings, and why he'd rooted himself on Manitoulin. When she left, she drove into Gore Bay, bought a bottle of merlot, and drove past the trailer park overlooking Lake Kagawong. She thought of last summer. Her Manhattan winter had been busy, working long hours in the office to make up for her time off, and dating, well, a few nice men. She was free, ever free, to keep learning. She sang the opening of "Sempre libera": "Ever free to follow my chances, in the game of folly and pleasure…"

The grass was freshly cut where she parked next to the working barn, the familiar buzz of insects greeting her as she stepped out of the car. The front door of the farmhouse flashed open. Will bounded out—heavier, and walking with a suggestion of a limp. He was clean shaven, but needed a haircut. A frisky German shepherd catapulted out of the door, brushing by him. "Don't jump, Lola!"

The dog nosed Lily, sniffing her boots. So this was her replacement, she thought with amusement. Will came close. They stood, not touching, greeting each other as if they were strangers. Slowly, Lily raised her arms, her open hands toward him. With relief, he opened his arms, bent down and enfolded her, the scent of his hair familiar.

"There's a bottle of merlot in the trunk." She handed him the key.

"Molly told me about your breast cancer on condition that I not contact you," he said. "You look great, Lily."

"Thanks Will. The book's done well. I'm fine and busy."

"You always were," he said. Waiting while he opened the trunk, she glanced at the small apple tree in the front yard. The tree feathered into larger branches reaching out.

"You saw that lightening almost cut the tree in half?"

"Yes," Lily said. He stood beside her and they looked up at the little apple tree.

"I've got to clear the bottom of the trunk. Would you mind? It'll just take a minute." He didn't wait for an answer but lifted the chain saw that rested on the porch. Off came the offending piece of trunk as chips flew across the field. He looked around for more to prune, but stopped and placed the chainsaw back on the porch.

"It's been bugging me all day," he said. "Some things you just have to deal with."

Lily took a deep breath. What had Violet said to her? Illusion was at the heart of most relationships? She looked up through the tree's reshaped branches at the clear, deep blue sky of May, and blinked back memory. She looked over at the farmhouse, the fields and the river. She watched Will as he came back to the tree, wondering how she had given him such authority over her life. The dog ran in circles, eager for his attention.

Inside the house, the two easy chairs sat in the mud room where they'd sat in the early days, watching lightning and thunder work their way across the field. Her sturdy boots still stood at the end of the row along one wall. His jackets and hats hung on knobs, layers for all seasons of the year. Her green plaid jacket was there, long forgotten.

She peered into the living room; its walls hadn't changed since last summer. The mood of the farmhouse enveloped her in gloom, its dark corners and unloved spaces seeming to reproach her, but she was unmoved. The dining room was empty, except for the piano, with the quilt over it.

"I took the table, chairs, and mirrors to Toronto," Will said. Lily pushed the quilt aside and touched a few keys of the piano softly, listening to the sound. Will poured two glasses of wine. Each window sill and wall was familiar, but strangely unchanged, distant.

"I sold *Northern Loon* last month, got an unbeatable offer," Will told her as she wandered back towards the kitchen and accepted a glass of wine. "I told Bart to sell everything, to keep a share for himself. He got a berth on a vessel bound for Australia."

"You loved sailing."

"I did," he said. Three beats of silence. "But I can fly to the BVI and charter any time." He looked at her. "You've turned back into a skinny New Yorker. Your hair's too short. Your boots are pointy. I forgot you're stylish."

"I know you call it surface, Will," she said. "I have fun in Manhattan. Manitoulin's a different kind of fun: no one cares what you wear, so long as it's practical and protecting. Each island has a different ethos. My islands complement each other."

"Ethos," he murmured, "the distinctive spirit of a people or an era. Maybe my study of philosophy rubbed off on you. Want to put on your boots and walk the back forty?"

"A bear will climb through a window while we walk."

He laughed. This was the first time, Lily thought, he'd actually laughed about the episode, which had always made him grumpy. She changed into her old hiking boots, and Lola galloped past them as they walked across the yard. In the breezy afternoon, the field offered the gentle rustling of leaves in the bushes, the cheerful twitter of birdsong, and the occasional lowing of the cattle. Lily's old boots held her feet with a familiar feeling. Lola's exuberance complemented Will's laid-back nature. This man and his dog made a fine pair, she decided, surprised to feel a gentle affection for them. As they passed the herd, she looked for faces of the cows she knew, her endearing audience, but recognized none of them. Precious back-forty air filled her lungs. They passed an ancient, decayed skull of a cow that Will refused to move. The dog stopped to sniff.

"That's not for you, Lola. She's into everything. Like you."

"I knew I'd be compared to her," Lily said, amused. As the path wove further into the bush, she watched Will, knowing his walk, even with the slight limp, the way he went. But she looked further ahead into the living colour of the bush.

"I need to rest a minute." At the end of the field, Will sat on a tree stump. "I'm relieved to see you looking good."

"I had great doctors in New York."

"It's lucky you were there."

"I've often thought you saved my life by dumping me. I hadn't gotten around to finding a doctor here, let alone scheduling a physical. It was the early diagnosis that saved me."

"I'd taught you as much as I could. I had to let you go."

"You didn't let me go, Will." He wasn't getting away with that. "You sent me away."

"I wasn't being understood. I couldn't keep up with you, Lily. We weren't a team. I could feel the distance growing."

"Isn't it amazing how our happiness is in each other's hands," she said. "I always came home."

"There would have been a time you didn't. Are you ready to eat?"

This time it was easy, abundantly clear. They walked back to the house in silence.

Lily set the table. "I made a Waldorf salad," he said, cutting fresh bread. They took their old places at the table. "How are Violet, Dahlia and Stuart?"

"Everyone's good."

"My Uncle and Violet have developed quite a friendship of cribbage, golf, and those long stories." Will stopped short.

"Will, I have a gift for you. I was going to leave it with Ollie." She went to the car, returning with a box. He slit open the cardboard, unwrapped the purple tissue paper to reveal six pairs of colourful suspenders, designed by Sartorious George.

"Cows, chickens, and fir trees on elastic? These are great!"

"Sarty designed the Mudge Bay Collection."

He laughed. "Do I get a royalty?" Will chose the cow design, taking off his worn red ones, snapping on the new. She helped him place one strap over his shoulder. She affixed it twice at the back. Their eyes met as she sat down. He refilled the wine glasses. He told her how Laura had picked out the dog for him, and Lily related how she had had to rent a Lear jet to fly a client's dog from Palm Beach to New York to the dog dentist. And back.

After dinner, they sat outside in the Muskoka chairs and watched as the clouds of dusk danced from blue to wispy gold, to pink, and then red and purple. It soothed her to sit still, to look at the sky, so full of rapture, like nowhere else on all her travels.

"Lily, I've sold the farmhouse." Will's voice was very quiet.

She stilled for a moment, unable to grasp it. "Sold?"

"I'm hardly here. Laura has work and a life in Toronto—she never wanted this house. A young couple with three children pulled in a few weeks ago. I saw the dream in their eyes. I took 'em through the house. The husband kept telling the wife he could fix this, fix that. I could see the things I'm never going to fix. He's a computer guy, she's an artist. The kids played out front. I could hear them laughing. That was it. I named a price. He said yes. We shook on it."

"How soon—?"

"September closing," he said, quietly. Then he added, "The new family has read your book. They said you're welcome to pick apples from the tree any time."

They sat in silence, and it darkened to night. Neither moved. Among the stars, a startling white patch scintillated above.

"Northern lights," she realized.

"I'd like you to have the piano," he said out of the darkness as white flowed to green across the northern sky. "I like thinking of you playing it, as you did during our long winter."

"I'm not sure—"

"I don't play," he said. "I never will. I only had it fixed for you."

"Will, you know I've got my father's piano. A Manhattan apartment doesn't have room for two pianos."

"I guess," his voice suddenly sounded tired. "I just wanted—"

"I'd adore it. I'll take it," she cut in, recklessly. "I'll ask Sophia to keep it. I'll play it when I come in the summer."

She felt the shadow in the chair next to her relax. "Good. That's good," he said. "It was my grandmother's. Of course you know that. And it'll still be here, on island."

"When Mom sold our home, she said it would open healthy space for all of us."

"Violet is a wise woman." His voice shifted, suddenly lighter. "How she ever had such a talky daughter…"

Lily laughed. "Just lucky, I guess. What will you do now, Will?"

"I'm in Toronto for the next few years. But I'll be buying land out in the west end near Meldrum Bay. A long way from everything. Someday, I'll build there; keep a boat in the harbour."

The colours overhead faded into darkness, and a half-moon rose in the east.

"Time to go," Lily said. "Thank you, Will."

"I'll deliver the piano to Sophia later in the summer," he said.

"Oh, my boots are inside." They went in. She sat, slipped off the old, and zipped up her pretty new ones. She left the old ones on the floor. She would buy new walking boots in the summer ahead. She walked to her car. From across the meadow, a subtle wind enveloped them. Will opened her car door. As she slid in, he lowered his head, and a kiss landed on her cheek .

"Bye," she said, feeling sudden affection. "I wish everything good for you, Will."

On her way back to Gore Bay, a deer bolted out of the bush onto Highway 540. It leaped in front of her car, a perfect arc, missing the left side by inches. She and the car were intact.

Chapter Twenty Five

Over tea on Molly's front porch the next afternoon, Lily watched the familiar glint of the sun on Mudge Bay in silent contentment. She was ready to return to Manhattan next week after she visited the Sheguiandah dig. It had been a busy week, as always, but this moment of stillness in the Manitoulin breeze filled her heart. Molly poured more tea, and then shifted restlessly.

"I'm so at odds this spring. Everett's an aimless bore, living only for phone calls from Florida. He walks around the bay, head down. He's scruffy and annoying. I'm glad he and Violet are such good friends, Lily, but a brother is hard enough to live with—let alone one who's only half here!"

"You need a change," Lily said. "Come to New York with me. We'll go to theatre."

"I don't know—summer's short enough on Manitoulin, I hate to miss it. I've been invited to Paris. My school chum, Nora Fraser, died a month ago, and her husband Maurice asked me to come. She left things for me. I've known them for years."

"Molly, never say no to Paris! Does he want to mourn with you, or court you?"

"Who knows? He's a nice man," Molly allowed. "But who'll see to my brother?"

"The minute you leave, your quilting ladies will invite him to dinner," Lily scoffed. "Paris! I'm arranging your ticket today."

"Did you just settle my life for me, Lily?"

"I'm great at planning for others." Lily picked up her tea and leaned back in her chair.

"What about your own?" For all her graciousness, Molly was not to be teased with impunity.

"I'm busy enough—plenty of interesting work and writing and travel."

"Ev reads your column every other week."

"And criticizes!"

"Ev criticizes people he loves. He's always felt you were only touching the surface."

"Not much more you can do in a newspaper column," Lily agreed. "I didn't know I'd be good at it." She gazed out to where the wind skimmed the waves of the bay.

"I don't think he's just talking about your column, dear," Molly answered.

❧

At dinner that evening, Anna's phone rang. "Your office said I'd find you there!"

"Joel, what a surprise! I'll be here for one more week doing interviews. I'm staying long enough to visit the archaeological dig in Sheguiandah. How was Western Canada? Hey, did you swim naked in the Pacific?"

"You bet, Lily, the Pacific Rim was fun. Great wrecks in Barkley."

"Wrecks?"

"Shipwrecks," he elaborated. "The divers here call Barkley Sound 'the graveyard of shipwrecks.' Excellent diving! I wish you'd seen it—gardens of anemone, fans, and sponges."

"Sounds like fun," Lily said, thinking of the many clients she'd sent to explore warm Caribbean waters. The travel agent in her was taking notes.

"Hmmm… Ocean's cold in early summer, off Ucluelet, but yeah, it was great. I'm headed south to California, now, where I can dive without a wetsuit." He paused. "I have a proposition for you."

"Oh?" Lily replied.

"Spend some time with me. Alexis gave me Anna's address. When a package arrives, study it. I'd like to take you where you've never been before."

"If it's group sex," Anna said when Lily told her, "you'll give me the details!"

The package arrived; Lily ripped it open to find two books, one with a yellow sticky note on the front cover. *I'll be there in August. Come dive Fathom Five with me. ~ Joel.* Lily pulled the note off the book. "*Dive Ontario! The Guide to Shipwrecks and Scuba Diving,*" she read aloud. She opened the book at the spot where a tasseled bookmark trailed. "Fathom Five Provincial Park." The second book was a scuba diving manual.

"Where's the Red Book, Anna?" she asked. "I need scuba lessons."

Anna came up behind her and peered over her shoulder. "Fathom Five? Well, well. You haven't done scuba diving yet. He knows you pretty well, doesn't he?"

"I could start learning now," Lily answered. "There's a dive shop in Gore Bay."

Scuba diving, it developed, could not be learned in her few remaining days on the island, but Lily made an appointment to interview the owner.

"Tobermory has some of the best freshwater diving in the world," she was told. "If you're planning on August, take your classes before you come back. You must know what you're doing. Some advice to start: when in doubt, get out. There are bold divers and old divers, but no old, bold divers."

Lily called Alexis that evening. "I'll be back in New York next week. Can you book diving instruction for me with that company we recommended to clients last winter? And send Molly to Paris."

"I can do anything, partner! Molly's going to Paris?"

"Molly needs romance."

"So do you, my friend!"

The next morning, Lily drove to Sheguiandah to meet a Laurentian University archeology professor who had worked on the dig for years. Silently, they followed a path through a tiny ravine, past verdant foliage and round grey rocks. "We've found remnants here of a nine-thousand-year-old culture, one of the earliest human sites in Canada. We think the people were attracted to the white quartzite for making stone tools," he said, gesturing to where Sheguiandah Hill rose above the fields. He pointed towards a ridge. "That was a beach, once." He picked up some stones and handed them to her. "That's debris from stone toolmaking. We look at them, and leave them behind."

Lily stared down at the shards of stone, imagining a hunter carefully chipping away at the stone to produce a blade that would feed his family or build shelter. She pictured him teaching children how to work the stone. She wandered around the dig site, imagining young hunters readying bows and arrows, and women kneeling at open fires, while small children raced about in play. How must the living descendents of these people feel, rooted for so long on this island? Lily felt like an outsider, but then thought, all of us are descended from people like this, doing the same thing, millennia ago, somewhere on this earth.

This afternoon was another gift in her learning about Manitoulin and its people and history. Those who studied the Sheguiandah site were tracing a long history of belonging on this island. She thought about the much shorter family history represented by her great-aunts' letters, but knew that, for her, the letters and the writing they inspired were a kind of digging, a way of exploring identity and belonging. She returned the shards of stone she held to the ground they'd come from. The professor reappeared, and they walked down the path back to their car, single file.

⌁

Back in Manhattan the following week, Lily went swimsuit shopping. There were special shops devoted to women who'd had mastectomies. She bought three bathing suits.

At the swimming pool, her scuba diving instructor taught her to hook up the regulator, attach it to the tank, and become familiar with the buoyancy control deflator button. On her first dive to the bottom of the pool, she floated up too fast.

"You have natural positive buoyancy," the instructor told her.

She grinned, "All my life!" He added fourteen pounds of lead weights to her weight belt. She found neutral buoyancy, kicking legs slowly, suspended in the pool. In the days that followed, she couldn't wait to leave work to come back and practice, chatting with the instructors and hovering in the blue stillness. Deep water diving was a revelation, an exacting and constant study. Lily was delighted to pass the written test with an 86%. Her fellow students spoke of vacations in Key Largo and Belize, working on their Open Water Certification, preparing for winter escape.

Joel, calling from California, was delighted at her progress. Lily tried to explain to him why even diving in a swimming pool was magical. "You can't do anything but experience that moment— not speak, not write. It's stillness, floating, breathing."

"I once hovered in the ocean off Fiji beside a humpback whale," Joel told her. "It moved with incredible grace. I'll have that moment forever."

Work settled into a creative balance as early summer arrived. Lily was thrilled to receive an email with pictures from Singapore. Bart, Will's boat manager, was happy beyond his dreams, as captain of a spectacular yacht owned by the president of an Asian airline. After days sending her clients to Europe and the Caribbean, Lily spent the evenings turning her Manitoulin interview notes into columns. She soon had copy enough to fill most of the summer, and one evening she dug out the manuscript she'd begun about the Boston sisters. Touching the papers, she remembered the cold, grey fall after she'd returned from Manitoulin, evenings spent writing about the Boston sisters' and their struggles for identity and fulfilment. That had all ended with the discovery of cancer. She sat down to read the manuscript, and her imagination was caught once more by the Boston sisters' lives. For the next few weeks, between arranging travel and dive practice, Lily returned to Boston and Paris of the nineteen thirties.

Then, one evening in early June, a frantic call from Florida: "Mom's got pneumonia," Dahlia said urgently. "How fast can you get here?"

Lily caught a predawn flight to Fort Lauderdale. She arrived at the hospital to find Dahlia by Violet's bed, trying to breathe for her. "I'm glad you're here," Dahlia said in a bright voice, desperate eyes meeting Lily's. "Yesterday I lost three games of rummy to Mom."

Violet's head turned, her eyes opening as her elder daughter approached the bed. The breathing mask prevented talk. She patted Lily's hand, her own fingers fluttering. Her eyes drifted shut in weariness. Violet seemed shrunken beneath the covers. Out in the hall, Dahlia whispered, "The doctors say she's improving, but she's not out of danger yet."

Lily and Dahlia traded shifts at the hospital in a world grown oddly unfamiliar. As the days passed, Violet imperceptibly grew stronger, from one breath to the next. Lily told Dahlia about Will selling his farmhouse and about the ancient stones at Sheguiandah, but the weight of passing generations and history was too heavy for their mother's bedside, and she turned the conversation to scuba diving lessons.

Finally, Violet grew strong enough to be bored, and they played fierce rummy in her hospital room. "She's on the mend now," the doctors told them.

"Girls, you've spent enough time here. I'm fine. Go back to your lives," the General decreed.

Lily, eying her mother, wasn't ready to leave. "Since I've been taking diving lessons, may I stay with you and finish my Open Water Certification here?"

"Of course you can, just don't fuss." The General was clearly tired of fuss.

Lily called a dive shop and joined a group of novice divers on their first open-ocean swim at Molasses Key, off Key Largo. Aboard the dive boat, she met vacationing Canadians from the Bruce Peninsula.

"Five Fathoms National Park is famous," they assured her when she shared her plans.

"Take your giant stride," the instructor told Lily, towering over her in his black wet suit. She took the giant stride, surrendering to warm Florida salt water.

"Do everything slowly," warned the instructor, when they surfaced. They descended to the bottom, swallowing to clear their ears every few seconds. Sunlight dappled the white sandy sea floor thirty feet down. A school of blue fish swam by Lily, and she floated in her sea dream, until the instructor motioned that it was time to do her drills. Lily repeatedly stood and knelt on the sea floor, showing how she took her mask off and replaced it. Thinking of Joel, how surprised he'd be at her competence, she lost focus, mixing up the deflator and the inflator. She shot puffs of air, forgetting her lessons in her hurry to correct, and forced herself to concentrate, completing the first drill. The instructor gave the sign for okay, the frown fading from his eyes. The class drifted over purple and orange flora and fauna, a new world shimmering below. A nurse shark swept by, oblivious to their presence. The instructor drew their attention to a large black and white spotted eagle ray gliding above them. Then he tapped his watch, signaling time to ascend, slowly.

That night, Lily played rummy with her mother, Violet often drifting into a light nap. The nurse reassured her. "She's getting better. She just needs rest."

A few days later, Lily's third and fourth dives were more comfortable, and she grew confident in her ability to navigate the underwater world safely, as Violet grew stronger. At last, Violet was re-established in her condo. Packing her suitcase, Lily gave Violet her first two chapters and a list of question about her Boston great-aunts.

"Mom, this'll entertain you while you convalesce. No golf tournaments without the doctor's permission!" She ducked as the General shook her fist in mock fury, her sister's quiet laughter following her out the door.

Lily boarded her return flight to New York, the precious Open Water Scuba Diver's Certificate tucked into her purse. In her luggage were her new mask, fins, and a black wetsuit.

She was sitting with coffee and laptop at her Manhattan kitchen table Sunday morning when Joel called from Toronto. "I'll be in Manitoulin in about two weeks," he announced.

"I'm certified!" she said.

"Crazy New York City certified?" he teased.

CHAPTER TWENTY SIX

LILY FLEW INTO SUDBURY, picked up her rental car, and by late afternoon she had crossed the swing bridge and arrived at the stone house on Whiskey Hill. Molly had stayed two extra weeks in Paris, but was back and glowing. They embraced, and then stood back to gaze at each other.

"You're Parisian blonde and beautiful, Molly! My mom was right!"

"You're in time for our dinner party. I've a surprise," said Molly, looking toward the kitchen door. "Come out, dear."

A strange gentleman came forward, a bit stooped, but tall and aristocratic, with thick grey hair and bright eyes. Lily was baffled.

"Lily, meet my new husband, Maurice Fraser!"

Her eyes went wide. "Congratulations!"

"Molly's told me all about you," he said smiling. His voice was rich and deep, with a slight French accent. "Thank you for sending her to Paris!"

"Being in Paris with Maurice made me feel younger than springtime," Molly said, meeting his eyes. "And Lily, your friend Sartorious was going back to Paris on business. Alexis placed him next to me on the flight. Such a charming young man—and then, when Maurice and I decided to get married, Sarty made my wedding suit!"

This was almost too much for Lily. As she followed Molly to her guestroom, Maurice trailing them with her suitcase, Lily eyed Molly's stylish Hermes blouse. Maurice wasn't the only elegant item Molly had brought back from Paris.

"How many people are coming tonight?" Lily asked, the planned dinner party suddenly gaining unanticipated significance. Molly would be introducing Maurice to her guests.

"Ten, dear," Molly answered. "And by the way, Will's coming. I thought I'd introduce Maurice to the island gradually," she said, smiling at Maurice as he placed Lily's suitcase on the bed in a room overlooking the bay.

"I'll see to the wine," Maurice said, retreating.

When he'd left, Molly said, "My brother's so jealous; he doesn't know what to do with himself. He could hardly speak the entire time he drove us home from the airport."

"He doesn't own you!"

"Maurice is already reeling him in. Ev's trying not to soften around him."

Uncle Mudge arrived shortly with a carton of fresh fish. "Puppy love at eighty is revolting," he sneered. "Molly and Maurice cook together...in two languages."

"I hear you're invited to Paris," Lily said.

"I'm going to Florida. Violet says she's back in shape for golf. Your mother's a real trouper. She mentioned your writing, read me a chapter. Keep going," he said gruffly as he turned away.

The evening progressed. Will arrived, looking fine with a fresh haircut and pressed clothes. Enhancing his popularity were the dozen bottles of champagne he brought. He put down the carton and quietly opened his arms to Lily for a hug, which she accepted.

"Lily, I brought you the last rhubarb preserves." She accepted three jars from him.

Molly and Maurice served up a feast: local perch and fresh island vegetables with added Parisian flare. Ray Cartwright, the commodore of the Little Current Yacht Club, and his wife Ellen, along with Ollie, Anna and Chris filled one side of the round table; the other included Uncle Mudge, Molly's friend Elizabeth beside him, then the happy hosting couple, and finally Will and Lily completing the circle.

"We'll live half the year in Paris and half on island," Molly told everyone. "Ev will care for the house when we're gone. You'll all visit, but not all at once!"

"Humph," Uncle Mudge responded. "And ticketey-boo!"

Talk led to Will's progress emptying house and barns. "Getting the stuff out of the farmhouse makes a difference," he told everyone. "I feel a thousand pounds lighter."

"You don't look it," growled Uncle Mudge.

"Go to Florida earlier, dear," Molly said, her eyes twinkling.

"My mother was thrilled to sell the Long Island house," said Lily. "She felt that getting rid of furniture, clothes, papers and more would truly free us. It took awhile for me not to see it as loss."

"The place has been in your family since before the turn of the century, Will," Ray said. "Doesn't it feel strange to be selling?"

"I bought the Carter place, fifty acres near Meldrum Bay," Will said. "I'll still have my feet on Manitoulin. I thought it would be tough to let go, but Violet was right. When it comes down to it, roots aren't about being tied to one piece of land or a house. It's more about being grounded in a place, knowing you, yourself, belong there." He looked up to meet Lily's eyes. "Lily understands me," he said with a quiet smile. "She knows how to belong to two islands."

Lily was surprised and smiled silently, as talk moved on to the annual Eaton Cup Race, taking place the next week from Gore Bay to Little Current.

"Lily, I want you to come sail with us next Saturday in the Eaton Cup," Ray invited her in his dignified voice, familiar from his summer morning cruising news broadcast to North Channel boaters. "You can crew on the *Quadriga*, and write up the race from the winning boat's point of view."

"I've never sailed the North Channel."

"No experience necessary," he assured her. "Be at the Gore Bay dock at eight."

🙰

"Lily, I'll have the same site at the trailer park as last summer," Joel said, his deep voice resonating in Lily's ear when he phoned her at the stone house in Kagawong. Relaxing on the couch overlooking the bay, she could hear a new relaxation in his voice that touched her deep inside. She closed her eyes. She could picture his face and see his long hair as he spoke.

"How is Violet?" he asked.

"The General is back up and managing her bridge club."

"And your writing?"

"The columns are pretty much as usual. But I'm back on an old project as well." She told him about her mother's aunts, and their willingness to fight for the lives they wanted.

"I've had my great-aunts' papers and letters for years," she said. "I planned to write something, eventually. I started that winter here with Will. The island's quiet in winter, not like Manhattan. I had this impulse to connect to my roots, when everything else here was so different. I spent the winter looking after Will's leg, as much he'd let me, making friends and writing about the Boston sisters."

"It sounds like your mother's aunts were way ahead of their time," he said. "Though knowing the General, I'm not surprised. Shall I consider myself forewarned?"

"I don't know that I've their courage, Joel," she said. "For a long time after leaving Manitoulin, I couldn't face that book again. That kind of writing demands so much, and then the breast cancer…" Her voice trailed off.

"But you've started writing again," he said.

"I'm determined." She paused. "Writing about art and happenings on Manitoulin deeply engages me. There's so much to share. But there's more to say about survival and courage."

"I look forward to seeing you again, Lily," he said.

"I look forward to you, Joel," She closed her eyes, imagining she could feel his warmth. "You've had a long year driving west."

"I camped in the Cypress Hills in October," he said. "They're down on the US border, between Saskatchewan and Alberta, an area of the prairie that the glaciers never covered. The land rises up in a forested plateau. The light was amazing. And I've never heard such silence."

"Did you camp through the winter?"

"I stored the trailer in Vancouver in mid-December," he said. "Flew back to Maine for holidays with my son, and spent January winter hiking in the Rockies. Lois always wanted to hike the Maligne Canyon in Jasper—the river's cut down thirty feet through the rock, very narrow. In winter you can hike down on the river's surface, past the rock walls and frozen ice falls."

Lily tried to picture it, sitting at Molly's home, in the warm morning sun of June overlooking the bay.

"This country's huge," he told her. "Everywhere I went, people told me about somewhere else I had to visit. I think I understand why you're a travel agent. How can anyone stay in one place, when there's so much out there still to see! But I'm ready to stay put for a while. When I get to Manitoulin, I won't leave until freeze-up. I feel like this winter completed something for me," he paused. "When Lois was diagnosed with cancer, everything changed. Our lives became about cancer: treatments, remission, more treatments, then fitting everything we could into those last two years. When she died, I lost her, but I also lost everything that I'd focused my life around. I was so used to making decisions in relation to what she could do. And I was angry," he added, "with no one and nothing to be angry at."

"I didn't think of you that way last summer," Lily protested.

"I'd worked through most of it by then," he agreed. "I've learned what it is to love without judgement, to have patience, to go on, day after day. I've seen the best of Canada, rolling down the highways. By the time I hit the Soo, last August, I realized I had stopped thinking about whether Lois would love to see this or that. Time on Manitoulin did wonders for me. I couldn't talk about Lois last summer, but I'd found myself again by the time I left the island. You and Violet gave shape to my time here, with your warmth. You brought me back to my own life."

"And now...?"

"The Ryans are always renovating, so anyone who can swing a hammer is welcome, and I have family all over the island." His voice lightened, "And for us, I've a list of wrecks we can dive."

"I'm ready and nervous."

"That's normal. I think you'll fall in love with the deeper world. I'm glad you've earned your certificate. When can we go to Tobermory?"

"I'm sailing in the Eaton Cup Race on Saturday," she told him. "We'll find the time…" Soon, she thought.

He chuckled, a deep rumble. "Last time the weather was lousy and I couldn't see anything on the *Emma Thompson*. She'll be a good wreck for your first dive. She caught fire and sank 80 years ago, 25 feet down. We'll find the treasures in her history firsthand."

"Yes, diving into history," she said, not meaning that at all.

He got it, his voice turning playful. "And maybe each other!"

CHAPTER TWENTY SEVEN

LILY HAD BEEN BOOKING HER SAILING CLIENTS to the North Channel, an inviting challenge for seasoned boaters, since her first summer on island. Her visits had never coincided with the Eaton Classic. Despite all her experience booking clients on boats in the Caribbean and Lake Huron, she hadn't sailed the North Channel herself.

Quadriga bobbed up and down, tethered at the Gore Bay dock, waiting to be let out to crisp North Channel winds. She remembered the day on the Virgin Gorda dock when she had stopped by *Northern Loon*.

"Ready to cast off!" Skipper Ray turned on the engine, while his friend Eric cast off lines. Within minutes, sails were up. *Quadriga* darted across the start line at the sound of the gun. Tacking their way out of the protected waters of the bay, *Quadriga* battled waves as wind picked up, the boat taking the huge troughs as they hobbyhorsed along. A wave splashed over the cockpit, drenching Lily's legs, clean, no salt—fresh Lake Huron! Ray handled the wheel expertly as he told Eric to trim the sails. Lily knew these fresh sapphire waters, whitecaps glinting in the sun of the North Channel, could be as challenging as any Caribbean inter-island passage. The wind embraced her; her pen fell out of her pocket and slid across the deck into the water. She laughed—simply sail this morning!

Seven boats were competing, four larger than *Quadriga*. The sailboats were close-hauled and sailing close together. Lily was in the wind and spray with friends.

Ray maneuvered the boat past Clapperton Island, pink granite rocks sliding away to the north. She remembered snowmobiling to Clapperton over winter ice. To experience Manitoulin, one had to be here in all seasons and see the island from surrounding waters. Ray pointed, "There're the Benjamin Islands and Croker, five-star accessible anchorages on the North Channel!"

Quadriga rounded the mark by James Foote Patch, where the water turned smooth, the wind behind them. Ray asked Eric to set the sails to go wing on wing. *Quadriga* moved forward, a majestic swan. Lily made her way to the bow, sat and dangled her legs over the side. She watched the water race by below her boat shoes. She had moccasins, sneakers, hiking boots, and slippers in her suitcase. All her high heels were in the back of her Manhattan closet. Later this week, she would be putting on her fins, and she and Joel would dive deep below the water as she now skimmed over it.

The swing bridge loomed before them. Three of the larger boats were ahead of *Quadriga*, near the buoy marking the end of the race. Black girders gleamed in the sun and sails shone as each boat slid past the marker ahead of *Quadriga*. The race was over.

Lily stood up at the bow, holding onto the rail. Ray would soon give the command to lower the sails, and then they would pass through the swing bridge. She remembered how Will had told her that once she crossed the bridge, she'd never be the same. She realized how much magic the swing bridge held for so many people. The bridge to Manitoulin had become her framework for change and growth. Lily had arrived on Manitoulin, in faith and love, awkward and so innocent of Ontario ways.

She'd always return to Manitoulin, allowing its mysterious power to transform her. Nor did she wish to escape from the embrace of Manhattan. Lily had pulled bounty out of Manitoulin. The two islands were now part of her, bridged by her own self across channels and waters and countries.

The old swing bridge cranked fully open. Lily looked at beckoning waters of the future, framed by the bridge as *Quadriga* moved forward between the open span and the shore. She glanced up at the line of cars waiting for the boats to pass through.

A familiar Chevy Silverado pulling a fifth wheel was parked first in line. She kept her balance and waved at the tall figure standing near the bridge. She giggled as he waved back. She remembered canoeing with this Canadian, and what he'd said about Canadians and canoes, and she thought of the sultry summer that lay before them.

"Take the main down," came Ray's order. Lily scrambled to the mast. The mainsail furled down into her open hands.

Summer felt celebratory; the future, irresistible.

Not *quite* the end…

Aunt Molly's Secret Recipe for
"ROMPING IN THE RHUBARB"
SOUR CREAM CAKE

Ingredients:

½ cup butter	1 cup sugar
Two large eggs	1 cup sour cream
1 teaspoon vanilla	1 teaspoon baking soda
2 cups flour	2-3 cups diced rhubarb, fresh or frozen

Heat your oven to 350 degrees F or 175 degrees C.
Grease a 9 x 11 cake pan

1. In a mixer or bowl combine ½ cup butter and 1 cup sugar.
2. Add two large eggs, one at a time, beating after each.
3. Stir in 1 cup of sour cream and 1 teaspoon of vanilla.

4. In a second bowl, mix 2 cups flour, 1 teaspoon baking soda.
5. Fold this mixture into the big bowl.
6. Add and fold in 2-3 cups of diced rhubarb, fresh or frozen.
7. If the rhubarb is frozen, thaw and drain. Don't squeeze.

8. Add this ambrosial mixture into your 9 x 11 greased cake pan.
9. Don't push the batter out to the sides.
10. Bake for 30 to 40 minutes, until a toothpick comes out clean.

Serve warm, with a dollop of whipped cream, and vanilla ice cream. Be sure to exercise next morning. Walk two miles in your old boots.

Acknowledgements

I wish to acknowledge my gratitude to the amazing people below, who have brought their talents into my life, and have a part in making this story:

On Islands and Cities North:

Sharon Alkenbrack, Donna and Klaus Bach, Ron Baecker, Constable Allan Boyd, Myril Lynn and Darcy Brason-Lediett, Brandy Birch, Lil Blume, Mike Brown, Sheryl Brown, Marni Cappe, Judy and Saul Cartman, Hindi and Randi Cartman, Roger Cazabon, Riita Clarini, Kevin Closs, Bruce Cowan, Margaret and Roy Eaton, Linda and Michael Erskine, Kevin Eshkawkogan, Brenda Fetterly, Lara Foucault, Mary Lou Fox, Father George Gardner, Kidane Gebrekristose, Rosemary Goldhar, Gloria Hall, Joyce and Dave Ham, Jean and Wilf Hardman, Susan Hare, Anthea Hastie, Ursula Hettmann, Hillary Higgins, Austin, Mike and Wayne Hunt, Boris Hyrbinsky, Marlene and Bill Jewell, Joe Kertes, Lisa LaFramboise, Sherry and Ray Lavigne, Joe Ann Lewis, Connie Lee-Reynolds and Frank Reynolds, Lois Lindley, Margo Little, Darren MacDonald, Don MacDonald, Brian MacLeod, Dawn Madahbee, Koki and Dick Maloney, Marianne Matichuk, Steve Maxwell, Rick, Julia and Alicia McCutcheon, Louise McKeen, Hugh McLaughlin, Jack McQuarrie, Sue Merrylees, Janet and Russ Moore, Rick Nelson, Kelly and Bruce O'Hare, Sarah Parlee, Shelley Pearen, Jo-Ann Philipow, Tania Renelli, Patricia Ross, Brent St. Denis, Tom Sasveri, Markus Schwabe, Marion Seabrook, Ken Seguin, Wanda Severns, Antanas Sileika, Joanne and Jim Smith, Almaz Solomon, Laurence Steven, Maryann Thomas, Kelly and Craig Timmermanns, Debby and Jib Turner, Guy Vanderhaege, Maxine Warsh, Mike Whitehouse, Jack Whyte, Dylon Whyte, Brady Wilson and Perry Wilson.

On Islands and Cities South:

Mandana and Eric Beckman, Nancy and Richard Beckman, Juanita and Richard Bleecker, Susan and Harvey Blomberg, Deborah and Ralph Blumenthal, Charlotte Brem, Cheryl Dern, Treva Farmen, Michael Green, Sharon and Mike Jackson, Amy and Steven Kotler, Hazel Penn, Marianne Peterson, Joe Sansivero, Marilyn and Stan Silverman, Sandra Stern, Michel Storch, Karin and Larry Rappaport, Grace Waters, Sue Wheatley, Christine and Alfred White, and Peter Workman.

©2012 David Beyda Studio

Author Note

A former travel agent, Bonnie Kogos travelled to more than 90 countries over her career. She studied literature and writing at Boston University, Radcliffe, and Humber College, published a travel newsletter, and was a contributor to *Travel Agent Magazine* and *Travel Weekly*. She has travelled between Manhattan and Manitoulin for the past 20 years, and her newspaper columns have appeared in the *Sudbury Star*, the *Manitoulin West Recorder*, and the *Manitoulin Expositor*. Her first book, *Manitoulin Adventures*, was published in 2001. *Manhattan, Manitoulin* is her first novel. Find her on Twitter @ MNTTNMANITOULIN and at BonnieKogos.com